# MOR*f*PHOLOGY

*Liv Reimers*

Morfphology

Liv Reimers

ISBN (Print Edition): 978-1-66782-622-6

ISBN (eBook Edition): 978-1-66782-623-3

*"... with wonderful craftsmanship he sculpted a gleaming white ivory statue... It appeared to be a real living girl, poised on the brink of motion but modestly holding back-so artfully did his artistry conceal itself... He kissed her, convinced himself that she kissed him back, spoke to her, embraced her..."*

Ovid, "Pygmalion and Galatea" Book X, Metamorphoses

**Morphology** (definition)

mor. Phol.o.gy (*n.*)

> The study of the form of things, in particular
>
> *Biology*
>
> The branch of biology that deals with the form of living organisms, and with the relationships between their structures
>
> *Linguistics*
>
> The study of the forms of words

**Morph**\* (definition)

> Verb:
>
> *Change smoothly from one image to another by small gradual steps*
>
> Noun:
>
> In biology, an individual of one particular form in a species that occurs in two or more forms

**Morfph** ™

> *A human being designed by Geneti-Search Technologies and Laboratories using gene editing to have the enhanced characteristics of being able to read emotions, thoughts and desires of one other human to whom they have bonded (their Patron). They have the added ability, need, and compulsion to change form (shape shifting) and emotions, to please and fulfill the desires of their bonded or Paired Patron.*

*\*Morph is derived from the word metamorphosis, which is a Greek word meaning "a transforming." As a verb, we have used it since the 1980s, when computers allowed animators to make things change shape seamlessly. As a noun, in the second definition, we have used it since after 2025 when gene editing was used to produce the enhanced humans described.*

# I

# CREATION

# EXCERPT FROM:

## *In Libro de Morfph*

## *The Morfph Compendium and Handbook*

(An unofficial and unapproved* manuscript outlining the history, genesis, development, and complete description of what they call the "Morfph project." The Morfph™ Project was an ambitious genetic engineering project created at, and run by, Geneti-Search Technologies.)

Author unknown* (acknowledged to be the late Alix Edison, Genetic Engineer, and originator and creator of The Morfph™ Project at Geneti-Search Technologies)

*Section E.5*

*At their Pairings, fully matured Morfphs at first appear genderless and unformed. And like mirages, they shimmer, as if not completely solid in form. Although everyone agrees they are lovely to look at, if you ask any Patron what their Morfph looked like when they first laid eyes on them, they cannot tell you—instead stammer and hesitate, then say they are just not sure. They shake their heads and close their eyes, as if to bring up a memory that will just not come. Patroni say, however, that before their Morfphs eventually come into complete focus, they were hard to look at—actually difficult to focus on. And the Patroni also all agree that their Morfphs glowed—literally shown with a light which was quite blinding in its brilliance.*

*Geneti-Search denies Alix Edison wrote or had any input into this compendium and claims that much of the information included is entirely untrue and fabricated.

# CHAPTER 1
## *The Unveiling*

*Pearl*

Pearl sank deeper and deeper below the surface of the dark, fetid water. She couldn't remember why or how, but her hands and legs were tightly bound and a heavy stone was lashed to her feet. All conspired to make her descent rapid and struggle futile. She held her breath as long as she was able—until it exploded from her lungs and sent a burst of bubbles upward to a sky she could no longer see.

Just as she knew she must breathe in the foul water to re-fill her emptied lungs, Pearl jerked awake, sat bolt upright, and gasped for air. Sweat and fear soaked the silk sheets of her bed. Laying her forehead on bent knees, she calmed her rapid breathing and pounding heart. She was safe, she told herself, safe in her own bed and in her own Niche.

The night of vivid dreams, however, had left behind a hunkered dread curled up tightly in her mind and body, and *it* was not so easily dislodged.

Then she remembered.

*It's my Pairing Day.*

A fresh wave of panic washed over her as another thought struck.

*And nothing will ever be the same again.*

---

She'd be the first of the Morfphs to go. They'd even had a party to celebrate. All twelve Alphas and their Caretakers dressed in their most colorful clothes and gathered in the Pod's Common room to eat cake—a rare treat—and to dance in whirling circles. It was the culmination of all they had all been working towards for so long. Pearl and her sister, Ruby, had sat out the dancing, held hands, and looked on with worried eyes.

"We're so proud," Pearl's Caretakers said when a Patron was chosen for her. "So very proud."

*Then why does it feel like I'm going to my execution?*

Pearl's official name was Alpha One of Twelve, and she was not only the first of them to go, she was also the very first Morfph. The first one born alive and healthy, anyway. And until about three months ago, she'd been fine—fine with all of it. Excited, even. But that was before Ruby—Alpha Two to the people at Geneti-Search—said all those awful things, using words like murder, annihilation, and bondage.

"Morfphs are just genetically engineered human sacrifices," Ruby whispered to Pearl one morning as they lay together in the beds they had pushed together the night before. "Sacrificial virgins offered to today's gods, the ones everyone seems to worship now—"

"Oh stop, Ruby. So much drama. Why do you say things like that? It's not true and you know it. We're not being *murdered*; we're being *Paired,* for Goodness's sake. To a *person*. A carefully selected one, but just a person. Besides, everyone at Geneti-Search loves us," Pearl had said. "They wouldn't let anything bad happen to us."

"Billionaires, Pearl. I meant billionaires and trillionaires and—What comes after trillion? Gazillion? Don't be so literal. I know they aren't actual gods," Ruby said and snorted.

"Okay, okay, Ruby. Geez, calm down. I just—"

"But only the super-wealthy can afford us. And do you really think Geneti-Search is doing all this because they love us so much? Out of the goodness of their hearts? They're grooming us, Pearl. They need us sleek, healthy and cooperative. Just getting us ready for the coming sacrifice. To increase our value."

"You don't think Mama and Papa love us?" Pearl said, appalled at the thought. "You think they're lying to us?"

Mama and Papa were the Caretakers she and Ruby shared. Papa had a soft spot for Ruby and let her have access to the unmonitored web occasionally. It was strictly forbidden, and Ruby and Papa could get in terrible trouble. Exactly what kind of trouble Pearl didn't know. But what she did know was it didn't seem to be doing Ruby any good.

Ruby's face slackened, and she shrugged.

"Oh, I don't know. Probably not on purpose, I guess. But they really have no more say in all this than we do."

And then, days later, Ruby said something else about the impending Pairing—something that hit closer to Pearl's fears and that chilled her to the bone.

"Afterwards, the person you are now—this minute—will be gone, you know. And someone else entirely will be in your place. You won't be *you* anymore. Your Patron, the person you're Paired with—*enslaved to*—will determine who and what you are. Everything down to what you think and feel. Their desires will become yours. Their wishes will be your wishes. Your very body will shape-shift to the form they crave. You will embody *their* desires. Forever. End of story. 'Bye, bye, Pearl,'" Ruby said, snapping her fingers.

"Not now, Ruby. Please don't start—"

"That's murder, Pearl," Ruby interrupted. "How is that not murder?"

Pearl really hated it when Ruby talked like that, but now, as she lay alone and isolated from the others in her Niche, she wished Ruby were with her. Until a month ago, before they had both fully matured, she would have been. The night before they would have shoved their two beds together and then, after talking for a while in low murmurs, they would have gone to sleep, wrapped around each other like two puppies from the same litter.

Last night Pearl had to sleep alone, just as she had done for the twenty-nine nights before. Not that she had slept that much.

––––––––––––

It hadn't helped, of course, when Pearl learned from her Caretakers who her Patron was going to be.

"What an honor," Mama said. "What a tremendous honor... for all of us. Who would have thought that they would pair you with The Mother of Morfphs?"

"No," Pearl said. "Not her. Anyone but her. Please. Not her."

Surprised, her Caretaker shook her head. "Pearl, sweetie, it's happening."

"No," she said again. She cried—a mewling, defeated sound. It embarrassed her, but she couldn't stop.

*Ruby would never act like this.*

"It will be good. Just wait and see. You'll be fine. Better than fine," Mama had said. She'd put her arms around Pearl and kissed her on the forehead. But even her Caretaker hadn't looked convinced.

---

Now, sitting rigidly on her bed, dressed and ready, Pearl rubbed absentmindedly at the small, mostly healed incision on the soft underside of her forearm. A red line marked where Geneti-Search had implanted the identification and tracking chip soon after they chose her Patron. A Morfph's identity was incomplete until that point.

She changed into the clothes she'd found folded neatly on her bed the evening before. They were all a loose, flowing, white silk, as was her veil. She'd worn the veil and gloves, unless she was alone, for a month now–ever since she had come into her full empathic and shape-shifting Morfph capabilities and was ready for Pairing. The veil prevented eye contact with anyone besides her Patron. Eye contact and touch were important parts of the chemistry of the Pairing, and she must make no mistakes.

There was a light knock on the frame of the door; the signal. It was time. She stood up, slipped on her white silk gloves, adjusted her veil, and walked to the door to slide it open. The section of the veil that was over her eyes was a mesh she could peer through, but it obscured her vision enough that all she could see of her two Caretakers were their outlines, standing outside her door.

She couldn't see their faces, but she imagined them wreathed in the strained smiles she'd seen before whenever the topic of the Pairing came up. They stepped forward. Each took one of her arms to guide her to the Pairing room where her Patron waited.

Before they left, they fitted Bluetooth buds into her ears. These would deliver a low-powered electrical pulse into her ear canals at a crucial time during the bonding process. The pulse would stimulate her vagal nerve and boost the powerful bonding effect already encoded into the Morfph's brain upon meeting her Patron. The surge of dopamine, oxytocin, and vasopressin flooding into her body and brain would increase and intensify.

Most of what happened next was a blur, a confusion. Her nerves and the drugs they had given her to aid in the Pairing were taking effect. Body vibrating, her legs loose and wobbly, she walked and walked—for what seemed a very long time. *Dead woman walking*, she thought fuzzily. Then an elevator ride and more walking. Finally, a new room.

Low, flickering light and the faint smell of vanilla. Soft music. Plush, thick carpet underfoot. And someone else in the room—waiting as she had waited.

"Step forward, Alpha One," Papa said.

Mama and Papa stood behind her, close, but no longer touching her. Through her veil, Pearl could just make out a dark figure a few feet away. But she knew who it was.

*The Mother of Morfphs. My Patron.*

Pearl's entire body quaked again.

Papa started giving instructions in a formal tone Pearl hadn't heard before.

"Okay, Alpha One, please take off your veil and gloves now. We're ready to start."

She peeled off her gloves and unhooked her veil.

"Drop them on the floor, Alpha One. And now, Patron, please stand right there."

As the veil and gloves slithered to the carpet, her Patron walked closer and stood directly in front of her. Now in crisp focus, she looked just as Pearl remembered—cold, brittle, and white.

"Alpha One, one more step forward, please. Take your Patron's hand and look into her eyes."

She did as she was told and then felt a tickle in her ears and a low buzz, like a small electric shock. *The Bluetooth,* she thought.

As she stared into her Patron's eyes, Pearl's vision narrowed and tunneled until a dazzling light blinded her. A loud swooshing sound, like she'd heard in audios of the ocean, filled her ears.

Was she melting? She felt like she was melting... no, dissolving—her very molecules flying apart, dissociating and swirling away in all directions. Then, suddenly, a coming back together—a re-forming.

But re-forming into whom? Into what?

With the clearing of her vision, she realized she was still gazing into her Patron's ice-blue eyes. Pearl's terror transformed. Where there had been fear was now bliss... and a pure, ecstatic joy.

It was no longer necessary that her previous Caretakers guide her, for she now knew exactly what she needed to do. She put her other hand out and her Patron took it, as she had taken the first. She looked as dazed, blinded, and confused as Pearl had been only moments before. Pearl leaned in, buried her nose in her Patron's neck and deeply breathed in her smell. With an exhilarating surge of strength and energy, Pearl knew then that her Morfphing was complete, and that *everything* had indeed changed.

She looked down at their four clasped hands. Two of them, her Patron's hands, were white with long, elegant fingers. The other two must have been hers... no, *his*. For these hands were now men's hands. Where before she would have seen her small brown hands, he saw two large men's hands—hands with dark hair furring the backs and the spaces between the knuckles. For the *she* she had been, had become a *he*—just as his Patron desired of him.

He flexed the muscles in his legs and arms. They rippled like the sinews of a powerful animal, a leopard maybe. He knew when he walked, he would swagger. And then he smiled an arrogant smile. What had he been so afraid of? This was marvelous.

He looked back into his Patron's face and gazed with fresh eyes. Here was the great Dr. Alix Edison, PhD, genetic engineer, Head of Research at Geneti-Search Technologies and Laboratories, and creator of Morfphs. *Genius.*

How had he not seen before how amazing she was? Magnificent. A goddess. She was now his very reason for being, and he must keep her happy. Nothing but that mattered now.

# 3 MONTHS EARLIER

# CHAPTER 2

## *Visitation*

*Pearl*

Four years ago, she and all her Pod-mates had aged out of the Creche and graduated to their own areas. Even so, Pearl and Ruby always moved their beds from their own Niches and put them together at night.

Every morning, after soft piped-in music woke them, and she and Ruby returned their beds to their respective spaces, Pearl carefully and neatly made her bed. Then, she joined her Pod-mates for a breakfast of fresh fruit and soy yogurt.

Their Niches wagon-wheeled out from a large round Common Area they all shared. This arrangement afforded some visual privacy, but sounds carried well and the Caretakers frowned upon loud noises of any kind. The builders enclosed the Niches on three sides by shoji screens—Japanese-style sliding doors made of heavy translucent rice paper. On the third side, it adjoined her sister Ruby's Niche, and on that side only a billowy white curtain divided the two spaces. Although she and Ruby shared no common genetics, they did share two Caretakers, and that made them "sisters" within the Pod.

Pearl lay stretched out on her back on the cream-colored silk duvet and the piled-up pillows of her bed. Elbows jutting out, hands behind her head, she sank down into the covers, luxuriating in the feel of the smooth silk. The coolness soothed the aching in her rapidly growing limbs. The growing pains were especially bad today. A sudden sharp stabbing had her grabbing one of the soft pillows. She pressed it to her face and screamed. Very little noise escaped from behind the pillow—she hoped. Luckily Ruby was, by then, well away and deep into the Natural area.

Most of the time the Morfphs left both their shoji screens and curtains wide open, welcoming company. But today Pearl had closed the paper doors and the curtains to show she wanted some alone time—time to think and, evidently, to scream. The eleven other Morfphs in her Pod were very good about honoring this arrangement, just as she was with them.

It was now Free Time and, if she had chosen, she could have gone outside into the five-acre natural enclosure just outside the door of their Commons. She had a favorite place to sit in the enclosure—right under a blooming fruit tree and by the stream. But today she wanted to hear the comforting sounds of her Pod-mates talking and laughing from the large, sun-filled Common Area. The room was high-ceilinged and painted a stark white, with an entire wall of floor-to-ceiling windows facing out to the Natural Area.

A few of the girls must be playing games. She could hear them from her Niche. Chess had become popular recently, but Bridge and Mahjong were also favorites with the girls.

She could picture them lounging on brightly colored, overstuffed pillows. It was midday, and they had all just finished their morning classes and Qigong session. After a light lunch and flow-dance class, there would be more group and individual learning sessions, followed by yoga and meditation before the evening meal. After dinner, it was their choice again. Most sang in their small chorale group.

The learning sessions took up most of their time now. There was still so much to learn before they fully matured and were ready for Pairing with their Patroni. Only a handful of months to go now. After the Pairing, everything would change–everything in her life and everything about herself. And it scared her, especially with Ruby going on and on like she did.

"No, no, Pearl," her Caretaker, the one she called Mama, said. "Don't be afraid of change. This is not a loss. It's more like a caterpillar changing into a butterfly. You will still be yourself... your *new* self. Just keep remembering what we've told you. After you're Paired, your capacity for perfect empathy with your Patron will activate and their desires will become yours. And even better, you will have the amazing capacity and the joyful need to fulfill those desires—body and soul. Your Higher Purpose is to relieve the terrible loneliness and disconnection that has descended on so many people. It is why you were created. Why they encode these special abilities into your very genetics!" Mama's eyes shone.

She held tightly to Pearl's hands.

"So, that is *exactly* who you are. You mustn't be afraid. It will be your happiness... your ecstasy."

Still, the niggling worm of doubt persisted.

———————

A commotion in the Commons brought Pearl out of her ruminations. The Caretakers were here. That was unusual. The Caretakers usually rested in their rooms in a different, but close, part of the building when they had time to themselves. Pearl heard a soft rap on her shoji screen and then her male Caretaker's voice. *Papa.*

"Pearl, so sorry to disturb you, but we have a very important visitor who has come unannounced. Would you kindly fetch Ruby?"

Pearl groaned, pushed herself up from her bed, and walked over to open the screen.

"Of course, Papa. I know where she'll be. But it might take a bit to get there and back."

"Thanks, Pearl. Do your best... but hurry!"

As she left to go outside, Pearl overheard the Head Caretaker.

"Will everyone please come join us in the Commons? We have a very special guest from Geneti-Search today. The Mother of Morfphs is here to meet you all!"

*Oh my god. The Creator!*

Here. Today.

Now.

*Shit.*

She froze and looked back to see what the famous Alix Edison looked like; she'd imagined her so many times. Then she ran to find her sister.

———————

Pearl found Ruby in *her* favorite place—close to a ring of tall oaks and beside the same sparkling stream they both loved. The trees were budding, coming out of the long winter and into spring. She took a deep breath. The air was still cool but was moist and smelled of lush life with a subtle underlay of decay. Her sister sat on a large mossy rock, staring into the water.

As usual, Ruby dressed all in black—a long-sleeved, turtle-neck tee-shirt over form-fitting yoga pants. If given the choice, Ruby preferred black and wore it all the time. She'd swept her long hair up in an untidy knot on top of her head, and Pearl could just see a small glimpse of the tattooed barcode at the nape of Ruby's graceful neck as she gazed down into the stream. Pearl had a similar series of identifying black lines on the back of her neck. They all did.

As Pearl got closer, she could hear the soft plops of pebbles, as one by one, Ruby threw them into the still frigid water. She seemed mesmerized as each smooth rock hit and disappeared with a splash, followed by radiating, slowly dissipating rings on the surface of the water. Ruby was already tall and angular, even though the Morfphs had not yet reached their full height or maturity.

Her skin was a smooth, tawny brown. Her hair was also dark, but her eyes were a startling hazel; sometimes bluish-green, sometimes brown and sometimes, somehow, both at the same time. She may have been of Indian, or perhaps Middle Eastern descent, judging by what Pearl had seen in the educational sessions and the many actual print books they had at their disposal. But Morfphs didn't have any information about their genetic heritages, and by some unspoken agreement, they never discussed it.

Pearl's skin and hair were darker than Ruby's, and her eyes were a deep, warm brown. She came up to Ruby's shoulders. Her male Caretaker had once referred to them as Mutt and Jeff, but she did not know what he meant.

*Something to do with the vintage comics he collected,* she guessed.

"Hey Sister," Pearl called. "There you are." She plunked herself down on the rock next to Ruby. "Move over, fat-ass."

Ruby laughed and moved over so they each had just enough space to get one bun on the rock.

"Not too hard to find, I guess. What are you doing here? I thought you were going to meditate in your Niche," Ruby said as she reached down and started rubbing her legs. "My legs really ache today. We just grow too damn fast. Sometimes I feel like I'm going to split out of my skin."

"I know, I know. Mine too, but listen. You'll never believe this, Ruby. You'll never guess who's here today. Try. Try to guess."

"Geez, Pearl. I'm not going to guess. Just tell me."

"Okay, okay. The Mother of Morfphs, that's who. The Mother of Morfphs is in the Common Room right now."

Ruby audibly gasped. "In the flesh?"

"Yup. In the *very white* flesh. I've never seen anyone so white. And she's even taller and skinnier than you are."

Ruby's eyes widened. She let the remark go, which was unusual.

"Shit."

"That's what I said. Or maybe I just thought it... Anyway, Papa wants us to come right away. We need to hurry."

"This can't be good. I keep forgetting how little time we have."

"You'll see. It's all fine. We'll be fine. You need to stop worrying... stop *catastrophizing* and just have faith."

Ruby reached out and took Pearl's hand in hers.

"Nice word, Pearl... *Catastrophizing...* love it." Ruby looked back at the stream with a grim look on her face.

"And I love you too, Pearl. I really do, but... sometimes you are so... so... naïve... so gullible. Spewing all their propaganda. Use your brain, for god's sake.

That's one good thing they gave us; freakin' amazing brains. You should try using yours."

Pearl dismissed Ruby's insult. That was just Ruby.

"I mean, is there anything we can do about it, anyway?" Pearl said.

"We could run away. They say we're free to go."

Pearl made a scoffing sound deep in her throat.

"But I don't know where we would go... or what we would do," Ruby said bleakly. "No idea."

"Well, then... let's hope for the best."

"I repeat... shit." Ruby laughed, but it was a sharp, unhappy sound.

It took them about ten minutes, but when they got back everyone had gathered, standing stiffly, their hands by their sides.

The Head Caretaker then spoke.

"Girls, we are extremely honored today to have a very special visitor. This is someone you have been hearing about your entire lives. This is your creator, Dr. Alix Edison, The Mother of Morfphs. She is the genetic engineer from Geneti-Search Laboratories and Technology who created the gene editing sequence for Morfphs."

They all stared, eyes wide, and no one said anything or even moved or shifted. Many were even holding their breaths.

"Doctor," the Head Caretaker said. "This is our complete Alpha Pod."

Alix stood up from the molded chair she had been sitting in and surveyed them. Her face was impassive, impossible to read, but she was definitely not smiling.

Then she said something under her breath. The Caretakers couldn't hear her, but all the Morfphs could... easily. "Goddam, they're just a bunch of pubescent *girls*." And it wasn't a compliment. Not at all. But surely it couldn't be a surprise.

Pearl looked at all her Pod-mates, all precious to her.

*Yes,* she thought, *all girls.* Pearl had heard a rumor that almost all the viable Morfph embryos were female. Most of the genetic males had evidently failed before they could even be implanted. And of the three males who had survived implantation, all of them had died in utero.

*The Creator* walked from girl to girl, looking at them closely, like bugs under a microscope, and shook each of their hands. Just as she had told Ruby, the woman was tall and very pale, but what she saw now was that everything about her was brittle ice.

She was jagged, knife-blade thin, but a thinness very different from Ruby's. Ruby was rangy and lithe. The woman's hair was white-blond, her eyes a frozen blue. And her skin... Pearl had seen no one that white before, ever. Like a ghost. The Morfphs and the Caretakers, too, were mostly brown and black—a few were Caucasian, but none were so white as she.

When The Mother approached, Pearl took the proffered hand and shook it politely. The hand was icy and bony, the handshake limp. The woman's eyes drilled into hers.

Pearl blinked.

"Hello, I'm Alpha One," she said.

"Ah, the first," the woman said. She stared fiercely into Pearl's eyes before abruptly breaking eye contact and going on to the next girl in line.

————————

After shaking hands and examining all the girls one by one, The Mother of Morfphs—Dr. Edison—stood to the side of the room and talked to the Head Caretaker known as Pi.

The Morfphs all called their primary Caretakers Papa and Mama. *A leftover from more traditional families,* Pearl guessed. They all seemed to like it. Caretakers were named according to their assigned Morfphs. Pearl and Ruby's Caretakers were officially "Male Caretaker of Alpha One and Two" and "Female Caretaker of Alpha One and Two." That was a mouthful. So, like the Morfphs, they also had their own Pod-names.

"They're not very impressive to look at," the Mother of Morfphs said quietly to the Head Caretaker.

Pi visibly bristled. The Morfphs loved their Caretakers, and the Caretakers reciprocated that love.

"Let me assure you, they are phenomenal. *Amazing,*" she said. "All of them are exceptionally intelligent. They not only grow and develop at an accelerated rate, they also learn incredibly fast. Even their coordination is amazing. Their senses sharpened—including their hearing," she said pointedly, then shook her head. "But why am I telling you all this? That's how you designed them."

"Yes, of course," Dr. Edison said dismissively.

"But beyond that, they are also wonderful to work with. Kind and caring of each other and to us. Intuitive, empathetic. Just lovely. Exemplary human beings—every one of them, in every way. I'm very fond of all of them."

"I really hope so. You can't possibly know how important this is," the Mother of Morfphs said.

She continued talking, but almost—it seemed—directed to no one in particular.

"We're working on arranging Patroni now," she said. "We will Pair this group inside the company for alpha testing. That's the in-house testing before beta testing. That way we can keep a close eye on them. If all goes well, then on to the Betas... and the Gammas."

The Caretaker's face creased in a worried frown.

———————

*I don't like this woman,* Pearl thought with a jolt. She'd been so excited; her expectations, despite her fears, had been high. They called her the Mother of Morfphs, but she didn't look like she could be a mother to any of them.

But, really, Morfphs had no mothers... or maybe they had many. They had Donators who supplied germ cells—the eggs and sperm. But they weren't really *donators*—they were paid. And well. Ruby said that was likely the reason so many of them were various shades of brown and so few were Caucasian.

"The rich always prey on poor people's children," Ruby had said. But Ruby said a lot of things.

They'd also had paid surrogates known as Gestators, or sometimes just Wombs. And for a year they'd had Feeders—lactating women who breastfed the Morfphs. None of the Gestators could also be Feeders, because they strongly discouraged attachments between Gestators, Feeders, and the Morfphs.

Despite the separation of duties, they did form attachments. Pearl remembered everything about her Feeder and the time they'd had together; snuggled into her, skin to skin, warm and cared for. They both cried the last time she fed.

Caretakers, however, were allowed a longer, loving connection with the Morfphs. But after Pairing, Pearl would never see them, or any of her Podmates, again.

For five years—*all of her life* — she'd known only these people, and she felt terrified of losing them.

But Pearl did *not* want this woman for another of her mothers, or for anything else. She was the one person Pearl hoped she'd never have to see again.

# CHAPTER 3

## *Counseling Session*

*Sara*

Alix Edison walked into Sara Wilde's counseling office.

"It's quite important you understand that I'm a genius," Alix said. She strode past Sara and sat down in a lavender colored leather chair.

"Thomas Edison was my great-great-great-grandfather. Or maybe my... oh, never mind. I forget how many greats." Alix swiveled in her chair and looked around. "Nice office," she said.

*It is a nice office,* Sara thought. She wanted it to be an oasis from the world outside. Oil paintings on stretched canvases lined the sage green walls. Blue skies, flowers, and calm azure oceans were the prevailing themes. She'd partially covered the glowing bamboo floor with a large rug woven in pastel blues, corals, and teals. Silky white drapes covered the windows. She used to keep the draperies open to let in the natural light and to see the large oak and the birds and squirrels the tree had housed just outside the window. But that tree had finally died two years ago; had given up the ghost, another victim of the prolonged drought and unrelenting high temperatures. Now it stood out there, like all the other dead trees, as a stark and skeletal harbinger. The light that showed through today was a dirty orange glow. She knew if she were to open the drapes, she would see the apocalyptic sun hanging in the sky, made blood-red by the fires burning—now getting too close for comfort.

"Why is it important I know that you're a genius?" Sara sat down facing Alix.

"Well, I should think that would be obvious. Also, it's important that you don't underestimate me. Other people have made that mistake."

Sara examined Alix: *tall, very blond, no longer young but beautiful, most likely with the help of cosmetic surgery. Alpha female. Used to getting what she wants—used to being in charge.*

"Hmm. Noted. But let's get back to that later. It's nice to meet you in person, Alix. I'm Sara Wilde, of course." Several years before, she would have shaken Alix's hand, but shaking hands ended when the rolling Pandemics had started. At least they could talk without masks on today. Usually, they only wore masks when in groups, and when the smoke was bad.

Alix stared at Sara with unsettling eyes, so light blue they were almost silver.

Sara cleared her throat.

"I know we talked briefly on the phone, but I know little about you. What is it you do, Alix? Can you tell me a little about yourself?"

"I'm a Genetic Engineer at Geneti-Search Laboratories—head of research."

"How interesting. Aren't you the ones doing all the designer baby work?"

"Yes," Alix said, sounding slightly bored. "We are one of the leading companies using gene editing to create what you're calling 'designer babies' for parents-to-be. They can choose from a variety of enhanced attributes for their child."

"Amazing."

"Not really. It's all pretty routine now." Alix sat up taller. "But I *am* working on a project that's... well, let's just say it's big and it will roll out soon. Finally. Been in the works for years. Can't really talk about it though. The NDA's—non-disclosure agreements—are brutal. That was my doing," she said and laughed. "But it will change everything... *everything*. You can't even imagine."

"How intriguing. But I wonder about the effect all this is having on society... in the long run, you know. Some of my clients have gone into terrible debt to go that route: the IVF, the gene editing, and the implantation. They're terrified to not enhance their kids. They're afraid they will become second-class citizens."

"Well, of course," Alix said. "They'd be at a tremendous disadvantage. Everyone who can afford it, does it now. But the price will come down as more and more places offer our services."

"Even so, there'd be many who..."

Alix shrugged, looking both irritated and disinterested. "Let's get back to me, please."

"Of course. What do--"

"I see that you have a PhD. That's important... I want the best. I don't have any patience for mediocrity. What's your degree in?"

"Counseling Psychology."

"I was a little put off it was from a public University. But you had superlative ratings. All five stars... people seem to like you. That doesn't normally matter to me, but I thought maybe I'd try something new."

"Can you tell me why you *are* here today? What are you hoping to get from counseling?"

"I just need to tune up my life a bit. Do you think you can tune me up, Doc?"

The question sounded sarcastic, but Sara answered seriously.

"Well, that's not exactly how it works. But maybe together we can work some things out. You'll have to give me a bit more information before I can know if we're a good fit, though. Maybe something a little more specific? What about yourself would you like to change... or work on?"

"Change about myself?" Alix laughed. "I didn't come here because I need fixing. I'm not like your other clients."

"I see," Sara said, smiling. "Let's start with getting a bit more on what's going on in your life then."

"Well, let's see. My daughter says I'm an emotional black hole and wants nothing to do with me. My partner—soon to be *ex*-partner—is sleeping with another woman *and* her thirteen-year-old daughter. The men at work hate me because I'm smarter than they are. I have no friends—but that's ok; there're very few people I can stand. Even my daughter, truth be told."

"Hmm," Sara said. "Sounds like you've got a lot going on. How about parents? How is your relationship with them?"

"Dead and gone. And good riddance."

"Okay. So, it sounds like relationships are an issue. We could address that if you would like."

"Yeah, I guess you could say I have people problems. So many assholes, so little time."

"Did I pick up that you've had counseling before?"

"I've had a couple of other therapists," Alix said. "They were helpful—" She snorted. "--for a while. They were all men. I decided I needed to see a woman this time around."

"I see. Why is that?"

"Oh, you know. Same old bullshit. One was patronizing. I can't stand that. The others just didn't get it."

Despite all her alarms going off, this woman intrigued Sara. And she needed something interesting—distracting—to sink her teeth into right now. She thought for a moment.

"Well, Alix, I think we could certainly try it if you are agreeable."

"Okay, good, good," Alix said absent-mindedly. Then she seemed to perk up. "Who is that man I saw in the waiting room talking to your girl? The tall, gorgeous one. Looks like he has a bit of Asian genetics. Does he work here?"

"Oh, Sam. You must mean Sam." Momentarily startled, Sara felt a small jolt of protectiveness. She felt surprise at her reluctancy to answer. But Sam's name was listed on the door and many other places for anyone to see.

"Sam Hamada. He's another therapist... in the office on the other side of the waiting room. There are four of us here."

Sara glanced at the clock on the wall behind Alix.

"Our time is up for today. This was just a ten-minute consultation. Would you like to start next week? I usually see clients weekly, but we can do whatever you want."

"Fine, fine. Weekly works for me."

"Let's set up a time, then. You can do that with my assistant, Tania, at the desk. She can also fill you in my rates and take your insurance information. Oh! And there's one more thing. I ask my clients to start a journal or think about it, anyway. I find they are quite useful."

"Put me in the category of 'think about it,'" Alix said with a scowl that disappeared as soon as it appeared.

Sara noted the scowl. *Interesting,* she thought. Most of her clients were really into their journals.

"Totally up to you, of course."

"Sure, we'll see," Alix said. She stood up and smoothed her pants with her hands.

"I'll walk you out. I look forward to working together."

Alix nodded and smiled thinly.

Back in her office, Sara tapped a pen on a pad of paper in her lap. Alix seemed different from her other clients. Angrier, maybe... certainly more arrogant. And almost certainly a Narcissist. She didn't get many of those in her practice. She saw more women than men, and if narcissism was involved, it was usually their partner's or some other close relative. She had quite a few of those. But mostly her clients were suffering from what she had started calling The Dread.

It had descended on *her* about ten years before. That was when the world had stopped making sense to her. Conflagrations, Super Storms, Pandemics... and then all the trees died.

The more recent increase of violent, well-armed, roaming militias and their large-scale kidnappings of young girls was the cherry on a chaos sundae.

The Dread manifested in several ways. The most common being unrelenting insomnia, nightmares, chronic worry, panic, depression, OCD, and PTSD. And then, of course, there was the sister of dread—rampant epidemic, soul-sucking loneliness. Mustn't forget the loneliness.

*Am I a fool to take on this woman... this self-proclaimed genius?*

It was time to make some notes, wrap it up for the day and go home. Home to Jack, her very own resident Narcissist. Something was up with him, but she wasn't sure what. She smiled, took a deep breath, and slowly let out a long sigh.

## Alix

Alix left Sara Wilde's office with mixed feelings. *All that flowing fabric covering her up. What's up with that?* But she seemed smart enough; at least smart enough to be amusing. It was going to be fun to have someone intelligent to talk to again. She hadn't had a proper conversation with anyone for a long time—since she threw Felix out.

*But journaling? Ugh, so boring.* She might do an entry or two to placate her.

And then her mind circled back to her Morfphs. She'd recently decided she would be the first person Paired with a Morfph. The decision seemed inevitable, meant to be—and she could monitor the project's success first hand.

She'd felt anxious after seeing the first batch of Morfphs. Disconcertingly, they'd looked like adolescent girls standing around their lockers at the local middle school. Especially the Morfph called Pearl. *Alpha One.*

Pearl couldn't possibly end up being what Alix most desired.

Of course, if all went to plan, neither Alpha One's appearance nor personality would matter an iota. After the Pairing, the Morfph would transform into Alix's heart's desire. That was the whole point.

Alix wasn't really sure what that would be, but it certainly wouldn't be the girl she had seen three months earlier.

Only four people at Geneti-Search, other than Alpha One and Alix, would even know of their Pairing. The two Caretakers who had nurtured the Morfph and raised her to maturity, Alix's wealthy investor and benefactor, and her boss. Everyone's boss. *The Big Guy.*

She wouldn't even be able to tell her shrink. Not yet, anyway. The project needed absolute secrecy for at least another year until they could launch to the public.

# CHAPTER 4

## *Just Friends*

### *Sara*

Sara Wilde was lost in thought as she drove home after the first appointment with her new "genius" client, Alix Edison. She analyzed her reaction to Alix's question about Sam, the counselor that shared the building with her. She hadn't liked it. Not at all. And it wasn't just protectiveness of a colleague's privacy.

Sara knew Sam loved her... had for years... even before his wife, Katy, had left him. Everyone knew it. He said nothing, but it was an open secret and he wasn't very good at hiding his feelings. Sometimes she worried she took advantage of Sam's feelings for her, but he was so different from Jack and she craved what Sam gave her—acceptance, encouragement, and yeah, praise and admiration, too. Those had been in short supply from Jack for quite a while. And Sam was so easy to talk to.

When he had taken Sara aside one day and told her Katy had left him, she was incredulous. "How could anyone leave you? You're almost perfect."

He gave her a skeptical look and said, "Well, she left me for *Beatrice*."

"Beatrice?" It took a moment to sink in. "Ahh, Beatrice. Huh. Really?" She'd met Beatrice but had detected nothing but friendship between her and Katy. "Well, that might be a reason.... I guess...," reluctantly conceding that maybe there could be at least one good reason.

Sam had listened to Sara agonize over Jack many times over the years. More than once she had cried on his shoulder when she suspected Jack was seeing yet another of his young students. Sam, unfailingly and patiently, consoled her, but rarely let on how he felt about Jack. He told her, however, more than once, that he thought she was too good for him. That's about as far as Sam usually went in criticizing Jack, though.

"I think Jack is seeing someone else—*another* one of his 'cupcakes,'" she said to Sam one day. "He denied it but all his female students just idolize him—treat him like a little Demi-god. He loves it. Eats it up. And they get younger and younger every year." She laughed a humorless laugh. "How can I possibly compete with that?"

Sam sighed.

"Well, number one, Sara, you shouldn't have to. And number two... have you ever looked in the mirror?" He paused and frowned.

"Scratch that last comment. I mean, it's true... but Sara, you're the complete package. Smart, funny, caring, beautiful..." He stopped, looking embarrassed. "I'm just saying, he's an idiot to risk that. I'm sorry, Sara, but he is."

She cut him off before he could say anything else. An uncomfortable silence followed.

"Well," Sam said, "come to think of it, maybe you are a little too skinny."

She laughed, pushing back a momentary irritation.

"Leave my body out of it, please," she said. "I get enough comments at home on that topic."

But Sam was the only one who could make those sorts of comments and not make her feel judged and defensive. She knew it came from a place of concern, as he worked a lot with eating disorders.

"Sara," he blurted, "just leave him. He's a bastard."

"Sam," she said, and shook her head. "I can't. I just can't."

"I'm sorry. I shouldn't have said that. I won't do it again."

Sam's feelings for Sara hadn't gone unnoticed by Jack, either. Another memory bubbled up into Sara's mind. One night before Katy had left Sam, Sara and Jack were on their way home from a barbeque at the couple's house. Jack was at the wheel, and Sara knew he was not happy. But it was a rare clear night with stars studding the sky, and Sara was feeling mellow after a very pleasant night with good friends.

She loved being with Sam and Katy and their girls. There had also been a handful of other friends, including her best friend, Tania, and Tania's partner, Alphonse, who had been in particularly high form.

Actually, everyone had seemed to be in a good mood... everyone, except Jack. Sara avoided looking at him in the car, savoring her good feelings for as long as she could, and choosing to delay the inevitable.

Finally, she glanced over and, as suspected, Jack's shoulders hunched forward and his knuckles blanched white on the steering wheel. Not a good sign. She sighed and shrugged. *Here we go again.* Deciding to wait him out, she remained silent. Maybe it would pass.

He was the one to first break the silence.

"That guy really bugs me. He's so fake sincere—so emo. Always talking about feelings. I'd swear he was gay if he hadn't been panting around you all night."

"Who?" she asked innocently, feigning ignorance. But she knew very well who he was talking about.

Jack looked over at her in the passenger seat and gave her an irritated look.

"You know who. Sam."

"He's not even a little fake. He's a therapist, Jack. Feelings is what he does."

She'd heard it all before and really didn't want to engage or listen to Jack's rant on Sam. Jack hated it that Sam and she often sat talking and laughing together. She knew he was jealous and could understand it, but it still irked her, especially since Jack had been a real asshole lately—critical and harping and "helping" her understand all her shortcomings.

It had been a relief to talk to someone who actually seemed to like her and enjoy her company. Besides, Jack really had no leg to stand on in the jealousy department, with his entourage of beautiful, young, and eager acolytes hanging on his every word at departmental functions. And he was the one who said he wanted an open relationship. *Only for him,* she guessed.

Sara smiled an annoying smile.

"You just can't stand that he's younger and better looking than you are." Sam was five years younger than she and fifteen... no, almost *seventeen*... years younger than Jack.

"If you like that type," he'd snapped back. His face had turned a beet red.

"What, the beautiful type?"

"Beautiful!" he sputtered. "Geez. That's just wrong."

"Back to the gay theory, Jack? Make up your mind."

"He's just trying to get you in bed. That's the reason he talks to you all the time and laughs at all your jokes."

"Oh, Jack, that's just not true. We've been friends for years and he's made no kind of move on me. Besides, I'm pretty damn funny."

"You're really not, Sara," he snapped back, his voice acid.

"Sam seems to think so." She couldn't keep herself from another dig. She was really tiring of this. Jack's last comment had done it for her, and she came back at him.

"I know what you're doing, Jack. Plain as the nose on your face. It's called projection. I think you've heard of it?" She smirked.

"You're talking about yourself. That's what *you* do. That's how *you* are... not Sam. Sam has a lot of friends who are women and he obviously enjoys talking to them and appreciates them as people with no ulterior motive. You judge everyone by your warped view of the world."

"Don't psychoanalyze *me*, Sara. Talk about as plain as the nose on your face. Sam Hamada wants you." Jack had been right, at least about that.

"He's in love with you, you know that."

"We're just friends," she said firmly, done with the conversation.

They drove the rest of the way home in a strained silence, both seething. When they got home, she went upstairs to bed, saying nothing else to him. Jack sat down in his chair in the living room, undoubtedly fuming. When he finally came up, she was still awake, but stayed scrunched well over on her side of the bed and silent until she heard him breathing deeply in sleep.

Sara had been so immersed in her thoughts she was surprised when her self-driving car pulled into their driveway and came to a smooth stop in the garage. She shook off the unpleasant memories and replaced them with a more pleasurable thought. Tonight, she and Jack were going to a wine tasting put on by their favorite restaurant.

# CHAPTER 5

## *We've Had a Good Run*

*"The majority of husbands remind me of an orangutan trying to play the violin."*

-Honore de Balzac

### *Sara*

Sara jerked awake. Her jaw spasmed and snapped shut with an audible snick of tooth on tooth. Her head and eyes ached, and the latter were crusty and scratchy after a night of intermittent crying.

She lay on the far-left side of a king-sized bed and stared blindly at a slowly whirling ceiling fan. The other side of the bed was empty and cold. Her tongue worried at her front tooth, now chipped.

Two days ago, five days after she had first seen Alix Edison, her husband of almost twenty years, Jack, had left her. An empty bottle of forty-dollar Pinot Noir she had liberated from Jack's coveted wine collection the night before hadn't improved matters.

*At least now I can get a dog.*

She'd wanted one for a very long time, but Jack hated dogs. "Too needy," he had said of them. He had little tolerance for what he perceived as weakness. But what did that matter anymore?

Through the pulsing throb, her mind raced—obsessively going over and over all recent, and not so recent, events—trying, with minor success, to make sense of it.

The night before Jack left, he had arrived home from his University job as a tenured psychology professor and joined Sara at the table. She poured him a glass of red wine.

The wood of the large Craftsman-style table and the old paneled walls glowed a warm mahogany in the late afternoon sun. It was almost summer, and the daylight was lasting longer into the day. They had bought the bottle at their wine-tasting group the Friday night before, and she'd been looking forward to sharing it with him.

With no lead up, no heat or nervousness, and completely out of the blue, he spoke precisely and deliberately.

"I've decided it's time for me to leave you."

*A joke, of course.* Just Jack being provocative or pulling her leg. That was something he liked to do. Thought it was amusing.

"Oh, really? And where are you going to go? Your girlfriend's?" She laughed.

He looked slightly taken aback, but didn't skip a beat. He took a sip of the wine and made an appreciative nod.

"Yes, as a matter of fact," he said.

She stretched back in her chair, swirled the jewel-colored wine in her glass, admiring the richness of its color, and gave him an indulgent look. *Such a kidder.*

"You know, then?" he said. "Well, that's a big relief. I didn't think you did... this time. But that makes it so much easier... for both of us, really." His expression changed from his concerned face to a more genuine, wide, cheerful smile.

"Good old Sara," he said. "You really have always been so reasonable. I'm going to miss that." Then he shrugged slightly, as if shaking off some mild regret. "But it has to happen. It's time."

"Wait... what?" Steel gripped her heart, but she shook it off.

"Oh, come on, Jack, stop it. You're making me think you're serious. That's just mean." She reached over playfully and cuffed him on the arm.

"No, I mean it. I *am* serious." A slight frown creased his brow.

He switched to his light and breezy voice.

"It's been great, Sara. Really great, but it's played itself out, don't you think? Come on, admit we've had a good run—I mean, my god, almost twenty years," and he smiled at her. His boyish, beguiling smile. The smile he'd always depended on to get away with his cutting insults and slights.

Her face felt frozen in a rictus smile and it ached with it. Actually, every muscle in her body felt like it had rigored. She seemed to have lost the ability to speak. She shook her head and drew in a deep, jagged breath.

*He wasn't joking at all.*

Somewhere, deep inside, she must have been waiting for this their entire life together. There was a sinking feeling of inevitability about it. She felt gutted— laying there, flayed open and bleeding.

Jack seemed to take her silence and apparent lack of reaction as acceptance of the situation, an agreement of sorts.

"We really have had a good run, Sara. A really good *long* run," he said again.

She couldn't move. So, Jack filled in the silence with his voice. He had never liked silence.

"And don't think that I haven't appreciated our time together. It's been great! *You've* been great. But you must see it's time that I move on—that *we* move on. No point dragging this thing out. One quick, clean yank and we're done here. Really, this marriage has lasted a lot longer than I expected and a lot longer than any other relationship I've ever had. You should feel pretty damn good about that. You really should learn to look at the positive."

He put his glass down and took it to the next level of surreal.

"I better not drink all this wine right now. I was thinking I'd take a run. Do you want to go with me? I'm not leaving until tomorrow."

"Jack, c'mon. You're leaving tomorrow? As in moving out? Where are you going?" she said, shaken.

"I told you... to my girlfriend's," he said, now with a twinge of exasperation, but still trying for patience, as if talking to a slow child.

"To your girlfriend's?" she said, still mentally flailing. "What are you talking about? Who *is* this girlfriend?"

"Jazz, of course. I'm going to Jazz's—for now. Her roommate just moved out. We'll probably stay there until you and I can get a divorce and split things up, I guess."

"To Jazz's. You mean Jazmin? Jazmin is your girlfriend? Since when? And since when did she become Jazz?" Her throat felt sticky and dry at the same time. She put her hand out, as if to stop herself from babbling. Stop this entire event from happening.

"Never mind. What does that matter? How old is *Jazz*? Like twenty-five? Jesus, Jack. Is this a joke? If it is, it's not funny. It's cruel. Stop it. Just stop it." She swallowed hard.

"She's twenty-nine... almost thirty. She's an adult, has been for several years. Old enough to know what she wants, and she wants me." His voice sounded prim at that point—self-righteous and indignant.

"Oh, an elderly twenty-nine, huh? Well, excuse me. And you only fifty-six. That's a mere—what? — twenty-six, twenty-seven years difference. Hardly anything at all."

"No need for sarcasm, Sara. You've never been good at it." He paused. Now his tone switched again. Back to reasonable, self-righteous Jack. "We're in love. There's no fighting love, Sara."

"It's Love, is it? Well, isn't that nice. Totally out of your control. You had no choice. No choice but to discard our marriage after twenty years—to discard *me*. Like so much milk that's gone bad, that's expired. Past my pull date."

"Actually, eighteen years," he corrected.

She made a scoffing, guttural noise in her throat and finally cried.

"Look, I'll always remember our time together fondly. But it's over. Don't be so dramatic, Sara. You're being histrionic, don't you think? Listen to yourself. You sound crazy. And I thought you were being so reasonable. I told you a long time ago what I felt about monogamy, and marriage, for that matter. I never pretended otherwise."

As she continued to cry, Jack's body posture softened a little, and he tried to come to her, his arms outstretched. She shoved him away. She was in no mood for pity—no mood for *his* pity, anyway.

He shrugged. "You'll be fine, Sara. You're still attractive... for your age. Anyway, you..."

Anger surged through her throat.

"For my age? Are you serious? I'm eleven years younger that you are, Jack. Eleven years!"

"Well yeah, but it's different for men, isn't it?" he said, now with an edge of spite in his voice. "Anyway, you make more money than I do now. But don't worry. I won't be asking for alimony."

That she made more money than he galled him and had become a sore point in their marriage. They usually avoided talking about it.

"Oh, Christ, have I fallen down some sort of rabbit hole? Who are you? Who the hell are you?"

Jack shook his head and smiled a thin smile. "I've never made a secret of who I am."

Eyes now squinted, she looked at him closely.

"She won't make you young, you know, Jack."

With that, she threw her half-full glass of wine at the wall and walked out of the room. Shaking, she went into the bedroom and locked the door to feel like she had some control, some agency. But she knew Jack wouldn't follow her. The last look she saw on his face was one of relief. Maybe he had thought it was all over—the issue all settled.

And now, looking back, she guessed it had been. The red wine stain was still in that light-colored rug, and it looked like blood had spilled instead of wine. Jack was lucky it wasn't.

As promised, Jack left the next day, taking only a couple of large suitcases.

*Was that only yesterday?*

"I'll come get the rest later. I think we can do the dividing of property thing without lawyers, don't you? We're both reasonable people."

She had watched him leave in silence.

# FLASHSTORY

*Right-Thinking Militia thought to be perpetrators in attack on middle school in which they kidnapped 20 girls between the ages of 11 and 14*

By June Garcia

12 June, 20** 02:30 PM ET

In the tenth such attack this year, men armed with semi-automatic weapons, and wearing body armor, invaded a middle school. Yelling and identifying themselves as The Right Thinkers, they rounded up twenty girls who were at cheerleader practice. They killed five school guards in the attack in a short but deadly shoot-out. Authorities believe the Right Thinkers took the girls as "Virtuous Wives" for men in one or more of their fortified compounds.

A young girl who escaped one such encampment earlier in the year described the conditions of the kidnapped girls.

During the initial period of captivity, reportedly called the *Adjustment to the Righteous Way*, "they beat us and starved us for… a long time… days… I was so hungry. They made us chant bible verses for hours and hours every day... wouldn't let us sleep. My friend… April… they put her in the whore house… they called it *The House of Harlots*. That was after all the men raped her… she wouldn't do what they said…

April was brave… I wasn't. I ran when they weren't looking… I was going to have to marry this old fat guy. He was gross and his breath stank bad. They kept saying they would kill us if we wouldn't… 'Adjust.'"

Of note, there have been multiple, but unsubstantiated, reports of executions within these compounds.

These alarming incidents add to a long list of atrocities as our country continues to go through an unprecedented upsurge of lawlessness, violent tribalism, and femicide. Many groups have already broken away from society and are living in well-armed and defended complexes, many in deserted warehouses, apartment buildings, or bankrupted housing developments. Some are groups of women escaping abuse and gender violence by retreating to *Femazon Compounds*. Most, however, are various Right-Thinking groups. These are often brutal, patriarchal groups of men. At this point, their "women" are predominantly girls that they have "liberated from sin," *i.e.* kidnapped and indoctrinated.

# CHAPTER 6

## *Mother of Morfphs*

*"A new species would bless me as its creator and I would be the father to a race of children."*

-from *Frankenstein: Or, The Modern Prometheus* by Mary Shelley

\* \* \* \* \* \*

**Morfph™** *(n.)* **Enhanced Human Genotype- EHG-ss/e (shapeshifter/ empath group)**

Human beings who have been genetically designed, engineered, and raised by Geneti-Search Technologies and Laboratories to have enhanced characteristics of: 1) Targeted perfect empathy (Super–Empath Characteristic or SEC), *i.e.* the ability to read perfectly one individual's (their Paired Patron's\*) emotions, wants, and desires; and 2) The capacity to physically, behaviorally, and emotionally transform into the embodiment of those desires (Shapeshifter Characteristic or SSC); and 3) An overriding drive to meet their Patron's desires (Pleasing an Other Characteristic or POC).

-from *Terminology* section of presentation made by Alix Edison to Geneti-Search board regarding the impending launch of Morfph program

### *Alix*

Alix willed herself to breathe slowly and deeply. Breathe in, *I am calm*. Breathe out, *I am focused*. Appearing nerveless and arrogantly confident was always important, but it was crucial today. Normally, she didn't have to work very hard at it—not anymore. After faking it for many years, one day, she realized it had become a reality. But today, that wasn't entirely true. Oh, she knew she was good—definitely the smartest person in the room—but she was nervy and these men would look for any weakness, any chink in her glossy, well-polished armor.

She stopped herself tap-tapping her long, lacquered nails on the gleaming wood of the table and from swiveling back and forth in her chair. Both were tells they would easily pick up on. As usual, she was the only woman sitting around the table. She was used to that by now, even took a perverse, smug pride in it.

Two days ago, she turned fifty-three, but looked a good ten years younger. At least that's what everyone told her. But the mirror confirmed it. Her eye job and face lift—an S-lift, they had called it at Aesthetic Kosmos—were both well-healed and had been timed to make sure of that. Oh yeah, she looked pretty damn good, which was especially important on this most important of days.

She sat in the black leather chair to the very right of the Big Guy, Arthur Riche. He was the CEO of the company and now presided at the top of the long conference table. Alix's well-toned, salon-tanned legs were crossed at the knee, and her posture studiedly relaxed... but not too relaxed. She maintained a neutral expression on her perfectly made-up face.

Everyone at the table knew something big was coming, and she was hyper-aware that all warily watched her for clues. Most of them looked at least slightly hostile, some seemed to be fairly bristling with it.

*They don't wish me well*, she thought. But that was too mild.

They were hoping to see Alix fall flat on her ass, or—maybe better—face plant. Hoping for total humiliation. But they won't get it. Not today, anyway. She was going to blow them all out of the water with this proposal. They'd be kissing her stiletto-shod feet soon enough.

There were nineteen men in the room, and then her, making an even twenty around the elongated-oval table. It was constructed of the highest quality cherry wood and, like her nails, polished to a high gloss. The attendees included the various top people—the nabobs, the big kahunas, the heavy-weights, the big-wigs, the fat-cats—of Geneti-Search Technologies. Alix counted Arthur as an ally—her ace in the hole—although she never referred to him as Arthur anywhere but in her mind. Most were, like her, the leading genetic engineers in the company.

One more ally, right across the table from her, was the in-house attorney, Matthew. The only brown face in a sea of white. Mustn't forget him.

Alix was the Chief Research Officer, the CRO, which didn't go over well with most of the other scientists in the room. *But sod 'em*, she thought. *None of them even comes close to my abilities... to my brilliance.* She fought a small laugh, hiding it with a cough into her hand.

The company had been going big into gene editing, creating Designer Babies. Rich mommies and daddies could choose from a smorgasbord of enhanced abilities, attributes, and appearances for their pampered and entitled offspring-to-be. The more characteristics specified, the higher the price. The leftovers, the rest of the population who couldn't possibly scrape up enough for any genetic enhancement at all, were SOL. *Not my problem*, she thought with a mental shrug.

But, as of today, that was all old news. Alix had gone way beyond Designer Babies for rich people. She had made another even more amazing leap into what they could do with engineering special humans. And she was here today to pitch—really, to present—her newest project. They had already put much into motion. The cost had been outrageous. But the money to be made was well beyond anything they had ever done before. Astronomical.

This was to be a top-secret meeting. All laptops, phones, tablets, smartglasses—everything that could connect to the internet or record in any way—were confiscated at the door. They thoroughly searched all attendees to make absolutely sure of it. Many protested, but in the end everyone agreed. This was a whole new level of secrecy, and it intrigued them.

Alix was the only one in the room, besides her boss, with a laptop, and someone connected it to the screen that filled the entire end of the room. Everything said and seen today must be for their eyes and ears only. Everyone signed strict NDAs with dire consequences at the meeting. Tension and anticipation were high.

Alix glanced briefly over at Matthew, who had written the confidentiality forms. He winked at her, and a smile twitched briefly on her face. She wondered if it looked more like a grimace. He was her only other ally here today and, a rarity for her, a friend.

They had formed an unlikely friendship when his wife died suddenly about six months before—*or was it closer to a year by now*? Alix had been uncharacteristically sympathetic and reached out to him. He differed from the others in more ways than his skin color. She actually liked him. Besides, it was always better to know more about other people than they knew about you. Never knew when that might become useful.

And Christ, he was easy to look at, she thought, but not really her type. Alas, she never went for the nice ones. Besides, he was still grieving for his dead wife, which, after this long, was getting irritating and smacked of a fundamental weakness that Alix had little patience for. Not to mention, he was at least twelve years her junior. She was one of the old timers at the party, practically ancient in this environment. Especially for a woman.

The Big Guy waited patiently until it was quiet and everyone was settled, then cleared his throat to speak.

"I'm going to hand this meeting over to Alix. She has something very exciting to present to you today, and I know you will give her your rapt attention. Alix...?"

Alix swiveled around in her chair to face them.

"As you all well know, it is now possible through gene editing to create very special human beings. And because of the loosening, or really the almost total rollback of regulations and oversite on corporations that started during the first Drumpf presidency, and now has continued into the Drumph Regime... I mean the Drumph *Republic*... we can now aggressively push forward without being restrained by previous ethical considerations or restrictions."

Before the meeting, the newest rumors circulated—rumors that Drumph had actually died several months ago, maybe years, and now they just trotted out his stuffed body and propped it up on the White House balcony for appearances.

*Ridiculous*, Alix thought. *But who knows?* Altered videos could show anything they wanted. What did it matter, really? Elections were just for show now, anyway.

"It's wide open now, folks," she continued. "Anything goes, as long as we don't step on the toes of the wrong people, of course." She paused.

"So here we are. Totally free, completely unfettered to use, to cash in on, our science. What's that quote? Something about, 'If it can be imagined, it can be reality'? So, if we assume that is true—and I do—our imaginations are the only limits we have. The only thing holding us back. What an exciting time to be in this field. And I have something truly amazing to present to you today."

Alix put both feet on the floor and both hands on the table.

"Our specialty up to this point has been to make Designer Babies. People are now used to choosing their babies' characteristics. Of course, at first there was the requisite uproar, but that has died down—as things do. We are an adaptable species. Outrage dissipates, the outraged get weary, and everything new and alarming quickly becomes normal. But what if we could go further than choosing our offspring's traits? Go to the next step? No, forget steps, let's leap, soar forward, upward to yet unimaginable enhancements to human beings."

She looked around the room at their faces. They remained silent but were listening carefully. She put her hands in her lap and sat ramrod straight.

"And I'm not talking Super-Soldiers. This is not about war. This is a totally different direction. Let's talk about 'Love, Not War', Gentlemen." A laugh bubbled out unexpectedly. Almost a bray. She smothered her astonishment. *Get it together, Alix.*

What she really needed to do today, her actual goal, was to appeal to them as men, not as scientists or even as entrepreneurs. She wanted to appeal to their fantasies, their feelings of entitlement, and to their emotions... and most especially... to their less-than-noble instincts and yearnings.

Forget their intellect, or any sense of social justice, or higher values of any type. She was aiming lower. She had to hit them in the crotch, titillate them with the erotic possibilities. That was exactly where the marketing would need to go as well, so that's where she was aiming today with her pitch. *But let's not forget their greed.* She had to make them realize this could make them all truly wealthy. She launched in.

"What if we could genetically engineer perfect companions, who are *exactly* what we desire, exactly when we desire it, *and* who can take any form wanted of them?" She looked around at the skeptical faces. Many of them made scoffing guffaws, but she had grabbed their interest and she knew it.

"Alix, sex-bots aren't new," said a man with thinning, well-moussed blond hair that almost, but not quite, covered his emerging bald spot. His fleshy face was smooth and pig pink. His voice dripped with derision. Jason Martin was his name. He was another genetic scientist, and Alix knew he thought he should be the one in her job. She also knew some other quite interesting things about him.

"Jesus," Jason Martin said, "half of us have them already. Hell, you probably have one." They all snickered. Even Matthew, *aka Judas*, briefly twitched a smile.

Almost all sex-bots were purchased by men. Women who had them were considered pathetic, desperate, and unnatural. And, if they were married, then their partners were objects of ridicule as well. So, Jason's remark was a blatant burn and everyone knew it. But what they didn't all know, and Alix did, was that Jason's wife had her own sex-bot. Alix had learned a great deal about old Jasey from his young lab assistant, Nadia.

But for now, Alix just smiled, ignored Jason's insult about sex-bots, and continued her presentation.

"Jason, I'm not talking about A.I. I'm not talking sex-bots here. I'm talking about real human beings with genuine feelings. Just as human as you or I."

She cocked her head.

"Or maybe a bit more human than you, Jason."

She got the hoped-for reaction. Several men hid smirks behind their hands, and one or two sniggered. Jason glowered at her.

Alix leaned forward.

"Freud posed the question 'What does a woman want?' So, let's change that question to 'What does a man want?'" She looked around, and now she was the one smirking.

"What do *you* want, Gentlemen? What do you really desire?" she asked. "Limitless sex exactly to your specifications? Infinite variety in your partners? A different exotic beauty every night? Or maybe it's true love that you long for." Alix snorted. "Maybe not. Adoration, then? Admiration? No demands, no judgement, or dissatisfaction with performance?"

Most of these guys, Alix believed, still clung firmly to the old mythology of the insatiable male libido. Or at least they seemed to want to be seen that way. Also, many of them had probably been awkward and less than popular adolescents. Alix could imagine them being continually rejected by the pretty girls, the ones whom everyone wanted. The ones whom at that point in their lives had a transient, short-lived power and who sometimes had grown cruel with it. As for these grown-up awkward boys, they were the ones who now had the prestige and the power and felt the need to make up for their past rejections. All this had gone into Alix's calculations for this presentation.

"So, I ask again, what *do* men want? But let's not be so narrow, not to mention sexist. What do men *and women* long for? And what would fulfill those longings?"

Alix paused for dramatic effect and finally answered her own question.

"I would wager for most men and *women*, the answer would be: a Morfph." *There*, she thought, *I've named them. Now let the rumpus begin.*

"A Morph? What the hell are Morphs?" Jason said, loudly and right on cue.

"Morfphs, Gentlemen—and that's spelled M-o-r-*f*-p-h," she said with emphasis, "are the whole reason we're here today." She paused theatrically and then continued.

"Morfphs are real, sentient, feeling, human beings—who love passionately and unconditionally—*if* that's what's desired. And who have the capacity of infinite variety beyond your dreams."

Once again, the room exploded in questions and scoffing disbelief. Everyone talked at once.

"Patience, patience, Gentlemen. I'll get there soon enough. I will answer all questions," she said loudly over their voices.

"Jason, as you astutely pointed out, sex-bots have become very popular, and again, as you made equally clear—especially for men. 'Virtual' relationships are also thriving, for both men and women. We usually avoid the disturbing topic, but pedophilia has also increased, as they see children to be... let's say, unsullied... and more malleable and accommodating than adults. Child sex-bots have also normalized sex with children. Sex crimes and sex trafficking of young women and children have also alarmingly increased. And then there's all those mass kidnappings of teenage girls..."

Alix glanced at Stuart across the table and glanced away. His daughter had been one of those kidnapped girls taken by a militia. At the time of the kidnapping, two years before, she had only been thirteen years old.

The authorities would not get involved in helping them get her back... or any of the other girls, either. Sympathy for their cause and values had infiltrated the powers-that-be, including the highest of places. By now she was likely married with kids—unless she was "an incorrigible" and relegated to the brothel, or worse. Best-case scenario was that she was well- indoctrinated and had adjusted to the Righteous Way.

Either way, she was lost to Stuart and his family forever. He looked down at his hands, apparently trying to hide his sudden flush of emotion. Despair and grief slashed across his face.

"But I digress," Alix said. Changing her tact and smoothing her tone, she continued. "Men... and women... still yearn for genuine relationships with actual people. I think most people still want, still long, to be unreservedly, unconditionally loved. We can't go one day without hearing about our 'epidemic of loneliness.'

"So, let's just put it in a nutshell. Go over it once again. People are, of course, not all alike. They have a variety of wants and needs, but what do many people crave—fantasize about? Let's think big here.

"What if there were *real* human beings with perfect empathy, who could sense—could read—your every wish? And what if those humans also had the extraordinary capacity to physically and emotionally *become*—transform themselves—into the very embodiment of those desires? Not only that, but their overriding need is to fulfill your yearnings. Every need, every fantasy, every craving, every kink completely sensed and fulfilled.

"Let your imagination run wild. Can you imagine a partner who could do all that, *and* who truly adores you, understands you and loves you unconditionally? Or maybe what you want is to be taken care of, pampered, waited on, and cooked for, and to have your taxes done... perfectly." Grudging laughter. *Hook set*, she thought.

"There are, of course, much less talked about, uh... predilections, darker ones. Don't worry, I won't talk about them now either. What person, or sex-bot, can possibly take care of *all* these needs... even if they wanted to?

"And it isn't just fantasy. It isn't A.I. and it's not someone pretending or being paid. It is a living, feeling, real human being who is exactly what you want, who feels, looks, and behaves exactly how *you and only you* want them to look, feel, and behave. These human beings have been genetically engineered to bond with one Patron and one only. I'll get to the terms and details later in the meeting."

Alix had been talking for a long time. She stopped and took a deep breath, as if she was coming up for air. An unnatural calmness had settled on the room. *The calm before the storm*, she thought. They sat in their chairs unmoving, staring at her, some with their mouths ludicrously gaping open—stunned or openly skeptical looks on their faces.

Alix broke the silence.

"And the answer to the question I posed? The answer to 'What human could provide all these things?' The answer, once again, is: A Morfph. A Morfph can. And now *we* can provide Morfphs. At a price, of course—an enormous price. But the number of multimillionaires, billionaires, and trillionaires in the world keeps increasing, as all the money continues to flow to the top. And that's the market we will go for."

"Alix, you're crazy." Jason flushed fuchsia pink. "Totally nuts. Are you off your meds or something?"

He looked toward The Big Guy.

"What you're talking about here is simply not possible. We simply do not have the capability of such a thing. I mean, *Shape-shifting*? Give me a break."

This was rich, considering what she had heard whispered about another experimental project—headed by Jason. There were actually rumors of making human "Blanks"--empty vessels to be used to transplant consciousnesses. *Ridiculous.* Straight out of the worst science fiction. But Jason was a ridiculous man.

She smiled guilelessly at them, enjoying the derision and scorn this time.

"Call it what you want, Jason, but it's real. Morfphs are real. And it's in the works as we speak."

Alix looked over at her boss and smiled. He smiled back. The go-ahead on this project went through over five years before, and twelve Morfphs had already been born and raised to maturity. And beyond that, one had been successfully Paired, as well. Her *Adam*.

She had intended to continue to call him by his official name, Alpha One. But the very first day, after they had been Paired and had returned to her condo, he had named himself—sort of.

"I am the Adam of your labors," he had said to her.

She had felt a shiver go down her spine. *Where have I heard that phrase before?* But It must have come from *her* brain... from her desire, but she just couldn't place it.

So that was how he become Adam. He couldn't have any other name.

The meeting broke out into chaos. The men tried shouting over each other, some yelling questions and others making incredulous and derisive noises and comments. Alix relaxed back in her chair with a self-satisfied smile on her face she didn't even try to hide.

After letting it go on for a few minutes, Arthur intervened.

"Everyone quiet down. It's time for you to all shut up and listen and watch." The silence was immediate. "Alix, please proceed."

"We are already there—as you'll see with your own eyes in a video and—"

Once again, the room erupted in shouted questions and exclamations.

"How can this possibly work?"

"It will take forever... eighteen years at least to grow and mature these... these people..."

"Okay, okay, I *will* answer that one," Alix interrupted. "We've genetically designed Morfphs to develop, grow, and mature at a very rapid rate. They complete gestation in three months and they grow and develop into maturity in five years, instead of the eighteen to twenty-seven years required by non-Morfphs or Freeborns. They become a fully functioning adult human Morfph at the end of that five-year period and are ready to Pair or bond with a Patron at that point. The choice to design Morfphs to develop rapidly *was* a business decision with the purpose to speeding up the profitability of the project."

As they shouted more questions, Alix raised both her hands, palms out, to silence them.

"I've talked quite enough. Seeing is believing. I've made a video that will make you believers. It ends with an initial meeting between a Patron and his Morfph—what we call the Pairing, or the bonding phase. You've never seen anything like this."

The video was a complete documentary of the creation of a Morfph, from the gene editing and implantation, to scenes of the raising of Morfphs, and ending, as Alix promised, with the Pairing of Alix and her Morfph. A technician had completely obscured Alix's identity in the video. It showed only the Morfph and its amazing transformation during the Pairing.

Many of the men audibly gasped. There was some grumbling over the Morfph's transformation into a man, which made Alix laugh and shake her head.

"Well, that is entirely up to the Patron and what they want. So, if any of you *do* become Patroni, be prepared to find out what your deepest yearnings really are." By the end, they were, as Alix predicted, all on the same page—more or less, anyway.

The rest of the Alpha Morfphs who were ready for Pairing soon would be. They would offer all the men in the room the opportunity to put in applications to Patron a Morfph if they so chose. And judging by the looks on their faces at the end of the meeting, many of them would. Alix would carefully consider all the applications alone. This thought really made her smile, a huge smile this time. *Why get mad when you can get everything*, she thought, relishing and basking in her power.

# CHAPTER 7

## *About Souls*

*"I believe the solution to a great many of our social ills will be these real human beings who don't need autonomy, who are infinitely easy to get along with, and who want only to please. And the name of that solution—the name of our saviors—is Morfphs."*

-Quote from presentation made by Alix Edison to Geneti-Search board regarding the impending launch of Morfph program

### *Alix*

Sitting alone at the bar, Alix swirled the remaining ice cubes and spent slice of lime at the bottom of her glass. She stared into it as if she could find the answer to some unfathomable mystery within it—or perhaps, as if they were tea leaves in which she could read her future. She had just finished her second gin and diet tonic and was mentally slowing down. Needing to unwind before she went home, she had stopped to get a drink in the lounge downstairs after the big meeting. *I seem to be drinking my dinner tonight,* she thought.

She reached for a happy-hour olive from the bar's bowl and mentally calculated its calories before popping it in her mouth. She'd been running on black coffee and sugarless breath mints since her breakfast of a three egg-white omelet. Balefully, she eyed the lime at the bottom of her glass once again. Well, at least she wouldn't be dying of scurvy soon.

However, she had a lot to digest. She was obsessively gnawing over the meeting that had just taken place upstairs. She knew in her bones that it had gone well. Very well. They were intrigued—practically salivating at the prospect of having their own Morfph—but trying hard to hide their avid personal interest and to stay totally professional. This project was extensive. Enormous. But if they could pull it off, take the risk, it could mean billions—maybe trillions of dollars.

And then there was Jason. *Bastard,* she thought as her jaw clenched painfully.

Alix knew a great deal about Jason via his old lab assistant, Nadia—the one he had eventually fired. He had no idea. Evidently, he had spilled his guts to her before he really put the screws to her—so to speak. He had eventually and inevitably threatened to fire her unless she had sex with him. And that's when she had come to Alix for help.

"Get used to it and deal with it yourself. I can't help you," Alix had told her.

Nadia had cried then. "I really need this job."

Put off and slightly disgusted, Alix had said, "I'm afraid I'm the wrong audience, Nadia. If you have sex with him, he'll tire of you soon enough. You might even get a promotion out of it."

Nadia had shuddered. "The bastard won't even agree to wear a condom," she said bitterly. "'Takes away from the pleasure,' he says. He *knows* if I get pregnant, that's it for me. I'll get fired and no one else will hire me. 'A woman's highest and primary purpose is to bear and care for her young,'" she said, mimicking the public service messages heard and seen everywhere now.

Alix had grimaced at that. And Nadia was also right about pregnancy. It would mean being let go and not being rehired... anywhere. Since abortion and then all female birth control had been made illegal, life was that much more precarious for women. *Lose-lose,* Alix had thought. She was too familiar with that particular choice. Nadia would be fired if she didn't have sex with Jason, and she would be fired if she did and got pregnant. Alix had seen the handwriting on the wall years ago. After she'd had her daughter, she got herself sterilized while it was still legal. Those tubes had been tied good and tight.

*But these young women need to toughen up,* Alix thought. *She* had. And really, why should she save Nadia? No one had ever saved her. She couldn't even remember the number of men she'd had to "do" on her way up. But she had been smart about it and she had kept score, too. That didn't even count the various "uncles" her mother had brought home when she was a kid. *Whatever doesn't kill you*... and all that B.S. Besides. If she had helped Nadia, they'd all be coming to her for favors. She frowned briefly at the memory.

She had, of course, not revealed everything at the meeting... not by a long shot. They knew very little about her Adam. That was her business; particularly the part about being his Patron and that theirs was the Pairing they had viewed on the video. And it had gone off without a hitch—perfectly. Even she was amazed at the process. She hadn't felt like this in years; well, really, ever. Adam was waiting for her at home right now. What was she doing here? she wondered. *Decompressing,* she answered herself. *Decompressing and thinking.*

The initial euphoria of success and power was wearing off a little. They'd gone for it. Now the real work would begin—and the gigantic risks.

Just as she was about to get up and go, she spotted Matthew. He had just walked in the door and was heading for her. She patted the stool on her right, inviting him to join her. He was the only one at the meeting who had seemed at all worried about the ethics of the whole thing. Well, she guessed, that was part of his job. But his concerns had not just been about the legality of it, but seemingly more about the right and wrong of it. His brow creased, and he wasn't smiling.

Since Matthew's wife, Lily, had died, he seemed to carry the weight of his grief on his stooped shoulders. He was a tall, lean man and fit-looking. He often came into the office after lunch, dripping sweat from his daily run. But his defeated posture irritated her, and she wanted to tell him, "Stand up straight. Just shake it off. It's time. Past time."

He sat down on the stool next to her.

"Let me buy you drink, Matt. What'll you have?" She started to call the bartender over, but stopped with his next words.

"Do Morfphs have souls, Alix?" he asked and looked her in the eyes.

"Geez, Matthew. You're not very good at small talk, are you?"

She caught the bartender's eye and tapped her empty glass with her long, varnished fingernail.

"Sounds like I'm going to need another of these," she said, ever so slightly slurring her words. "Uh oh. Thank god for drone taxis."

Matthew didn't laugh and wasn't deterred from his question.

"This whole thing troubles me, Alix. Really troubles me. Just because we can do it doesn't mean we should. What would we be messing with here? Can we even hope to understand the consequences of this? Do we have the right? '*Only wanting to please*'? Jesus. It's creepy. Like something out of a nightmare."

The bartender brought Alix her drink and she took a big swig. She shook her head and barely hid her impatience.

"Hmm. Okay. A lot there. Well, let's see. Back to the soul issue. If *anyone* does indeed have souls, then so do Morfphs."

"Then how can we sell them if they are just like us?"

"Wait a minute, big boy. I didn't say they were just like us. Oh, not at all. They differ from us in many crucial ways. Besides, we do not sell them, Matthew. We Pair them—bond them." She poked his chest. "And they are completely free to do as and what they choose."

"Well, if they are not sold, then what is this huge price to be 'Paired' with one?" He made air quotes around the word Paired, probably mimicking the gesture Alix had made at the meeting.

"We need compensation for the R and D, of course. And the raising of them, and their education... and all of it. It's all very expensive, as you can imagine. But they are *not* slaves. They have total freedom to do and come and go as they please."

"But they can only want what their Patron wants, isn't that right?" Matthew objected.

"Precisely!" she said, poking him again.

"Then that is not freedom. They have no choice. They have no free will." He took a breath, and said, "... and what about consent? I would think you, as a woman, would have concerns about sexual consent."

Alix shook her head slowly back and forth and said, "There is no issue of consent with Morfphs. Morfphs always freely give consent... to their Patron, that is."

"But the question is: *can* a Morfph give consent?" Matthew persisted. "If they are created genetically to always give it, then they are incapable of not giving it. If you are incapable of not giving consent, then that is *not* consent."

"Why are you nit-picking this issue, Matthew? I didn't take you for such a prude. Don't we all have the right to a satisfying sex life? And come on—regarding the whole free will thing—do any of us really have free will? Morfphs are as free as we are. As capable of satisfaction and happiness in life as we are—maybe more. We think we have free will in our choices—in what we choose—but do we, really? Why and how do we choose what we choose?"

They both sat rigid, not looking at each other.

"Maybe we're all puppets, but *we* just don't know it," Alix said, muttering darkly into her drink.

"What?" Matthew said sharply. "What did you say?"

"Just something I read somewhere. Maybe Morfphs are freer than *we* are. Puppets who *know* they are puppets. And not only that, Matt, Morfphs truly love their strings."

He shook his head impatiently.

"Morfphs are as free as any of us," Alix repeated. "And they are completely un-conflicted. Are you un-conflicted? Can't say I am."

Matthew just shook his head again, harder this time. The furrow between his eyes deepened into a crevasse.

"C'mon Matthew, give this a break. The history of humanity is particularly checkered when it comes to forcing *others* into doing our bidding. I mean, the *otherness* could be the color of skin," and here she waved her hand around his face, "or maybe religion, class, or... surprise, surprise... gender. Women... like all those kidnapped girls... have been coerced and forced into being virtual Morfphs in the service of men's libidos and whims for... well, forever. How is that ethical? Where was... where is... their free will in that? At least Morfphs *want to* Morfph, want—no, *need to*—please. You're concerned with free will? Free will is overrated... if it exists at all."

She took another drink. "Just think of all the ways people with power or just the most guns, have forced, paid, or coerced other people to fulfill their desires." She could see he was still unconvinced by her argument. Impatient and exasperated, Alix continued, now definitely slurring her words.

"My god, women have been bullied, shamed, and coerced to fit one mold or another—someone else's idea of what and who they should be—for... for... mill... millennia. Just think of foot-binding... or corsets or... genital mutilation or..."

Matthew cut her off mid-sentence.

"Alix, take a breath. I'm not disagreeing with any of that. And believe me, it isn't just women who are pressured to fit into someone else's mold of who they should be. But I have seen no bound feet or corsets around here. That's ancient history."

*Not so ancient history*, Alix thought, as the little scars behind her ears that marked her latest surgery seemed to tingle. But what she said out loud was, "Easy for you to say, Matthew. You obviously have never had to stuff yourself into a full length Spankx body smoother. Feels like a sausage in a too-small casing."

Matthew's only response was a glum stare.

Alix shrugged. "Okay, so I give up trying to make you laugh tonight. But really, Matthew, think about it. Wouldn't it be better if there were people who wouldn't suffer when other people's will is imposed on them? And who, in fact, have an infinite capacity to change everything about themselves and... and... who actually finds their *joy* in the pleasing?

"Wouldn't it be a better world with Morfphs? People who *want* the role the Patron has assigned them? No force. No coercion. No resentment. No cutting. No starving. No damage to them at all."

"Okay, okay, Alix, but..."

"And this time, women—that is, women with the money—" She laughed, aware her argument wasn't quite flawless on this point. "—will get to have it their way, *our way*, as well. It won't just be men who get to call all the shots, who get it all their way," she said, bitterness creeping into her voice.

"I think this would clearly come into the territory of two wrongs, Alix," said Matthew, unconvinced. "It's still wrong. They have no choice."

*Jesus, he just cannot get off this choice thing. This is really getting tedious.*

"What if the so-called Patroni don't even know what they want?" Matthew asked.

"The Morfph will know what the Patron wants, even if they don't," Alix said shortly.

"What if a Patron is conflicted, ambivalent? Wants two or more opposing, even opposite things?"

"I don't know. We don't have all the answers. I guess we'll find out."

"What if the Patron wants something that is painful or harms the Morfph?"

"Protections will be written into the contract, Matt. You'll help write those."

Matthew frowned harder. His normally pleasant face had turned into a mask of disapproval and anger.

"You're playing God, Alix. You're playing with real people's lives. As you said, these Morfphs are actual people. As are the Patroni, as you call them. They are not chess pieces on your board to play with and manipulate. This won't end well. This will end badly. Have you ever read *Frankenstein*?"

Alix stiffened. *Where in the hell did that come from?* She jerked her head to look directly into Matthew's face. Then it hit her. *I'm the Adam of your labors,* Adam had said... the very words the monster had said to Frankenstein. Alarmed and stung, her hurt quickly turned to anger.

"Yeah, Matthew, I've read *Frankenstein,* when I was about eight. What are you getting at?"

She, of course, knew exactly what he was implying. Matthew always was a pious son of a bitch. But he had hit a little too close to Alix's own doubts, which was the real spark for the sudden flash of fiery rage she felt. And when she got angry, she went for the jugular, went directly, unerringly for people's weaknesses. So that is what she then did, almost without thinking. And she knew very well about Matthew's weakness. He had made the foolish mistake of telling her.

But despite the rage, or maybe because of it, it had seemed to clear her mind nicely. Alix was still able to calculate rationally and plan. And her brain was spinning a plan now. *Multitasking—women are wonderful at it*, she thought, grimly amused. She had developed that particular skill a very long time ago. And she was single-mindedly determined to make this project—her baby—successful.

She had thought for quite a while that Matthew would be an excellent candidate for becoming a Patron. And ironically, it seemed he might be the last hold-out. She needed to sell him on it, but she also now wanted badly to cause him some pain for his judgmental, holier-than-thou stance. Maybe she could use his loneliness and grief, *his weakness*, to her advantage. *That's the place to slip in the thin edge of the wedge,* she thought.

"Think about it, Matthew. You could have her back," she said with a cunning look on her face. "You could have her back," she repeated. "You could see her again. Touch her. Be with her."

Matthew snapped his head around and his eyes drilled into her. "What did you say? What did you say, Alix?"

"You heard what I said," Alix said, the alcohol making her more reckless than usual. "Get Paired with a Morfph and you could end that tedious grief of yours right now. You could have her back in your bed in a matter of weeks."

At this, Matthew's face suffused with blood and both his hands convulsed into fists where they rested on the bar. His body was a ramrod, his posture no longer slumped.

Alix reflexively flinched away from him and put her hands out in front of herself in a gesture both placating and self-defensive.

"Shut up, Alix, just shut up! You're talking about Lily, aren't you? Christ. You'll stop at nothing to get your own way, won't you? It wouldn't be her. It would just be someone imitating her, trying to get it right," he retorted. "It wouldn't be her."

"Are you sure, Matthew? Are you so sure of that? It might as well be her. Believe me, you wouldn't be able to tell the difference."

"It wouldn't be her," he yelled loudly this time. Everyone in the bar stopped talking and looked at them. This was a Matthew she had never seen. He was always the epitome of benevolent politeness. She tingled with a pleasure tinged with lust.

Matthew got up abruptly, toppling the bar stool to the floor. After glaring mutely at Alix for a moment, he stalked, stiff-legged, out of the bar. But Alix was confident her worm had successfully dropped into his ear. If she knew anything, she knew how to exploit people's weaknesses. *Yeah,* she thought, *that ravenous little worm is already at work; munching and burrowing its way right into his brain.*

# CHAPTER 8

## *Matthew's decision*

*"We are born alone and die alone, and it terrifies us. And
the loneliness and separation continue to bedevil us in life—
especially at night as we lay in the dark with our racing
thoughts as cold company."*

-Anonymous

## Matthew

Leaving the bar, Matthew hurried to his car, taking the stairs two at time to the parking garage under the Geneti-Search building. Just a handful of years before, he would have been taking the high-speed train from the city and walking home from the station... to his beloved wife and to their beautiful old house.

But everything had changed. His wife was dead, his house sold, and the roaming bands of well-armed militias and burgeoning number of desperate and angry Unfortunates—the unemployed and unhoused—made the train less than safe.

He slammed the car door and banged the steering wheel over and over with the palms of both his hands. Finally spent, hands throbbing painfully, he stopped and lay his head down where he had been hitting. *That damned woman. What was I thinking, making friends with her? I should have listened to everyone else.*

"She's a snake," everyone had said. "Careful what you tell her. She'll use it against you first chance she gets... whenever it benefits her or, maybe, just when it suits her."

But he had thought he knew better. Being one of the few people with any pigment in his skin at Geneti-Search, he'd felt a certain kinship, a sympathy for her otherness.

"It's hard being a woman in this business," he'd said. "She's okay."

Surprising him, she had been the easiest to talk to of everyone at work after Lily had died, asking how he was and really listening with a seemingly genuine, but dispassionate sympathy that Matthew found soothing. *I guess she really was just storing information up to use against me, after all*, he thought.

He pushed the ignition button, and the car came to life. He set it at level zero—no automation. He wanted to drive, wanted complete control over the car tonight.

Matthew tried to push away what Alix had said, but he couldn't stop thinking about her words. The poison she had injected was doing its work. Her words kept repeating over and over in his head, "You could have Lily back. You could see her again. Touch her. Be with her."

*Talk to her... and have her talk to me.* There was so much he wanted to tell Lily, to pass by her. Nothing felt quite real without her.

*No, I won't. I will not. I can't.* His heart raced.

Driving through the city, his foot heavier on the gas pedal than necessary, he passed through the outer edges of a vast homeless camp, a squalid, crime-infested city within a city that went on as far as the eye could see. Hordes of ragged, dead-eyed men, women, children, babies, and even dogs and cats sat around or picked their way through the rigged-up tarps and tents, shopping carts, broken bicycles, and piles of trash and sodden clothes. It went on for miles and increased daily as more hopeless refugees from environmental degradation and unemployment arrived.

It used to be mostly men, often mentally ill and drug addicted, but not anymore. Matthew's eyes watered, and it was not only from the stench of human waste and garbage that emanated from the camps and wafted through his closed windows. *There, but for the grace of God...*

His mental war waged the entire thirty-minute drive home. The lights of the hemorrhaging city paradoxically looked beautiful in the distance as he crossed the large span of the Bay Bridge. He hardly noticed, after passing through the security gate with an eye scan, arriving home and pulling into the driveway. It was the same condo he had shared with Lily... after they had decided they needed to sell their lovingly restored house. The pain of the loss of Lily washed over him once again, like it was brand new—like it did every time he came home. He felt like he was drowning in it. *It's supposed to get better. Right? But when will that happen?*

He walked into the dark and empty condo and sat down heavily in the big red armchair, not bothering to turn on any lights. He closed his eyes, remembering when he and Lily had bought that chair together. At the time, it had stressed their budget, so the decision seemed important to them. He had wanted the brown leather, she the red. Now even the chair caused him pain.

He was so weary of the ever-present dull ache and loneliness. It only lifted when he was broadsided by the sharper waves of grief. It had been a kind of relief to get so angry at Alix at the bar. At least he felt alive. But now the adrenaline had worn off, replaced by a profound exhaustion. *I need a drink,* he thought. *Or six.*

Matthew turned on a video of himself and Lily together—a picnic next to a river somewhere. He put it on repeat so he could continue to hear her voice, and especially her laugh, as he fell asleep. He didn't make it to the bed that night. He rarely did. What was the point? She wasn't there.

He dreamed about Lily that night, as he did most nights. But the dreams were changing. In this one, he discovered she wasn't really dead, a fact that had been kept from him because she just didn't want to see him anymore. He woke most days to a fresh jolt of grief when he remembered his loss anew, but this dream put a slightly new twist on the daily morning rush of pain. Besides the lingering feelings from the dream, Alix's words from the night before kept going through his mind—just wouldn't go away. And like his longing and grief, he couldn't shake them.

### Alix

*So much drama,* Alix thought irritably.

After finishing her drink, she grabbed her phone off the bar and told it to fetch a drone taxi to pick her up. She then slipped limply off the bar stool onto her noodle legs. She had to get back home to *her* Morfph. Separation from their Patron was hard on Morfphs, and regardless of what people thought of her, she was not a complete sociopath. A Morfph's sense of self depended on continued close contact with their Patron. *And that would be me.*

She had left a video of herself and of them together repeating in a loop on the screen that filled an entire wall of her living room and he had her nightgown with her scent on it, as well. She knew that brief separations really posed little a problem; it was long separations that could cause intense stress and possibly even a shortening of lifespan. She was anxious to get home.

The armored drone taxi was waiting outside the building by the time she stepped into the bullet-proofed enclosure outside the door of the bar. The two doormen, armed with semi-automatic weapons, sprang forward and escorted her into the driverless vehicle. She was grateful for the help, as her adrenaline surge was rapidly wearing off and the alcohol was hitting her hard. She was suddenly exhausted.

"Take me home," she said to the taxi as she slumped into the seat and closed her eyes.

Immediately her head started spinning and her stomach lurched until she popped her eyes open again. After the spinning stopped, her mind went back to the first time she had seen her Morfph, back to their Pairing. As he had stepped forward, his somewhat blurry form seemed to solidify and transform into her desire, into *her* Adam. He'd had a smirk on his face and a swagger in his step. He actually looked a lot like Matthew with his dark-eyed, honey- skinned good looks, only bigger, more muscular, more dominant looking. And Matthew had never had that arrogant look on his face.

Interesting, she had thought, very interesting. That was obviously what she desired in her man. Shouldn't be surprised; the Morfph had become an amalgam of her exes. Later she would find he was as arrogant as he looked and as bitingly witty. Just what she always chose. Hence her "bad luck" in men.

At that point in the Pairing, she had been momentarily stunned. *Amazing*, she thought. That little girl had managed it somehow. She had turned into this beautiful, swaggering stud of a man.

The Morfph had taken her hands, pulled her to him, leaned in and smelled her neck. Then he pretended to bite her like a lion with its prey. He had even growled softly and laughed at her intake of breath.

"Mine," he said, and laughed.

After they completed the Pairing, he put his hand on her back and steered her out the door to her car.

"Throw me the keys," he said as he slipped into the driver's seat. "I'll drive."

He looked over at her, smiled his arrogant smile, and said, "Let's go home. You belong to me now."

After he sped up and shifted with a jerk, he said, "I'll have you tonight and every other night, if I say so." He was smiling when he said it, watching her reaction.

She had felt her face heat... *and other regions too*, she thought hotly. She looked over at him driving and knew it was true. And had smiled, too.

*Her Adam. Perfect.* She'd be home with her Adam soon. And even in her drunken state, she flushed with excitement.

### Matthew

Finally—inevitably—after many days of fighting it, the worm Alix had dropped into his brain bore in deeper and finished its work. *It wouldn't be her,* he told himself. But it would be the closest thing he could ever get to her. Ever. How could he turn that down? How?

"I'm sorry, Lily," he said out loud. He realized then he was actually going to do it; he was going to get a Morfph. "I'm so very sorry," he repeated to the air.

He knew very well that she would hate it, hate everything about it. *But you're not here, are you? You're not here.* Then—and he was ashamed to admit this to himself—he felt a surge of hot anger. But not at Alix this time—at Lily.

*You left me, Lily. You left me so alone.*

A month later, Matthew went to Alix's large, glossy office. The view was of the bay on two of its wall-to-floor windowed sides. As he sat in the chair in front of her glass desk, he could see her long legs crossed beneath it. She waited patiently for him to speak, looking as perfect and glossy as ever, but also, he thought briefly, as shatterable as her glass office. He promptly dismissed that thought as patently ridiculous.

"I'll do it, Alix. I'll become a Patron."

Alix smiled broadly, obviously pleased but unsurprised. To her credit, she didn't show any signs of gloating, either.

"Well, very good Matthew. Let's finish up that work on the final draft of the contract for Morfph Patroning then. As soon as it's completed and we get you thoroughly screened, you can sign, and we can Pair you and your Morfph. You won't regret it. I can promise you that."

It ended up taking two and a half more months to make it real.

"Marvels such as this are worth the wait," Alix had said.

# CHAPTER 9

## *The Unnaturalness of Monogamy*

*Sara*

"I feel like I'm trading up," Jack had said to Sara one night at the very beginning of *their* affair. Because that's how it had started twenty years before, as an affair. He had still been married to his first wife, Sally.

*Like I'm a better grade of used car,* she remembered thinking. She had called him on it, but with no real heat or rancor. He'd laughed, apparently finding it amusing—finding himself amusing. He had always prided himself on being outrageous—edgy and clever. Besides, it would have been obvious to him and anyone else paying attention that she was hooked and not going anywhere. She had still been flying high in that "chosen one" glow.

Inevitably, it had now become her turn. And just as Jack had alluded to that last evening before he walked out, he *had* told her very early in their relationship that he couldn't even imagine never having a sexual relationship with anyone but her for the rest of his life. And he had said it again. The second time was right before they had moved in together.

"Monogamy is completely unnatural," he had said. "Don't you think?"

Her mind had shrieked in fear, but out loud she stammered something stupid.

"Well, while I can intellectually understand what you are saying... I... I mean... emotionally I... um... the thought of it is... well, let's see... it's... a little difficult." *More like devastating,* she had thought, but hadn't said.

Another time, not long after that, he had said, "I enjoy moving from person to person in love relationships... giving them the special thing I offer them. Helping them reach their full potential, boosting their confidence and sense of well-being, then moving on to the next person who needs me."

They had been in bed together when he had busted out that particular line. Tears had sprung to her eyes, and she went silent. Jack was too busy preening over himself and his "oh-so-very giving nature" to notice.

But she had married him, anyway. Even then, it had been against her better judgement. Judgement, however, had had nothing to do with it.

Much later, not long before he left, he had said it again or something quite like it.

"Do you think you have a magic dick, Jack?" she'd snapped.

———————

So now, once again, Jack was trading up—bringing in the newer model. This one was, of course, another of his graduate students. Admittedly, Jack was still handsome, but not the young Wonder Boy anymore. And not nearly as handsome or youthful-looking as he imagined himself to be. He had lost his new-penny shine, she thought. Time to plug into a new, young energy source.

Sara had met this new one—Jazmin—a few times. What kind of name was Jazmin, anyway? Was she named after one of those old Disney Princesses? Or possibly a defunct birth control? And when had she become Jazz, for god's sake?

They had talked for quite a while at one of the many tedious department gatherings, and Sara had liked her—even told Jack so on the way home. He had said nothing in response. That alone should have tipped her off. Now Sara almost felt a little sorry for her, even as she reeled with hurt, humiliation, and betrayal. She couldn't really blame her—could she? Well, maybe a little. Maybe she could, a little.

Yeah, she definitely blamed that devious bitch. Tears stung her eyes again.

*Damn you, Jazz. Damn both of you.*

———————

Jack and Sara had first met when *she,* like Jazmin, had been a graduate student in Counseling Psychology. Sara had been twenty-five years old and had just been admitted into the program at the university where Jack taught. She was smart enough, but prone to a self-sabotaging anxiety that reared its head at the most inopportune times. She called her anxiety her 'Enoch'—a private joke she had with herself.

Enoch was a little demon in a short story by Robert Bloch. When she was a kid, she had found a forgotten, worn out paperback of horror stories while she was snooping around her two older brothers's room. She took it and read it secretly at night when she was supposed to be sleeping. Enoch was invisible and sat on his chosen victim's shoulder, continually whispering evil things in their ear. The story stuck with her. Like Enoch, her anxiety spoke into her ear and her brain. But instead of insisting she murder, the voice hissed panic and self-doubt. She joked about it, but often it was anything but funny.

The first time she saw Jack was at a "meet and greet" for graduate students and faculty at the beginning of her first fall term. She could not keep her eyes off him. She didn't know this yet, but he was a thirty-six-year-old Assistant Professor in Psychology, barely holding onto his Wunderkind status, at least in his own mind.

What she knew was that he was what her best friend's grandma would have called, "a man with too many choices." Meaning he was too handsome to be trusted. That had turned out to be pretty apt, she thought later. It was very unlikely that hers were the only female, and probably male eyes, too, focused on Jack that afternoon... and many other afternoons, as well.

As she surreptitiously watched him, he looked directly at her, and he winked. She sloshed wine over her hand as she almost dropped her glass. Sara felt her face flame red, smiled an embarrassed twist of a smile, and peeked down at her glass. She was standing alone and awkward on the edge of the room.

Since she was looking away from him after the wink, she didn't see at first that he was edging his way towards her, slowly crossing the room. Once she looked up, she saw he was making steady, if somewhat slow, progress in her direction. She still didn't imagine he was doing it purposely. He kept stopping to talk animatedly with people as he walked by, patting them on the back and smiling at what they said. Always the charming extrovert, he left people laughing in his wake.

But then there he was, standing right in front of her, smiling. His eyes were a piercing, startling blue, and she felt pinned, deer-in-the-headlights paralyzed by their intent gaze. She did not know at the time that he knew very well the effect of his baby blues. Later, she couldn't even remember what they had talked about. Probably nothing special—maybe about what classes she was taking.

"Oh, Abnormal Psych? You'll be taking that from me," he may have said.

He made her feel like she was the only person in the room. She realized later that that was one of the finely honed skills he had cultivated, and of which he was very aware and particularly proud. He made everyone feel special and heard as he listened closely to their words. After an initial panicky awkwardness, he made her feel comfortable... and fascinating. She had flushed even redder with pleasure at his unexpected, engrossed attention.

With that wink and smile, the obsession had taken firm root. She had no idea that he was married *and* had a little boy—an adorable tow-headed four-year-old named Seth. His wife and Seth were not there that day, and he never mentioned them. Even after she knew (someone else had pointedly told her), he did not talk about them at all.

By the time she found out, however, she was hopelessly infatuated with him and did not ask for details. She just didn't want to know. When she did finally ask about them, he was dismissive, especially about his wife... but also about Seth.

Months later, when she finally met his wife, Sally, she seemed mousey and a little dim. Sara, for the life of her, couldn't figure out how Sally and Jack had ever gotten together. They were so mismatched, she had thought—conveniently. Jack was affable and outgoing and laughed and joked with everyone. And he had a laser-sharp wit that made her laugh; made everyone laugh.

Much later, it occurred to Sara that Sally wasn't dim at all. More likely she was just depressed and feeling helpless and beaten down by Jack's treatment. Sara was not the first young female student he had made to feel so very special.

Sara had Jack for Abnormal Psych. She would linger after class to ask him questions along with rest of his harem. They dogged him like eager little puppies, wanting a pat on the head and a tummy rub. But she was the one he answered most carefully and completely. He would tell her that her questions were especially astute and intelligent.

"You have an especially deep grasp of the subject—much deeper than the other students," he had said to her after the other girls had given up and left.

And she ate it up. Every flattering word. He would often ask her to his office after class to continue the discussion. As they discussed her paper or psychological theory, he would stare into her eyes intently and with a clear, deep interest. He would sometimes lean toward her and touch her lightly on her arm or hand to make a point. All of it would make her light-headed with pleasure, and she would lose track of the conversation. It didn't seem to matter to him. After these meetings, she always felt giddy and couldn't stop smiling.

It, their affair, actually started later in the year—during the holiday party at the department head's house. She walked in alone. It was in a pretty 1930s bungalow, which was in an area called Riley's Addition. They built all the houses in the area about the same time in a very early planned community. This area was sought after for a good reason. She loved those charming old houses.

As usual, she felt slightly uncomfortable as her social anxiety kicked in. Large parties were especially troublesome. She greeted some friends but stayed to herself and scanned the room, looking for Jack. The room was dark, lit mostly by candles and little white Christmas lights. Her eyes slowly adjusted to the dimness.

Sara *did* know what was going on between Jack and her. She may have been a bit naïve and somewhat inexperienced, but she was not a total idiot. Sara went there hoping to talk to him and maybe something more she hadn't quite admitted or articulated to herself. By that time, she thought about him constantly and felt antsy and completely unable to focus on anything else.

When he walked into the room, she knew it immediately, even before she saw him. Something had changed in the air. As she stood there for several minutes, she continued to monitor where he was in the room. Every once in a while, she would look over and he would stare back at her. She'd smile and look down, though not really trying to be coy. What she was feeling was an attack of discomfort mixed with a giant flush of excitement at being caught. Just as at their first meeting, he finally threaded himself through the room to make his way over to her.

He smiled one of his already familiar, beguiling smiles, pointed at her empty hands and asked, "You have nothing to drink. Do you want something? "

"Sure," she said. "That would be great. I could use a glass of wine. This whole thing makes me a little anxious." She looked around and laughed nervously. But she felt much calmer with him beside her. He had that effect on her—even then.

He then took her hand and led her across the room. There was an immediate frisson of feeling. Her hand tingled at his touch. He led her into the darkened and empty pantry, allegedly to find a bottle of wine. He then turned to her and buried his face in her neck and took a deep, sighing breath, almost sounding like relief.

"You smell so good," he said. "And not of perfume, of you." He kissed her then—deeply and slowly. And then he did something totally unexpected—to her, anyway. He reached down and unrepentantly pinched her nipple lightly through her thin sweater.

His smile had changed; not so much lecher as imp. He seemed both proud of his outrageous behavior and confident she wouldn't mind or seriously protest. She was slightly alarmed, certainly surprised, but she was also vibrating with excitement and her knees went weak under her. Desire shot through her like an electric charge. She had certainly never felt like that, and it wasn't she who pulled away. He was the first to separate. They just looked at each other and both grinned. She leaned forward again and put her mouth to his ear.

"We really need to be careful," she breathed into his ear, but feeling reckless and wild.

He laughed at that outright, a guffaw really. "Yeah, we're being really careful."

When they walked out of the little room, she was flustered and felt flushed. They hadn't even gotten the bottle of wine. No one seemed to notice, but in retrospect that seemed unlikely.

It progressed rapidly from there. She still couldn't believe that he had chosen *her*. They started sneaking out together during the day to hotel rooms. There was a Vacation Inn very near campus, and they spent long afternoons in bed, naked and wrapped around each other.

"Like hot ham and cheese," he said, laughing.

After making love, they talked and laughed, as they lay pressed together, her head in the hollow between his neck and shoulder, and her leg thrown up on his thigh. They would eat, spilling crumbs on the bed and all over his chest, which they used as a table, and then make love again. She was giddy with love. Looking back, she wondered how he had gotten away for so many hours. She certainly hadn't asked. Her grades suffered some, but she pulled it off without getting kicked out of the program. Sometimes he'd read to her, and she'd doze off feeling warm and safe. It was lovely. She was totally infatuated, over her head. Weekends were torture for her, days only to be endured until she could see him again.

But along with these memories there were others; less happy ones that left her feeling uneasy. She remembered once sitting with several of her graduate school friends. They had all happily stuffed themselves into one of the coveted horseshoe-shaped, wrap-around booths in the university student union café. Someone had bought a dozen donuts, and they were all eating them. They were laughing hard at something and then laughing more as donut crumbs sprayed out their mouths and noses. She couldn't remember now what they were laughing about, she just remembered the laughing and the fun they were having... until Jack had walked up to the table. He saw what they were eating and said, also laughing, but with an edge of derision in his voice.

"Better take it easy on those donuts, girls. You wouldn't want those muffin-tops to get any bigger, would you?" He was looking directly, pointedly, at Sara as he spoke. Her friends sat frozen and one of them gasped at the rudeness. Sara's face blazed as she put down her half-eaten donut and looked down at the table. She couldn't look her friends in the eye; it was so obviously directed at her. That was the day she started dieting. And she hadn't stopped since. She'd hardly eaten anything for a month and quickly lost fifteen pounds. Jack was pleased and praised her to the skies.

She hated obsessing over each bite of food she took, which was what she needed to do to maintain her new leanness. But she did it because Jack liked women thin and young. And young, thin women were always available to him, always flirting, which had kept her jealous and off balance from the beginning.

From this, she learned she was fundamentally flawed and must work at being, looking, and acting just as he wanted or she would lose his love. Sometimes she felt like one of the ugly stepsisters, trying desperately to fit her grossly oversized foot into a shoe that was just too small. But so much was good between them, she had reasoned, that it seemed worth it—worth anything—as she counted every calorie and second-guessed every bite of food she took. What she hadn't known then, but would soon come to understand, was that Jack's comment about her food choices was just the beginning of his "helpful" guidance.

# CHAPTER 10

## *Perfect Apple... Except Those Pesky Worms*

*Sara*

Sara sat in her home office, catching up on paperwork and typing notes on her client, Alix Edison, on her laptop. She usually took brief, scribbled notes with pen and paper during sessions to avoid missing any of her client's subtle body language or facial expressions. The rest of the house was empty and dark. There was no jazz playing from the speakers that Jack had installed in all the rooms of the house. And there was no clatter of dishes as he prepared one of his gourmet meals. All those sounds were now being heard by Jazmin at the house she and Jack shared.

Paperwork was not Sara's favorite activity, so she often put it off. But it did consolidate her thoughts about her clients and helped her decide where therapy might need to go. Tomorrow was another session with Alix, but today she was having a hard time focusing. Her own problems kept sneaking, unwanted, into her thoughts.

Staring at the screen, she opened her eyes wide, pushed her hair behind her ears, and determinedly started typing.

**Counseling Notes on Alix Edison, Sept 12, 20\*\***

<u>Client:</u> Alix Edison, Caucasian, cis-gender female, heterosexual, age 54.

<u>Profession:</u> Genetic engineer

<u>Diagnosis:</u> Narcissism with traits of Borderline Personality Disorder (BPD)

Relationship problems consistent with diagnosis.

*Parents deceased. Won't discuss mother other than to say she was verbally abusive and critical.*

*Problematic relationships with various partners including her first ex-husband (father of her daughter) and with her only child, a recently estranged daughter, Clare, age 21.*

<u>*Relationship status:*</u> *Divorced x3, currently single, recent break-up with live-in boyfriend*

Sara's fingers paused on the keyboard. She could readily imagine what another therapist might write about her and Jack's relationship and history... and what it would look like on the computer screen, in glaring black and white. Not good.

Jack had discarded his first family to be with her, and he had done it both efficiently and easily. He dispensed not only with his wife, Sally but also with his young son, Seth. Seth had been only five years old; a very cute little boy with a mop of white blond hair and his father's startling blue eyes. Jack and Sara gave up trying to hide their relationship and moved into a rented old house near to the University. No one at the University was really surprised. Their relationship was an open secret by then. Some of Jack's friends wondered, however, "Why this one?" There had been so many others before her. But everyone, even if they disapproved, liked Jack... and her, too, Sara thought. Jack had always been popular, even as friends and acquaintances would shake their heads at his behavior.

Sara had been ecstatic and couldn't believe her amazing good fortune. They married two years to the day after they had first met. A year later, after she finished her PhD, Sara put up her "shingle" and went into private practice. They then bought their own house. It was in the same old planned community and very near the house where they had first kissed. It was the house they still owned and, until he left, had lived in together.

Shaking her head, she went back to Alix's notes.

*Impressions of Dr. Edison:*

1. *Brilliant, often charming, even disarming. Can be scathingly sharp-tongued, and bitingly funny.*

2. *At times exhibits extreme anger and resentment.*

3. *Negative affect especially elicited when sense of self and strong ego defenses are threatened.*

4. *Very attractive and much younger in appearance than her chronological age. Addicted to plastic surgery. Has had multiple procedures.*

5. *Probable Anorexia Nervosa, but she will not discuss. Admits to "disciplined diet, and fitness routine."*

Sara inwardly winced as she typed these assessments. Did she have any right to judge Alix? Throughout their years together, Jack had expected her to stay greyhound lean, and she had. This was difficult for her, as her body naturally verged to fuller curves. But Jack gladly "helped" by carefully monitoring her body and her eating.

Somewhere during those years, she came to think of her own body as her nemesis, a foe she must dominate. She wore herself out running and was often hungry. She thought about food constantly—when she was going to eat next, what she shouldn't have eaten, how many calories she had already consumed that day, and how many she had left. But pleasing Jack was a priority... for both of them. Though it wasn't only her butt and abs that were whittled down with her hard-fought leanness, it was also her breasts... and, of course, Jack preferred those big. So, not long after he started making fun of her "boy" chest, she made an appointment. Her new breasts were a full C-cup, just as Jack requested.

Their friends often referred to them as the "perfect couple." When she heard those words uttered later, it made the hair on the back of her neck stand up. They were so often portents of relationship doom. It's what people said about a couple five minutes before they announce they are breaking up.

But *Sara* had also thought of her life with Jack as perfect. A perfect shiny red apple. But even back then, she wouldn't have denied that. In the shiny apple, there may have lived a worm—one that Sara couldn't entirely ignore. She had seen it as her fault because the worm was of her making... at least Jack would have said so. It was, after all, only she who longed—desperately—for a baby.

She had gone off the Pill and started trying to get pregnant when she was thirty-one. At that point, they had been married for four years. Jack was not thrilled about the idea or the reality of a baby, but she was happy and surprised that he didn't insist she use birth control. When she didn't conceive, he was, however, vehemently opposed to any sort of fertility intervention. She lobbied hard, but he wouldn't budge.

Sara concluded it was she who couldn't get pregnant and resigned herself to it. There were, as Jack also pointed out, definite perks to being childless. And she was thrilled with Jack. Happy with their otherwise charmed life. Happy with their friends. Happy with their life together. Some things just weren't meant to be.

"It's better this way, Sara," he had said. "Kids ruin everything. They suck up all the oxygen. Everything changes after a baby. You'd be completely focused on it, and I want you focused on me." He'd laughed like it was a joke, but it wasn't.

Also, they had nephews and nieces she loved to spoil, and then there were her friend Sam's two little girls whom she adored and who adored her back. Yes, life had seemed good.

Jack had also warned her that a baby would be completely her deal. And she believed him, as he rarely saw his son, Seth. He had been such a sweet little guy when they first married. He later become an angry young man who loathed Jack. One could hardly blame him. He was—what now? Twenty-two? Twenty-three?

Seth had had some scrapes with the law and barely made it through high school, and not because he wasn't capable. He was a bright boy. Sara still felt guilty about Seth, but she would have been very happy to welcome him into their home in any way they could have worked it out. It was Jack who had no interest. And he resented the child support he paid. Sally was odd, but she had been a good mother—still was. She and Seth were close. Seth just seemed to be adrift... sad and angry.

Sara had never re-started birth control pills after that. What was the point? Jack obviously hadn't been at fault, as he reminded her—often. He had fathered Seth with Sally, after all. And female birth control eventually became illegal.

*Focus,* she thought angrily, as she wiped tears from her eyes. She again started writing her notes on Alix.

### Notes:

1. History of child and adolescent sexual abuse alluded to, but no details yet. All attempts to explore it have been brushed off. Alix abruptly changes the subject when the topic is broached. Sexual harassment and coercion in the workplace have also been reported but dismissed as unimportant.

2. Morbid fear of abandonment, which has become self-fulfilling prophecy, as she drives people away with abusive treatment and neediness. Very lonely individual. Describes fits of rage that "other people cause". Has been to four other therapists. Tells this therapist she feels empty inside. Verbalizes that all her pain is various other's fault.

3. Floundering in her personal life, but very successful and driven at work.

4. *Often refers to a personal history of "morphing" to please others, i.e. men. Morphing, in her parlance, evidently means changing how she acts, what she looks like and who and what she is, to please men. Some confusion on this therapist's part, as she also has let slip that she calls her "top secret" genetic engineering project at work "the Morph project."*

5. *Proclaims she is done "morphing" herself for others and that now she has someone who will change to her desires. No specifics on the new person in her life. This therapist fears new relationship is unlikely to be successful or long term. Client has so far only been attracted to narcissistic bullies. She will likely perceive an individual who changes according to her desires as weak and boring.*

Once more, her dispassionate notes—her judgements—of Alix and her relationships hit a nerve... or maybe two. Alix's idea of morphing to please another made one direct hit but, as had become quite clear after Jack left, there had been one other rather big fat, juicy worm deeply imbedded in their shiny apple of a marriage. And that worm Sara had tried very hard to ignore. She'd metaphorically closed her eyes and pretended with all her well-developed skills of denial that it wasn't there.

Jack still had his following of forever-young, mostly female, adoring students, and he loved it—thrived on it. Sara called them his cupcakes. Vampire-like, he seemed to feed off their youth and their adulation. When she kidded him about it, sometimes good-naturedly, sometimes not, he said they kept him edgy, which was very important to Jack.

So, deep down, even back then, Sara had her suspicions about Jack's relationships. And considering their shared history and his warnings about his aversion to monogamy, it wasn't much of a stretch. Sometimes he would get very happy, seemingly inexplicably. She had stopped asking about these giddy moods because he became evasive and, truthfully, she really didn't want to know. Just the thought of it plunged her into a swirl of despair.

Jack had told her once that he had no interest in talking to a woman unless he wanted to sleep with her. Actually, what he had said was, "unless I'd like to fuck her." Not that he fucked every woman he talked to, he assured her—as if that made the comment any less disturbing.

With a deep sigh, Sara ended the report:

6. *Every time Alix leaves this therapist's office, she says she is not coming back. So far, she has returned weekly since starting therapy.*

**Sara Wilde, PhD**

**Clinical Psychologist**

With that, she closed her computer with a firm snap.

# CHAPTER 11

## *Another Session*

*Alix*

**Entry in the personal journal of Alix Edison:**

**September 12, 20\*\***

I read somewhere that loneliness and longing do not mean you have failed, it simply means you are alive.

What would happen to our humanity if we were to never again feel loneliness or longing? What if my Morfphs could wipe loneliness and longing from the human race?

Would the place in our souls where it had lived fill with something else? Something darker? Would we get so bored, so restless, with our happiness... our satisfaction... we would sabotage ourselves in order to feel that ache again? To feel the intensity again? To feel painfully alive again?

Well, I say let's find out.

To hell with loneliness and longing. To hell with self-loathing and despair, too.

They've never done anything for me.

---

The next day, Alix sat in one of the lavender recliners in her therapist's office and stared out the window, studiously avoiding looking at the other woman who was sitting across from her in the matching chair. Sara Wilde *was*, however, intently studying Alix. They'd been there half-an-hour already, but they had discussed little.

"I suppose I'm a shit mother," Alix finally blurted out. "But my mother was no prize either, let me tell you."

"Okay, so, two topics there... What do you want to talk about now, Alix? Your daughter or your mother?"

Alix thought about her mother and scowled. Unbidden, a memory floated up to her consciousness.

*Twelve-years-old, standing in Mother's bedroom in front of a big full-length mirror. She is anxious.*

*"Okay, Alix dear," her mother says. "Take off all your clothes, please. NO, dear. ALL of them." Impatient, exasperated. "Good. Now stand right in front of the mirror. We really need to look at your body from top to bottom... see what needs work." Mother laughs.*

*She obediently stands and looks. Alix wraps her arms protectively around her chest. She sees her soft, round adolescent belly, and long skinny legs below. Shivering, mortified, ashamed.*

*"Alix, put your arms at your sides." Mother's voice cracks like a whip, making her jump. She jerks her arms down.*

*"Oh, dear," Mother says, sadly shaking her head and pursing her shiny crimson lips. "It's even worse than I thought."*

*Mother pokes Alix's exposed belly with the long, shellacked nail of her index finger. She sees the half-moon indentation Mother's nail has made on her tender skin.*

*"Don't cry, dear," Mother snaps, voice jagged ice. "It's for your own good. God knows I don't enjoy this." Mother waves her hand in a circle, indicating Alix's body, face distorted with disgust.*

*"Just imagine how humiliating it is to for me to have such a fat little girl."*

That was when Mother had started calling her Piglet, and also when she started locking up all the food in the cupboards and refrigerator. And also a few months before her step-father had started visiting her room at night.

Alix looked up to the corner of Sara's office ceiling, squeezed her eyes shut, and let out a little puff of breath. Memory banished, she lowered her eyes, looked directly at Sara, and answered her question.

"My daughter. Let's talk about my daughter. To hell with Mother. I'm done with her. The bitch is dead. Let's keep her that way."

Sara gave a small shrug.

"I'm not sure we should finish with her yet, but we can definitely leave it for another time, if you prefer. How *is* your daughter, Alix?"

"I don't know. She won't talk to me anymore," Alix said, her tone flat and expressionless.

"So, you haven't talked to her since that day you called me?"

A couple of weeks before, Alix had called Sara on her personal cell. Alix knew it was breaking "therapist boundaries," but she paid her good money to be accessible She had a guy that could find out anything about people and Sara's personal cell number had been easy. Besides, Alix had been desperate.

Sara had answered the phone immediately, sounding anxious, maybe even a little frantic. As soon as Alix had identified herself, Sara didn't even reprimand her about calling. She simply seemed to click into her therapist mode. She listened and made appropriate, soothing responses. But, thinking back, Alix realized Sara had been off; distracted and vague. At the time, Alix hadn't wondered about it. She had more pressing things on her mind. In fact, she had been totally beside herself after the fight she'd had with her daughter.

"No. That was the last time." She sighed, bored with the question. Alix looked more closely at Sara.

*She looks terrible. No makeup, pale, dark circles under her eyes. Has she even brushed her hair?* Ah hah. *No ring on her finger anymore. Just an indentation.*

"But hey, Doc, how's it going with you? I notice you're not wearing your wedding ring."

Sara flinched, curled her hand into a loose fist, and pulled it close to her body. She answered with ice in her voice.

"As you've reminded me before, we're here to talk about you, not me."

"Okay, okay." Alix laughed.

"Are you ready to talk about it?"

"About what? I've lost track."

"We were talking about your daughter."

"Oh yeah. Sure, why not? It doesn't really matter. I'm fine now."

"Okay, good. I think it might be helpful, anyway. I know it quite upset you and I know she said she didn't want to see you anymore. Will you tell me more about what happened that day?"

Alix sighed again.

"She said I'm an emotional vampire. She, and I quote her, 'won't be pulled into the void of neediness, despair and rage that is you.' Referring to me, of course.

"Oh, and she also called me 'an emotional black hole,' pulling everybody within reach 'into your swirling despair—into the howling void that is your inner life.'

"She said I was sucking out her soul and her joy. So melodramatic, my daughter. Then, she called me her personal dementor.

"I said, 'Make up your mind, Clare. Am I an emotional black hole, an emotional vampire, or a dementor?' Whatever the hell that is. Then, I called it all moronic psycho-babble."

"And?" Sara prompted.

"And then she said something like, 'It doesn't matter, Mother. They all suck. They all suck a fat one. Just like you.'"

"That must have been very hurtful. I'm sorry, Alix."

"Not really. I've heard it all before. But there's more. I threatened to cut her off financially. I had been paying for her college."

"How did that go?"

"She said she didn't want my money. She would never take my money again. It came at too high a price. She wanted nothing from me.

'Daddy will help me with school.'" Alix mimicked her daughter's voice.

"She's always called her father Daddy... called me Mother," Alix said disgustedly. "Said she wasn't a child anymore. Wasn't at my mercy. No more insults, no more name calling, no more belittling. Said she had finished with me this time... and evidently, she was... she is.

"Why would she treat me like this?" Alix's eyes drilled into Sara's, as if challenging her to come up with a good reason. "I always praised her to the skies. Told her she was special... all the time. My mother never said one nice thing to me or about me... ever. Well, once she said I was lucky to have her beautiful blonde hair. I don't think that should count. Do you?"

Alix crossed her legs, then her arms.

"Are you sure I can't smoke a cigarette?" she asked.

"Yes, Alix, still sure. But you say you don't understand how she could treat you like this. Would you like to explore that a bit?"

"I suppose." She looked at Sara, eyes slitted, wary.

"Tell me about the names and the belittling your daughter referred to..."

"She'd always make me so angry... *tried* to make me angry... always disagreeing and arguing. Maybe I did say some things..." Alix looked at the ceiling.

"And then there were the boys... I mean, she would bring them over after dates... take them downstairs... to her bedroom. I know what they were doing down there. I'm not stupid."

"When was that? She went to live with her father in high school, didn't she?"

"It was after that. When she went away to college, she would sometimes stay with me during her vacations. Said she wanted to see if we could mend our relationship or something. It didn't go well. She was just as hard to get along with as ever. Blamed me for everything."

"So, during college? What names was she referring to?"

"I don't even remember. Why do you keep harping on that?" Alix demanded. "Why is it so important? It was for her own good." Alix stopped talking, looking slightly discomfited. She vaguely remembered shouting slut and whore at her daughter. *But she had been acting like one, hadn't she?*

*A*nother memory of her mother surged forth.

*"You just keep getting fatter, Piglet. Maybe you've graduated to Sow, darling."* Her mother slapped Alix's ass—hard.

*"No man will ever want you, you know."*

All for her *own good.*

But her mother surely knew that at least one man had wanted her. Her stepfather's night-time visits to Alix had continued until she left home.

"Sometimes, just for fun," Alix finally said, "I try to picture what anger looks like. Sometimes I see it as an iridescent green and black, like the oily sheen of anti-freeze spilled onto dirty roads. Other times it looks like vomit when you've emptied your guts and there's only bile left to spew."

Alix stood abruptly, grabbed her purse, and headed for the door. Dr. Wilde was really getting irritating—just like all the rest. Might be time to move on.

"This is a waste of my time," she said. "You better up your game, Doc. There are a lot of therapists out there. Oh, and by the way, I tried that journaling thing. It's a no go. I don't have time for that shit. Besides, I'm writing a whole different kind of journal.... a handbook or maybe a compendium.... hmm. Anyway, maybe you'll read it someday. It should be pretty interesting."

# CHAPTER 12

## *Matthew's Pairing*

*"And the two shall become one flesh."*

*Mark 10:8*

### *Matthew*

Before Matthew had made the startling decision to Patron a Morfph himself, the ethics and morality of the Morfph Program was, in his mind, an insurmountable problem. Now everything had seemed to change almost overnight—simultaneous with his decision to get a Morfph. He had now made it his personal mission to make it all work. He was totally in. But the moral precariousness of this shift in his thinking and in his goals in no way eluded him. He had simply chosen not to think about it.

It pleased his parents when he had decided to become a lawyer after he had graduated from the state university in Santa Marina. He had met his wife, Lily, while he was there and she had moved with him so he could attend law school in another part of the state. She quickly enrolled in graduate school on the same campus and then got a job there after she graduated. And until she got cancer and died, their life had gone mostly according to plan. Even after things had changed so dramatically in the country, after the terrible fires and the daily threat of violence had become a reality of life, they had been happy... happy together.

Lily had taught Gender Studies... when it was still being taught. They lived in a rambling, three-story, old house within walking distance of the school. Matthew had taken the RTT, the rapid transit train, into the city every day to work at Geneti-Search. That was when it was still safe to take public transport, when the roaming bands of thugs, militia, and violence were still infrequent. Matthew and Lily had eventually and reluctantly left their beautiful old house and moved into a guarded and gated community about four years before she had died.

Lily had been everything to Matthew, and he had loved her beyond reason. She'd had red-gold hair that shone a bright strawberry in the sun and porcelain skin with very few freckles, except a sprinkling on her shoulders that increased with summer and sleeveless shirts. She hated being called a "ginger," but that's what she was. Her eyes were a startling clear aqua. He found her pale, smooth skin and bright hair, exotic. She laughed at that.

"Gingers are *not* exotic. At least I'm a day walker," she had said emphatically.

He had laughed, wrapped his arms around her, and squeezed her round bottom affectionately.

"I'll be the judge of that, little lady."

"Little lady! Oh my god." But then she laughed too, grabbing his ass in return.

———————————

On Halloween day, two months and sixteen days after Matthew had told Alix he would take a Morfph, he sat in his condo, staring into space, his coffee undrunk and cooling in the ceramic cup on the table in front of him. It had been another dream-filled night, this time with a disappointed Lily playing a prominent role. The enormity of what he was doing this morning hit him again… hard.

Today was the day. He would get his Morfph and bring her home to live and sleep in the home he had shared with Lily. He already thought of his Morfph as a *she*, even though he knew that although all Morfphs started out life as sterile females, after Pairing a Morfph's gender and sexuality were totally fluid and based entirely on the Patron's desires.

They would, however, remain sterile, regardless of their Patron's preference. Geneti-Search certainly didn't want Morfphs reproducing. No way of knowing how that would go, not to mention the possibility of cutting into future profits.

After Matthew committed to Pairing with a Morfph, he had signed the contract he himself had written with Alix's help. One stipulation was that he must provide "proper care and succor" to his Morfph. Geneti-Search provided detailed instructions, especially for the emotional care of his Morfph, and he had undergone several interviews to assure his clear understanding of a Morfph's unique needs.

So, he had carefully prepared a room for her—the spare bedroom. She would also have her own bathroom right next door to her bedroom. He hadn't really changed much of the décor of either of the rooms, but had supplied them with what he thought she would need. That included the essentials: toothbrush, toothpaste, hairbrush, the lilac soap that Lily had loved, shampoo and conditioner... and all Lily's clothes.

As he neatly folded the clothes and before putting them in the dresser drawers of the Morfph's room, he pressed them to his nose. Lily's scent still clung to them. He really had very little idea what belongings the Morfph would come with and what she would need or want. That part hadn't been outlined in the contract. After he found out who she turned out to be, they would go shopping.

In the months and weeks before this day, he had cycled through multiple emotional states, and his mind was still at war with itself. It had cycled from guilt and shame, to anxiety, fear and doubt, and finally to a heady excitement and anticipation. But he couldn't completely shake the uncomfortable knowledge coiled in the back of his mind that this decision might be a stunning betrayal of Lily and everything their relationship had been. What he had done would certainly have horrified Lily.

Lily had been a beautiful and amazing force to be reckoned with—lush of body and warm of heart but also fiercely independent and sharply intelligent, with a clear vision of who she was and what she believed in. They had both thrived on the intellectual give and take of their relationship and she had been the very of antithesis of a Morfph. She had never molded herself to fit his ideas of who she should be, and she had never held back her feelings, opinions, or her views. He had depended on that.

Her love for him had been fierce, too. Fiercer, even, than her passionate opinions and clearly defined sense of justice that was based on kindness and compassion. Her red-headed temper flared quickly, but it was usually a brief storm that blew through quickly and replaced with her usual warm-hearted nature. His grief hadn't lessened in the months since he had decided to Pair with his Morfph. It was always lurking, and could still knock him down in sharp waves of pain.

His decision to get a Morfph continued to surprise him. It had come from some place in his gut, but it hadn't taken long for his head to justify the decision his gut had made for him. He told himself over and over, until it became a mantra, that the Morfph would not be Lily. *Not at all. She will be a completely unique person.* He felt clear about that. He told himself, in no uncertain terms, that he didn't even want it to be Lily. So, if he didn't want it to be Lily, it wouldn't be. Simple as that. He didn't want an impostor Lily—a counterfeit. He had loved the real Lily and had loved that she had never compromised herself to please him. So, really, getting a Morfph was not a betrayal at all. Lily had even said before she died to find someone else to love. Although she could never have imagined this...

So, he was bonding—*or was it Pairing?*—with an "Alpha" Morfph, a literal human test model, in about four hours, at 9:00 am. For Matthew, they waived the enormous fee that the later wealthy Patroni would pay, as this was a trial run to test for any problems that may be lurking. But Alix assured him over and over that the process was working perfectly. He was pretty sure she had gone through the process and had her own Morfph, but she hadn't told him that outright.

---

Matthew arrived at the Geneti-Search building at the appointed time of 0900 and took the elevator to the top-most floor, where he had never been before. When he stepped into the hall, he jolted out of his haze and looked around. This floor was nothing like the rest of the white-walled, sterile-looking Geneti-Search building. The hall was lit softly with elegant wall sconces and lined with large, abstract oil paintings. His feet trod quietly on thick Persian rugs woven in beautiful, soft pastels. He entered a large, airy room—The Pairing Room—which was also expensively decorated in understated, muted colors. Again, the large carpets were thick Persians.

He sank into one of the plush chairs, but immediately shifted forward to the edge of the seat. His legs jiggled convulsively up and down, up and down, in a rapid, agitated rhythm. This room was lit softly, this time with the light of at least two dozen flickering candles lining the edges of the room and tucked into many nooks lining the walls. They must have been those battery-operated candles as he saw no smoke in the room–but it smelled delicately of vanilla. Everything about the room was soft; soft carpeting, soft colors, soft furniture and soft music playing—maybe some kind of South American flute? He knew it was all meant to be relaxing and soothing, but he was well beyond any music's ability to calm him. His entire body vibrated with nerves. He clamped his sweaty hands onto his knees to stop the shaking.

He jumped when a door in the wall he hadn't noticed before opened up and two attendants, one a youngish woman and the other a mild-looking, middle-aged man, walked in. They gently and solicitously led a shimmering, white-clad figure into the room. All the clothes the figure wore were lustrous, white, silky, and loose-fitting. They comprised a pair of wide-legged flowing pants and an oversized sleeveless tee-shirt. There was also a silky veil hanging softly over her? (his?) upper face with gauzy see-through netting over the eyes. Matthew looked at the attendants questioningly. *Caretakers*, Matthew thought. *These must be her Caretakers.*

"The veil protects from first eye contact with anyone but you. At this point in their development and preparation, they will bond with the first person with whom they have prolonged eye contact," the male Caretaker explained softly.

The attendants wordlessly indicated that Matthew walk towards them. The female attendant then leaned forward and removed the veil and stepped quickly back, being careful to remain totally out of sight of the white-clad figure—his soon-to-be Morfph.

Mesmerized, Matthew walked even closer as the attendants motioned him forward. As he got nearer, he rubbed his eyes. In the candlelight the Morfph's skin glimmered and glowed so he couldn't really focus on her, almost as if the light had gotten into his eyes and was blinding him. He couldn't tell what she looked like, not even a shape or size. Even though from the beginning he had thought of his Morfph as a "she," at this point the figure standing in front of him really seemed quite genderless.

He took her extended hands into his as she looked deeply into his widened eyes for several seconds. Then she unexpectedly put her hands on his shoulders and nuzzled her nose into the side of his neck. She took a long slow breath in through her nose, breathing deeply, as if savoring his personal scent. She sighed a deep, gusty breath, took a step back, and languorously gazed into his eyes again, appearing almost drugged this time. The Morfph slowly pulled what looked like earbuds from her ears. The female Caretaker stepped forward, still being careful to stay out of the Morfph's sight, took the earbuds, then immediately drew back again.

Matthew's vision had cleared, and he could finally see her, really see her. His Morfph had now clearly become a "she." And as he continued to look deeply into her eyes, they became the clear blue-green of his wife's. Her body had also formed into his wife's figure. Shoulder length, red-gold hair shone vividly against her white shirt.

He realized, in amazement, that in every way he could discern, this *was* his dead wife standing there, newly hatched—resurrected—and very much alive. Her skin was smooth and pale, and her bright hair gleamed in the light—the same coloring he had found so exotic when he'd met her so many years before. The Morfph still seemed to emit a slight glow, but not nearly as blindingly as before. He had been told all Morfphs glimmer, and she did have a slight iridescent glow that was hard to describe.

Matthew stood there with both her hands in his, amazed, stunned. He felt tears form in his eyes and an intense release from the deep grief he had been carrying with him since his wife had died. He also felt like laughing with a giddy joy. But he neither cried nor laughed. He, instead, just stood there, unmoving, almost paralyzed.

She continued to stare into his eyes, looking quite solemn, until finally a slow smile spread across her face. It was, of course, his wife's smile. "Hello," she breathed in his wife's voice. "It's a pleasure to meet you, a real pleasure."

### *Matthew's Morfph*

*Inside the Morfph's body, imbedded into her very genes, the correct hormones and pheromones surged, and as a baby bonds with her mother and a lover bonds with his beloved, the Morfph bonded with Matthew. And so, eyes gazing into eyes, skin to skin, and pulse to pulse, they fell into the ecstasy of love... as hormones cascaded, nerve endings sparked, and their hearts beat as one in a rhythm of the blood. And in all things, Morfphs react rapidly and intensely. They formed the strongest of bonds, and the Morfph became Matthew's—body and soul.*

### Matthew

As he left with his Morfph, after the required exit interview that outlined his obligations, Matthew held her hand protectively in his. Her two Caretakers came and said goodbye. They wiped their eyes and kissed the Morfph on both her cheeks and hugged her for a long time. They had essentially been her parents for the five years since she had been born and had been with her every day of her short life.

They murmured their goodbyes to her.

"Treat her well," the man said to Matthew earnestly, like any loving father would ask. "She has been gently raised."

### *Matthew's Morfph*

The Morfph returned the hugs, but she was not sad. From now on, she only had eyes for Matthew.

# CHAPTER 13

## Matthew's Morfph Becomes Aspasia

*"What's in a name?"*

William Shakespeare

### Matthew

Late that night, Matthew lay sleepless in bed next to his Morfph, churning with feelings. After they had made love the second time, Matthew held her in his arms until they both drifted off to an exhausted but contented sleep. But he woke with a surge of anxiety a couple hours later. As he looked over and saw Lily's bright hair spread on the pillow, he finally admitted to himself what his subconscious had been planning all along. And he felt a stab of shame. His Morfph had immediately turned into the exact doppelganger of Lily in the Pairing room because that's exactly what he had desperately desired, what he had in mind all along.

Before it happened, he hadn't let himself realize it consciously—had completely blocked it out—even actively denied it to himself. But his wife had come to life again right before his eyes. Everything about her was Lily as he remembered her—her mannerisms, the expressions that flitted across her face—even how she absentmindedly tucked her red-gold hair behind her ears. Her touch was Lily's touch. Her voice was Lily's voice; not just its sound, but also the cadence of her speech and the very words and turns of phrase she used. And then there was her scent...

During the Pairing, as his Morfph started shape shifting into Lily, he caught the subtle fragrance first, before it even registered in his consciousness. He smelled the unique honey apricot smell of Lily. Not perfume or lotions—her animal-body smell. The delicate, sweet fragrance of Lily's skin had been slowly fading from her clothes and from his mind, but now it emanated from the woman lying in the bed next to him.

His chest constricted, his heart painfully squeezed. But, quickly, that feeling faded, pushed aside, and the same heart that had felt the guilt and shame, filled with a buoyant joy. Being together again was euphoria. He sank back into the sensation—the bliss—of having her back in his bed and back in his life.

And with Lily's seeming resurrection and homecoming, the idea that she would sleep separately and in her own room had vanished along with Matthew's denial of his own deep desires.

But he still would not, could not, call her Lily. He couldn't cross that last line of total self-deception and what he knew, deep in his bones, was his betrayal of the real, of his own sweet Lily.

### Matthew's Morfph

In the morning—their first morning together, Matthew and his Morfph sat silently drinking coffee at the dining room table. It surprised her to find she loved coffee... lots of cream, no sugar. She never had before. Matthew had also made toast, and she nibbled a corner of her piece, waiting for Matthew to ask the question she knew was forming in his mind.

"I've decided to call you Aspasia," Matthew said. "Is that okay? Do you like it?"

"Of course. I can't help but love it," she said and laughed his wife's throaty laugh.

He laughed too, charmed.

"And it's so much prettier than my Geneti-Search name," she added, pulling a face—another of Lily's expressions. She knew he couldn't bring himself to call her Lily—not yet—and she knew why.

"But," he said, "I really want to know what you think about it. I want to know what you really feel and think about everything. Would you rather I call you something else? I thought I heard your Caretakers call you something else, but I couldn't make it out. It's okay if you would rather use that name."

Her jaw reflexively clenched when she thought of her old name. She studied Matthew closely through Lily's aqua eyes, exact images of his dead wife's.

"No. I love it, you know. It's a wonderful name," she said. "And I know where it's from—the name. I know who Aspasia was." She could read it all from him—her perfect empathy functioning perfectly. She also knew it had been his joke pet name for Lily and why.

. "You know who Aspasia was? How would you know that? Do you remember?" Matthew said, looking surprised and a little alarmed. He shook his head. "No, no, that's not how this works," he mumbled.

Aspasia answered his question, trying to explain and to smooth him down.

"No, you're right. That's *not* how this works. I only know who she is to you, Matthew. Of course, I don't remember it. You *know* I'm not Lily. That's why you can't call me by her name. I understand."

"I know that Aspasia... the original Aspasia... was a Greek Hetaera—a courtesan," she continued. "But the Hetaera were very special kinds of courtesans. They were educated and groomed from a young age to be perfect companions to the wealthy and elite Athenian men. She was much loved by Pericles, the governor of Athens. But it was against the law for him to marry her... to marry any Hetaera."

She looked at him pointedly, straight on. It was also against the law to marry Morfphs, as they were not Freeborn. Although, technically, they only lost their own wills *after* Pairing.

*But I had it—freewill. Before. Didn't I?*

"Matthew, do you want me to go on about Aspasia and the Hetaera?" she asked, coming back to the moment. It was the sort of question Lily might have asked. She understood he needed the equal interchange, the give and take of conversation and ideas.

"I want to know what *you* think about Aspasia—about the name and about you being named after her."

"Well, let's see now," she said after a pause, exactly as Lily would have, with just a little exasperation. And her words were also very like what Lily's had been—how Matthew remembered them, anyway.

"Matthew, I know the idea of a beautiful, outspoken woman who has a mind of her own appeals to you. But I think you are romanticizing history and—as you really well know—that was clear to Lily. Maybe Aspasia and the Hetaera *were* freer than other Athenian women. They were bright, educated, and encouraged to have opinions... to speak their own minds. But their fates depended on men... on pleasing men. Once they stopped... perhaps by saying the wrong thing, or getting old, or disfigured, or just gaining weight from eating too many baklavas or.... whatever... they were toast."

She held out her partially eaten piece for emphasis and continued.

"But, let's be fair—in Aspasia's case, Pericles did die... but you get my point. A bit precarious, don't you think? Maybe not totally unlike my situation, really."

But Aspasia had left out some of the conversation Matthew previously had with Lily. It was hard to know how accurate his recollection actually was, but she could read what *he* remembered of it.

"The Golden Age of Greece? Hah! It was only golden for wealthy *male* citizens." Lily had practically snorted in that old conversation. "Not so golden for the foreigners, or the slaves, or for almost *any* woman."

"What about the Hetaera you're always talking about?" Matthew had asked, deadpan, baiting her good-naturedly. "What about Aspasia and... what was that other one's name?... oh yeah, Phryne. What about them?"

And Matthew's Morfph knew that had gotten Lily going again, just as Matthew had thought it might. That was when Matthew had started jokingly calling Lily "his little Aspasia."

Now the Morfph slipped a sideways look at Matthew, waiting for his response to what she had just said, just as his wife would have done. She knew what his reaction had been that day with Lily—knew he had briefly been taken aback, a little defensive, but ultimately pleased that she'd presented an idea which he had not yet thought. Matthew was pleased today, too... pleased with Aspasia. She beamed at him.

So Matthew's Morfph became Aspasia. Not "the Morfph" anymore—Aspasia. And she did like it. She loved it.

She really had no choice.

## Matthew

Although Matthew was pleased, giddy even, he felt unsettled to an equal degree. *This is going to take some getting used to,* he thought. The conversation he'd just had with Aspasia was almost word for word the same as he'd had with his wife only months before she'd gotten sick. The men in the history department had earlier kicked Lily's Women's History classes out of the History department and into Gender Studies. Woman's History was, evidently, not "genuine history." Then, they dropped the Gender Studies department entirely; supposedly it merged with Sociology, but all Lily's classes were eliminated, and to her grief, she was eventually let go.

Not long after that, she lost her right to vote as well, when the Head of Household voting law took effect. A few months later she was dead.

*This person is not Lily,* he reminded himself over and over. *This is not her.* But then the mental mantra turned quickly into a defiant, *I don't care. I don't care. I have her back.*

"I have you back," he whispered. He walked over, took her into his arms, and kissed her. She even tasted like Lily. He let out a deep sigh and pulled her even closer.

And *I won't ever let anything happen to this one,* he thought fiercely.

# CHAPTER 14

## *Pygmalion and the Perfect Woman*

*"... there lives on earth no one beautiful person who could not be more beautiful."*

—*Albrecht Durer*

### Sara

Towards the end of Sara and Jack's relationship, before Jack's exodus, they lay in bed, naked and entwined. It felt like old times, and Sara was buoyant. This was a rare event, and she was enjoying the rosy afterglow of some passionate sex. It hadn't been quite that good for a while.

Her finger traced the familiar crescent-shaped line beside his mouth.

"I love to kiss you right here," she said, and then did.

As she lay, replete and happy, with her hip pressed firmly against his side, Jack reached over, grabbed her rounded belly, and jiggled it back and forth. Surprised, she laughed with embarrassment.

She pushed his hand off.

"Stop it, Jack. What are you doing?"

"Where did this come from?" he said, laughing but deadly serious. "Geez, it's like Jell-O or something. Look at it shake."

She inhaled sharply, spun away, curled up into a fetal position, and stared blindly at the wall next to the bed.

"God, don't pout. It's so irritating," he said.

She sat up abruptly, lurched out of bed, a pillow held to her middle to hide her maligned belly, and trotted into the bathroom.

When in the bathroom, she stared at her body in the mirror. Then, as Jack had done, she grabbed the pooch of her belly in both her hands. But she went further than Jack and squeezed hard, hard enough for the flesh to squish up painfully between her fingers.

*He's right*, she thought with a burst of self-disgust. *But I'm forty-five... or almost. Isn't it inevitable? Why should I feel shame for getting older?* But she knew quite well, with a shiver of dread, that Jack wasn't one to give women a break for getting older and for showing it. It seemed like he took women's aging as a personal affront—saw it as a lack of self-control on their part. And Jack thought of himself as an expert, an arbiter, of women's looks. His judgements of the few not-so-young actresses still in movies or on TV were brutal.

As she stared at her reflection, her mind in a turmoil of self-loathing, the more flaws she saw—the strands of white peppering her dark hair, and the start of sagging around her jaws and under her chin. The longer she stared, the more removed from herself she felt. A painful shame filled her. She'd been here before—too many times. What to do? What to do? It's not like she hadn't tried. She'd tried hard—obsessively, even. She'd done it for Jack or, at least, because of him.

"I just want you to be the best you can be," he'd said later that day. "Don't be so sensitive. Just do something about it. You'd feel better about yourself if you did. You know that."

Maybe his idea of an apology? The next day she made an appointment for her tummy tuck and lipo-suction.

———

Later, when she remembered that day, the day he had grabbed her belly, a realization hit her square in the gut; Jack had almost certainly been sleeping with his new upgrade by that time. Of course he had. How stupid and blind she was. She really should have seen it coming from miles away. Because *what goes around comes around.*

———

For weeks after Jack left her, Sara had obsessively checked and rechecked her phone to see if he had texted or called. She kept thinking, hoping, he would come to his senses and tell her he had made a mistake.

"I'm so sorry. Please take me back. I can't live without you," he'd say in her fantasies. She would then make a show of not forgiving him. But, of course, she eventually would and then everything would go back to normal. And she would have her life—their life back.

Even though it made her feel crazy and defeated, she kept looping back to the same ruminations. Every time she checked her phone, and he hadn't called or texted, the feelings of loss and pain washed over her anew. In her saner moments, she contemplated getting a new number so she wouldn't keep torturing herself, but she never did. She couldn't face cutting off that last possible channel of communication.

Instead, she composed text after text meant for him as she cycled through various painful emotional states. Sometimes they were rage-filled diatribes. Other times they were sad and begging. Sometimes they were longer—mini-essays— addressing things they had talked about and disagreed about in the past. Often, she wrote out whole broken-hearted poems. Sara composed these texts, essays and poems at night as she lay sleepless in bed and as she took her daily walks. Sara composed them as she drove to work, as she brushed her teeth and as she made toast.

And through it all, Jack remained the audience in her head and her internal mirror. Sometimes when she peered into an actual mirror, she half-expected no one would reflect back. Her life was so changed she didn't really know how to live it anymore.

*Who I am without Jack?* she wondered with despair.

She'd read that sometimes when limbs were amputated, they became phantoms. An arm was severed, but the amputee still felt like they were flexing their fingers, or making a fist, or reaching out to touch a loved one's hand. But it was long gone—the arm and the hand. Burnt up in the hospital's incinerator. That's what she felt for Jack, that their love was like a phantom limb, her heart a phantom heart.

When she wasn't composing angry or sad texts and poems, other familiar and persistent thoughts bubbled up out of the quagmire of her grieving brain. She felt powerless to shake off the overpowering feeling that if she could only be what

Jack wanted her to be... look the way he wanted her to look... everything would go back the way it was.

Rationally, though, she knew it was an illusion, a *chimera*. And, as she had told countless clients, all the surgery, all the exercise, and all the dieting in the world would not fix what needed fixing within.

*Counselor, heal thyself,* she thought. *Heal thy effing self.*

She did, however, have enough sense left not to send any of those texts. In fact, she had stopped contacting Jack at all.

---

Alix came back for her next counseling appointment. Sara had gotten used to her saying she was quitting therapy. That was how she ended most sessions... often walking out early, then complaining next time for being charged for the entire hour. It had become a ritual of sorts, and sometimes almost a joke between them.

Today, sitting across from Sara, Alix almost made it through a whole forty-five minutes saying nothing of substance. But then Sara focused on Alix's abrupt digression.

"I used to follow him, Doc... my boyfriend. I stalked him. I would wait and watch outside his house. At first, I was just cyber-stalking him on my phone—you know, things like watching where he went, reading his texts and emails, listening to him—that sort of thing. But then I needed to see him, you know?" Alix was a lapsed Catholic and often seemed to use her sessions as confessionals.

"Who, Alix? Are you talking about Felix? I thought you had finished with him. You said you thought he was having sex with his new girlfriend's young daughter, as I recall. We talked a lot about this. I know he's a... a... well, a terrible person, really... but it's an invasion to read people's personal texts and emails. You did that with your daughter too, didn't you? It rarely goes well... for anyone. I'm not even going to ask you how you do it."

"Yeah, I am done with him... done with that, too. No need for it anymore. But I learned a lot that way, Doc. Kept one step ahead. I found out he was on dating sites. I found out about Selene." Selene was his current girlfriend.

"Alix, you already knew he was no good for you. He was abusive, verbally *and* physically. I really don't think you needed any more information than that. But that's in the past, isn't it? You're not still doing it...?"

"No, I already said... it's over," she said, obviously exasperated. "But I did, though—I needed to know. I can take pain. God, maybe I even like the pain. There must be something I like about it, right? I mean, I seem to seek men who will supply it. What I can't take is the leaving. But they all leave. Everyone leaves. I need to know when it's going to happen."

With that admission, Alix's face collapsed—crumpled in on itself—and suddenly she looked every year of her age and many more besides. Sara reflexively leaned forward in her chair to touch Alix's knee, to comfort her physically. But just as quickly as the anguish had flashed onto Alix's face, it had disappeared again and she physically jerked away from her therapist's hand.

"I told you—I'm done with all that. I don't have to worry about that. Not anymore," Alix muttered in a low voice, more to herself than to Sara. Sara wasn't even sure she heard it right.

Then, just as suddenly, Alix's face lit up and a sly smile stretched her lips.

"Maybe I should engineer a perfect boyfriend, a perfect husband. One who would worship me and never leave. What do you think?"

Sara laughed. "I think it's an interesting fantasy."

"But what if it's not a fantasy? What if I've already done it? What if it's my last chance?"

"Last chance? Done what? What have you done, Alix?" A note of alarm made Sara's voice a little shriller than she had intended. Alix had talked about her Morfph project in other sessions, but Sara had dismissed it as some sort of odd bragging or just Alix blowing smoke. She never dreamed Alix or her company could pursue it. Even if it were possible, which she sincerely doubted. There *must* be some limits to these things.

"Doc, you know I've only been able to tell you about my project because you're bound to confidentiality. Right? I'm breaking the company's NDA by even mentioning it to you. "

Sara shook her head in bewilderment. "Of course. Of course, Alix. I'm professionally bound to keep your confidences. So, we're talking about your Morfphs again... The Morfph Project?" she asked. "Pretty hard to believe, really."

"Well, believe it. We've done it. *I've* done it. They're real. They're not just a pipe dream. Not anymore."

"Sounds more like a nightmare." Sara said darkly.

Alix ignored Sara's last comment. Or maybe she had just filed it away. She did that, Sara knew. At any rate, she continued without a pause.

"Who says you can't buy love? I mean, we see it every day, don't we? Every time we see some rich old man with a pretty young thing on his arm—and by implication, in his bed—we see it. Sometimes the old men even think the girls love them for themselves.

"But with Morfphs it's different. You can buy *actual* love. And with none of the messiness of relationships with regular human beings. So much tidier, so much less fraught with rejection and heartache. So much better. You can have exactly what you want, exactly when you want it. And all to your specifications. It's fucking great. In so many ways."

"Alix, are you saying that you... Do *you* have one... of them?" Sara said, eyes wide.

Alix abruptly stood up and smoothed her creased pants.

"See you next time, Doc. Gotta run... Really though, I'm not sure if I'll be back or not."

Alix smiled as she walked out the door... a cat-who-ate-the-canary kind of grin.

---

It was at their next session when it all came out. Bit by bit, one revelation after another, the complete story of Morphs... spelled "Morfphs" Sara had learned... spilled out. Alix couldn't seem to help herself, even though the NDA she had created herself strictly forbade it.

"Have you ever heard the story of Pygmalion?" Alix asked.

"Of course." Sara nodded.

"It's an illuminating story, don't you think? The goddess, Aphrodite, brings Galatea to life for Pygmalion. He has sculpted her, Galatea, his perfect woman, out of marble. Made her to his scrupulous specifications. Perfect because she is his creature. Alive and now human, but free of the pesky flaws that humans inevitably have. Perfect, likes Morfphs are perfect. And she, like a Morfph, has no choice but to also perfectly love him, regardless of *his* pesky human flaws.

"And that *is* what is expected of the perfect woman... to be lovely and to stay lovely, to be gentle and accepting, to be sexy but not *too* sexual, to be modest but eager to satisfy, to never be angry, to be intelligent but not *too* intelligent, to always acquiesce to their man's needs and to love and adore him unconditionally with no demands or needs of her own."

"Alix, what—?

Alix continued single-mindedly.

"Pygmalion created his perfect mate, the perfect woman, and lived happily ever after with her. Don't you see? It's what Morfphs are. They are our unique individual creation, the personification of our perfect mate, our soulmate come to life. Perfect. Real. Human. Loving. Devoted. Or not. They are whatever is desired most."

"But what does this have to do with—?"

"Let me finish. Most men seem to want women to be exactly what *they* want them to be. And what they want them to be often changes from day to day... maybe from minute to minute. Well, Morfphs can do that... and will do that willingly... not just willingly, enthusiastically. To be fair, I suppose we could say the same about women—I mean the part about what they want from their man... or their whatever... let's say their mate. But I don't feel like being fair. Fuck fair. Fuck it in the.... never mind."

"Alix, lets..."

Without missing a beat, her mania seeming to propel her forward, Alix rasped out a laugh.

"Hey," she said, "that reminds me of an old boyfriend. Did I ever tell you about Joe? Always wanted to do that. Ugh." Another manic laugh.

"Alix, I think we should try to..."

"I need to make you understand. This could mean the end of the battle of the sexes. The end of disappointments in love. The end of forcing others to conform to our desires. Isn't it better that Morfphs *want* to please?" she asked defiantly.

"Why do I keep asking myself, and other people, that question?" she said, almost to herself. "To calm my own doubts? That's what you'd say... but no. I have no doubts. You're the doubters. Small thinkers, all of you."

"Why do you think you keep asking that same question? Maybe you *do* have doubts."

"See? What did I say? No. No, no. That's not it. Don't you see? We all morph ourselves for others to get what we need from them—from life.

"'Oh honey, I love you so,'" Alix said in a high mimicking voice. "'What can I do to make you love me more? I know, I'll pretend you're so much smarter than I am. Or, I've got it... I'll have my boobs cut open so that they can shove big plastic bags of saline water into them. Would you like that, dear? Would you love me more?'"

Sara flinched.

"Morfphs just do it so much better," Alix said.

"*Exactly* what do they do better?" Sara said.

"Morph, of course... morph," Alix said. "They're the Mercedes of morphing."

Even after Alix had explained so much about Morfphs, Sara hadn't completely believed her. Not yet. But then she started spotting the occasional unsubstantiated story on the web. Then the stories started appearing with increasing frequency. Many claims were being made. Some, Sara knew, were exaggerated. Others were simply lies, and often particularly salacious ones. But most of them jibed with what Alix had told her.

*Maybe it's all true.*

And then Sara wondered about something else, and it was an equally uncomfortable thought.

*Am I horrified?* she wondered, *Or am I envious... envious of a Morfph's ability to so easily and thoroughly please their beloved?*

The answer further appalled her. *Both.*

# THE DAILYBEAT

Arnold Hidalgo

Posted 5 minutes ago

Nov 18,20**

There are yet unsubstantiated reports that a genetic engineering company named Geneti-Search Technologies has successfully engineered enhanced human beings aptly named Morfphs.

An anonymous source reports that these enhanced individuals can read minds and shape shift to any form desired of them by a Patron to whom they have been Paired.

Geneti-Search, and individuals rumored to be Patroni, were contacted for statements. Geneti-Search and all other individuals contacted declined comment.

When asked about these reports, Dr. David Rubins, PhD of Stanfield University, succinctly replied, "Ridiculous and patently impossible."

# II

# MORPHOSES

# EXCERPT FROM:

## *"In Libro de Morfph"*

## *—the Morfph Compendium and Handbook*

Author: unknown (generally acknowledged to be the late Alix Edison, Genetic Engineer, and originator and creator of the "Morfph" project at Geneti-Search Technologies)

### *Section H, 1-4*
### *Production of Morfphs*

*The first group of Morfphs engineered, implanted, and born were the Alpha group, which comprised twelve individuals. They bonded these individuals to high-level people at Geneti-Search who had applied and qualified. They were and continue to be closely monitored. Geneti-Search waived payment for Patronage in this initial testing group.*

*The Second wave of twelve Beta Morfphs were mature just a month after the initial twelve, and were paired with a select cadre of influential, wealthy men. Geneti-Search offered these men a Morfph at a special, much reduced price. The wealthy evidently love saving money—love feeling they are getting a special deal because **they** are special, smarter, and just better than everyone else. This decision was a marketing strategy, as we've determined that word of mouth is the most cost-effective marketing strategy for this elite niche market.*

*After the second (Beta) batch of twelve were Paired, more Morfphs came to maturity. These also were reserved and their contracts pre-paid, which provided billions of dollars, enabling production to continue.*

*Production rate increased to about one hundred twenty per month. Not all matured Morfphs were Paired immediately upon maturity, but most were—at full cost.*

*Within six months, we had paired almost seven hundred mature Morfphs with wealthy clients. As of this writing, the production continues at that pace. It will probably slow somewhat in the future, but so far, demand continues to exceed production.*

# CHAPTER 15
## *The Kiss*

*Sara*

Sam and Sara kissed for the first time on Thanksgiving Day. Katy and Beatrice invited Sara to their house, and of course, Sam and the girls were there. It had been a wonderful day and a good vegetarian dinner, much of which had come from their vast backyard garden. But it was getting late, and Sara had already called a taxi to pick her up and take her home. Sam was staying longer to tuck in his girls, who were still up but were flagging fast.

As Sara stood to leave, Sam jumped up.

"I'll walk you out," he said.

After she retrieved her coat and shrugged into it, Sara companionably took Sam's arm in hers. They walked out the door and stood on the wide, covered front porch. Lights strung from the eaves bathed the porch in a cheerful glow. They were both happy and full—full of nuts, legumes, berries, various sauces, homemade cider, and wine—and full of good cheer. Just content to be together, they waited arm-in-arm and watched for the taxi.

Sara patted Sam on the arm she held and then went up on her toes, intending to kiss his cheek. Sam turned his head to meet her. His mouth met hers tentatively, softly, as if he didn't want to scare her away.

Startled, Sara tensed and almost jerked away. But she didn't. Instead, it felt so good—so sweet and warm—that she leaned in. When Sam came away, he looked searchingly at her face, and that's when Sara went up for another one. This kiss was longer—deeper and more passionate—almost urgent. It surprised her how her body reacted to it—to his kisses. Evidently, her body knew more than she did about her feelings for Sam.

With terrible timing, the taxi arrived and almost immediately started making a repetitive beeping sound, like a truck backing up. They knew it would not stop until Sara opened the door to get in. A little mewling sound of frustration escaped her lips as she finally, reluctantly, pulled away from Sam.

"I guess I better go," she said, feeling a little embarrassed now.

But Sam laughed happily.

"Sara, you are amazing. You don't know how long I have wanted to do that."

"Oh, I think I might," she replied and laughed too, the discomfort broken. "I'll see you soon."

"I'll count the hours."

"Oh, shut up," she said, and laughed again.

"You wound me with your laughter," he said, clutching his chest.

At the taxi, Sara turned.

"Sam?" she said.

"Yeah?"

"I'm going to the animal shelter Monday. I've decided to get a dog."

"Oh, that's gr—"

"Do you want to come with me... help me pick one out?"

Sam beamed.

"That sounds fun. I love dogs. As a kid, we always had dogs."

Sara smiled back.

*He loves dogs*, Sara thought. *Of course he does.*

———

Knowing how Sam felt about her, it wasn't really a surprise when he finally kissed her. She adored Sam, but not in the way she still craved—obsessed over—Jack. And she had been scared, too. Scared if she dated him, she'd lose her best friend. So, until the kiss, she had put him off. Consistent with his generous and patient manner, he didn't push or get mad or back off from their friendship. He was just always there for her.

Going and picking out Fergus, a goofy, gangly, half-grown poodle- Heinz 57 mix, was their first date. Choosing Fergus from the rest wasn't hard, but leaving the others behind was. They were all so eager to please, to be petted, and to be loved. Even the scared ones looked on with beseeching eyes.

Fergus had been well-loved and taken care of, but his owner had suddenly and unexpectedly died, leaving Fergus orphaned. His eyes were a deep, melting brown and his tail never stopped beating a rhythmic tattoo of his sweet nature. They all three fell in love at first sight. When they brought him home to Sara's house, he curled up in the new bed they had bought him on the way home and sighed a deep sigh of utter contentment.

On their second date, this one a "real date," Sam went all out. He got tickets for a popular musical that was brimming with merry songs, colorful costumes, and energetic dancing. Afterwards, driving by the sprawling homeless camp on the way to Sam's house didn't dispel the high leftover from the show. But the hopeless scene hit Sara in the gut every time she passed it. It reminded her how very fortunate she had been so far in her life.

Once they got to Sam's, he heated a dinner he had prepared for them earlier in the day. After margaritas, he served fried purple potatoes and onions, some sort of nondescript cultured meat, and then ice cream, or something quite like it. Sara wondered if she'd ever stop longing for the real things. But the margaritas and potatoes were good.

Despite the faux-meat and odd ice cream-like dessert, it was a wonderfully fun evening. Giddy on the drinks and honestly, sexually parched as well, the inevitable happened. It was also very sweet. Not quite the earthquake sex she had with Jack, especially in the beginning, but very nice. He was an ardent and, not unexpectedly, a very generous lover.

When they become an acknowledged couple, everyone seemed pleased. "*Perfect,*" they said. "*Finally!*"

---

After Sam and Sara had been dating for a little over two months, they were again contentedly sitting around a dining room table, this time in her house. They had just shared a large dinner, much of which had come from her thriving garden now covering her entire back yard.

The draught-resistant plantings had become a lifesaver, as vegetables and fruit were getting scarcer and, even when available, were outrageously expensive. She felt very lucky to have her large garden patch; she got a larger water allotment for it. The grey water system she had installed a few years back meant she had enough water to keep her garden producing during the persistent draught and the often-searing heat. She'd gotten enough blueberries to make a large tart today.

They both had the top buttons of their pants undone to give the dinner they had just eaten more room to settle. Sara felt mellow and happy... and quite satiated, with food and with life. Her new dog, Fergus, lay draped over both sets of their feet, seeking constant connection with his saviors. Fergus was always exuberant, and a bit ungainly on his huge puppyish feet.

"He's going to get even bigger, you know. He's not quite full grown yet," the kennel attendant had said.

He had turned out to be the perfect choice. When Sam had arrived that evening for dinner, Fergus had whipped himself into a frenzy of ecstasy. His tail wagged his entire body.

"Stop making a fool of yourself, Fergus," Sara said with a laugh.

"No, you're fine, Fergus. I love you too, bro," Sam said, reaching down to rub the dog's exposed belly.

Now the remains of dinner were still on the table, and they were sipping small glasses of some blackberry liqueur Sara had made months back from fresh-picked blackberries—also from her garden. They had wine at dinner, as Jack's wine cellar was still full and she and Sam were freely sampling it. Jack had earlier made noises about collecting his wine, but Sara hadn't heard from him for quite a while.

"You're quiet tonight, Sara," Sam said.

"Mmm. I'm good. Just thinking about a client."

Sara had seen Alix the day before, and she was still thinking about what Alix had disclosed.

Sam quirked his head.

"Sorry, can't really discuss it."

Sam nodded his head.

"I'm stuffed," he said. "Wish I hadn't eaten so much. That tart was... so good... amazing. Everything was."

He leaned back in his chair, unbuttoned another button on his pants, and groaned.

"No self-control, that's your problem. Why don't you get fat?"

"It's my youthful metabolism," he said and grinned. "Maybe when I get to be your age..."

"Okay, okay, asshole, enough of that," she said, laughing.

As she stood and started clearing the table, Sam jumped up.

"Let me do that. You cooked."

She handed him a plate. "We can do it together."

"I read this weird article about sex-bots today," Sara said, as they worked side-by-side at the sink. "It's amazing how many people have them... men, mostly. Would you ever want one, a sex-bot?"

She had searched the topic and read the article because Alix had brought them up them during her session.

"What? No. Yuck. What a question. They freak me out. I saw something about them, too. Probably the same article. They say they're so real now it's hard to even tell they're A.I. One model is actually named Frigid Fanny. 'For only 19.95 you too can have a fem-bot of your very own to rape to your heart's content.' Very disturbing."

Sara pulled a face. "Prices *are* coming down, Sam, but I'm pretty sure you still can't get one for $19.95. Seriously, though, I agree. Very disturbing. I bet Jack would love one of those. Maybe he has one." She paused. "Maybe not. He has always been proud of being able to attract real human females."

Sam grunted and frowned, as he did whenever she mentioned Jack.

She handed him a rinsed dish to dry.

"Okay, no robots then. What about a genetically engineered, real live person who can become exactly what you want? Perpetually young and beautiful, completely fluid, shape shifting into any form you desire?"

"Oh, oh. You're talking about those... those... What are they calling them? But that's just crazy rumors... isn't it?"

"Those glasses go on that shelf... right over there."

"It is, isn't it?" Sam repeated as he wiped out a glass and stacked it on the shelf she pointed to. "Does this have something to do with your client? Do you know something you're not telling?"

"Mmm. Can't say."

"Wild. But becoming—literally changing into—exactly what someone wants? What does that even mean? What if I want... what's the name of that actress I like... oh yeah, Alexandra Muñoz?... Hey, please stop hitting me, I just said *what if.*"

"Sorry. It's a good question, really. And yeah, you could have Ms. Muñoz. I mean, not the *real* Alexandra, but..."

"Ah, they would be the perfect sex slaves, wouldn't they?"

"There you go. Straight to the heart of the matter," she said and then frowned.

"I'm just kidding, you know. You mad?"

"No, no. You didn't say anything." Sara had become obsessed with Alix's Morfphs and she really needed to talk about it, but she couldn't tell Sam the whole truth since it involved what Alix had told her in therapy.

"Let's go lay on the couch, watch a mindless show and make out," she said.

"Well, normally that's not an offer I would refuse, but... something's eating you, I can tell. Spill."

Sara took a deep breath and looked at him.

"Well, there's probably not much I haven't told you about Jack but... um... he was... he could be... very... judgmental. Especially about women's appearances... about *my* appearance..."

Sam looked irritated.

"You're beautiful," he said. "In every way."

She shrugged.

"Jack," he said disgustedly, shaking his head, "what an idiot. He had no appreciation for what he had."

She was still skeptical.

"Well, thanks, you're very good for my self-esteem. But he often left me feeling if I could just alter myself, change myself, improve myself enough, he would love me more or just keep loving me. I always felt like I was competing with all his beautiful young students. Well, I'm not blameless in all this. I was one of those young students, you know. Anyway, I was right, he left me for someone younger—'a finer specimen.' Brand spanking new."

Sam made a scoffing grunt in his throat and, saying nothing, he walked over to Sara and wrapped his arms around her. She buried her head in his chest as he gathered her in.

"Sam, would you want one of those shapeshifters? I mean, if they existed?" she asked, her voice slightly muffled against his body.

She waited for his answer, her breath held. This was important to her. Sara had already had one man she loved leave her because... because why, exactly? She wasn't really sure. Was she not young enough? Sexy enough? Flawed in some basic way? She had tried so hard to get it right.

"Well, let me see, hmm, maybe for a weekend," he answered softly into her hair. She struggled out of his hug as his chest and arms shook with laughter. "But really, no. How boring. It would be like dating myself. I mean, I don't mind an occasional fling with my hand, but we're not really *dating*..."

Sara continued to struggle, and now she was laughing, too, but Sam kept her pinned.

"But no, my love," he said, his tone serious. "My real answer is, no. I wouldn't want a sex-bot or a shapeshifter. I want to be loved completely and *voluntarily*. I don't need perfect. I need real... *actual love*. So, a... a... whatever they're called— wouldn't work for me."

"Good answer, Sam. Very good answer."

# CHAPTER 16

## *He's Back*

### *Sara*

Jack had gone silent for months. Sara knew she needed to contact him about proceeding with their divorce, but kept putting it off. She didn't want to have to sell the house, and she couldn't afford to buy him out. Not yet, anyway. The house had skyrocketed in value since they had bought it almost twenty years before. And then there were the extra costs of the security walls and gates built around their community and the armed guards who needed payment.

But out of the blue, not that long after her relationship with Sam was getting more serious, Jack started texting her. It was classic Jack. Somehow, he must have found out about Sam, and he needed to reel her back in. The balance of power and control was out of whack now—out of his comfort zone. He had always needed her adoration. If she was suffering from his absence and pining for him, Jack was happy. This relationship with Sam was probably more than a little alarming for Jack.

*It's like he has a sixth sense about me and Sam.*

Maybe someone had told him, but she couldn't imagine who. It's not like she had posted it online or anything. She supposed one of his friends could have seen them having dinner together or something. But it wasn't a secret... not really. She just didn't feel ready to deal with any of his B.S.—not yet.

He had started with texting brief messages. Just breezy little things, like, "Been thinking about you," or, "Just wondering how you are," and soon progressed to, "Missing you." Then he started texting some minor complaints about Jazmin.

After ignoring him for a few weeks, Sara started texting back terse notes.

"I'm fine," "No complaints," or "Work is going well."

Then his texts started getting longer, his complaints becoming missives. Jazz didn't seem as appreciative of his talents and his specialness as he liked. Often the complaining texts made her laugh, which was not the hoped-for reaction, she was sure.

*It's coming apart already,* she thought. She couldn't help feeling an uncharitable glee.

He then moved to saying he'd like to come over to get something. Some vinyl record he'd forgotten, his binoculars, wine... whatever. She resisted. She had dropped a few things off at his department office at the University to avoid his visits. But she held firm with not allowing him to come over.

---

One night, after he had been texting for several weeks, Jack-like, he came over anyway. Sara was at home alone with her dog Fergus, who was, as usual, asleep and flopped nervelessly over her feet under the table, acting as her personal furry foot warmer. He was close to full grown now and *had,* as predicted, gotten large... eighty-five pounds the last time he was at the vet.

Sam was not coming over that night, as he was busy playing some game (city league volleyball?). The dishes left from the dinner she had made for herself—cultured salmon, baby potatoes, and grilled asparagus, both from her garden—littered the table.

The salmon had been a bit off-tasting—something about its texture. With bitter-sweet nostalgia, Sara remembered the abundance of real, beautiful pink-orange wild salmon that used to so readily available. She also remembered the Farmer's Market tables laden with piles of colorful local produce—purple, orange, yellow, red, blue, green. Peppers, eggplants, carrots, blueberries, raspberries, oceans of lettuces, kales, and greens.

She sipped a glass of her favorite wine, a Sauvignon Blanc from another bottle she had lifted from Jack's stash. This was one she had chosen and bought. The bottle had been dusty, but the wine was still good. She was writing in her journal, feeling quite relaxed and content. She remembered similar evenings with Jack when they'd sit in their dining room sipping wine and discussing their day.

After a brief twinge, she came quickly back to the knowledge that she was glad he wasn't there. She was feeling more at peace than she had for a long time. Her relationship with Sam was sweet and calm, without drama. She had gotten over feeling that there should be fireworks. She felt calmly happy and balanced when she was with Sam. When she needed to talk, it was him she wanted to talk to. Jack was all but exorcised from her head. Sam was the kindest man she had ever known. She felt blessed.

Just as she was writing about Jack's texts in her journal, she heard someone fumbling with a key at the door. Fergus jumped up and ran at the door in a frenzy of ferocious barking.

"Good boy," she breathed. They both stared anxiously at the door as the scrabbling sound continued. She went to the drawer where she kept her stun gun and pulled it out to hold in her hand as she walked to the front door. Then, over the loud barking, she heard Jack calling her name.

"Sara, Sara, it's just me. Answer the door. Why doesn't the key work? What did you do? What in God's name is that racket?"

"Shit," she said under her breath. She still didn't move. She just sat there, trying to decide what to do. After the initial relief she said to Fergus, "This is not good. This is not good at all."

"Sara, please. I just want to talk a little about the house."

"Shit," she said, aloud this time. She didn't want to have this conversation. Sara had been living in their house and paying most of the mortgage, but not all of it, since Jack was still a co-owner. She loved this house and wanted to stay put.

Against her better judgement, she finally let Jack in. At some level, she must have known she was risking letting him back into her life as well. But the house was Jack's Trojan horse in this transaction. He was clever.

Fergus, still doing his rabid dog impression, ran menacingly at Jack.

Jack backed up.

"You got a dog. You know I hate dogs," he said with disgust in his voice.

"Like that should still matter," she said.

"He better not be peeing on my Persian rugs."

Fergus knew a dog-hater when he smelled one. He barked until Sara pulled him off. "Quiet, Fergus, he's a friend. Sort of."

Fergus sniffed Jack's pant legs, still growling deep in his throat. Jack gingerly tried to push Fergus away from him with the side of his foot. Then he sidestepped past the dog to Sara and came in to kiss her on the cheek, prompting Fergus to growl more loudly.

Sara jerked back. Jack missed and kissed the air by her face. The potent smell of whiskey wafted in her face. Which was unlike him... used to be, anyway. He had never been much of a drinker unless it was a particularly excellent wine. And he looked less than well-groomed, disheveled and unshaved. Again, quite unlike him, but it could very well have been part of a ploy.

"What's with the lock?"

"I had it re-keyed."

"It's still my house, too, you know," he said, sounding peevish but not pursuing it further.

He then walked past her and into the living room. She followed him. He kicked his loafers off his sockless feet and plunked down into his favorite chair, a cushioned brown leather one from Pottery Barn. Fergus was right behind Jack, following closely on his heels, watching him closely. He obviously still didn't trust this guy.

*Better judgment than me*, she thought.

"Watch out, Jack. He might hump your leg."

She laughed as he pulled his legs back and grimaced.

"Gawd, Sara, that's disgusting. Does he do that?"

"Calm down, Jack. No, he doesn't. He's neutered. And he's *still* better in bed than you are. Quite the cuddler."

"Oh man, he sleeps with you? In our bed?" he said, outraged.

"My bed. It's my bed now, Jack."

"Yeah, well, I wouldn't want it back now. Between that mutt and Sam, it's probably infested with fleas."

"Ha ha. Good one."

He was fishing. She doubted he really knew whether Sam and she were sleeping together at that point. But she didn't bite—just looked at him blandly. Jack had dressed in faded jeans and a rumpled brown tee shirt with some brewery logo on it. His jeans hung on him like he had lost weight, but there was a new unhealthy-looking beer-belly swelling under his cotton shirt that she hadn't noticed before.

His hair was getting quite grey, and it was messy and longer than usual. And were his blue eyes a little less blue... a little faded? They were definitely watery and bloodshot. *Worse for wear and looking his age*, she thought.

She stood there, unmoving, for a few beats, trying to figure out what she should do. He had relaxed into "his" chair with a contended sound, somewhere between a moan and a grunt. She felt irritated, and a little amused, but the initial sense of foreboding remained in the mix. She finally took pity on him, sighed, and offered him a glass of wine.

"This wine is overrated, in my opinion," he said, his brow slightly wrinkled. "Are you draining my wine cellar? I really need to come get it. Wine is getting outrageously expensive. The vineyards are drying up."

She made her own face and immediately felt less sorry for him. He knew it was her favorite wine, the Sauv. He had to get his dig in. She *had* drunk more wine than she should after he left, but tonight she was not drinking to dull anything. She had really been enjoying relaxing, feeling good, and sipping her favorite wine. Before.

*"Our* wine cellar. Not yours."

The real reason for the visit surfaced pretty quickly. Jack started complaining bitterly about Jazmin. It relieved Sara to know it wasn't really about the house. The wine had mellowed her, so she just sat back and listened.

*What's the harm?* She was used to listening to people talking about their problems, so she just let him go on. Sara had, without totally realizing it, kicked into her therapist mode. But after more wine, things took a turn towards the silly.

They started laughing about ridiculous things. They'd always enjoyed laughing together and shared a sense of humor. Things continued to get funnier and funnier as she opened another bottle of wine. She noticed he didn't complain about the next bottle.

His top grievance seemed to be that Jazmin didn't like his music. She had made fun of his collection of vinyl jazz records, of which he was so proud.

"Sara, she called it old people's music... all that classic music," he said, obviously outraged.

*Jazz didn't like his jazz,* Sara thought, and smirked.

"What did you say to that?

"I said it was like fine wine; it just got better with time. Her response was, 'Whatever,'" he said, mimicking Jazmin's voice. "Like the entire conversation bored her. She asked why I wanted to listen to that tedious old music on a turntable. 'What a lot of bother,'" he mimicked her again.

"Then she said it was *pretentious.* Said that about my music collection, about my turntable and about me."

At that, Sara laughed so hard wine snorted out her nose, making her cough and sputter. By this time, they were both quite drunk and everything was hilarious. In the past, she would have just stifled a smile. At least she'd changed that much.

He threw her an aggrieved, *"Et tu,"* look, which made her laugh harder. He smiled a little self-deprecatingly at that. But then they looked at each other and broke down into helpless laughter. It started building on itself and became more and more hilarious. They were both holding their sides, tears streaming down their faces and eventually rolling around on the handmade Persian carpet they both loved... having hysterics over Jazz and his vinyl jazz collection.

Finally, their laughter died down to a few little bursts of giggles as they lay side by side on their backs, staring up at the ceiling. She looked over at him and startled to see him staring back, his eyes so dilated they looked black in the dimming light.

He abruptly sat up, took her head in his hands, and kissed her. It was not a gentle kiss, but an aggressor taking possession. A little yip escaped her commandeered mouth, but to her shame—not then, but later—she didn't stop him. She kissed him back with a passion that matched his. Desire for him filled her, and it felt like coming home. Something broke loose, pleasure tinged with panic, pain wrapped in ecstasy.

"You belong to *me*. Not to him. You know you do," he rasped into her ear. He rolled on top of her, pinning her under him. He held her hands down onto the floor over her head and kissed her again. This kiss was as possessive, but not as rough as the first.

Her heart leapt, and she knew. This was what she had never stopped wanting... so familiar... so yearned for. He finally understood, finally figured out they were meant to be together. But the next feeling, pursuing on the heels of the last, was a flare of rage.

She struggled to get away, but he kept her pinned to the floor.

"Then why did you leave me? Why?" Her voice raised to an angry, anguished wail of pain. "I even let you have your damned 'cupcakes.'"

"Shh, shh," he said and kissed her again, successfully muffling her wails. "Calm down, my darling. I know just how to love you, Sara. Does he? I bet that pansy hasn't got a clue."

He pressed his mouth to her neck and kissed the smooth skin just below her earlobe. It sent an electric current of passion through her. She stopped struggling and arched up to meet his mouth with hers. Only then did he let go of her hands to lift her to a sitting position. He efficiently pulled off her sweater and then her bra. She frantically helped him.

"Sara, you *are* gorgeous," he said as he cupped her full breasts and kissed them one after the other, with real or feigned reverence.

Her hands shaking, she unbuckled Jack's belt, unzipped his fly, and slipped her hand into his pants to caress him. With a sharp intake of breath, he pushed her gently but firmly back down to the floor. Travelling down her body, he peeled off the rest of her clothes, kissing goose-fleshed skin as he went.

When his mouth reached the desired destination, Jack said, "I'm going to make you forget all about anyone but me."

She left him to his work until she was moaning with pleasure and then reached down, took his head in her hands.

"Come up here. I want you up here with me," she said.

When his face was level with hers, she kissed him deeply and tasted herself in his mouth.

"Fuck me, Jack. I need you inside of me now."

"Oh, sweet darlin', I do love it so when you talk dirty to me," he said into her hair as he proceeded to do as he was told.

"Do you never shut up?" she said with a gasp and a single throaty laugh.

Wave after wave of building pleasure ended in an explosion of ecstasy and left them both sweaty and breathing hard.

"Oh my god," Sara said.

"At your service, Ma'am."

Sara laughed. "Always so humble."

"They don't call it the little death for nothing."

Lying next to each other, still on the floor, Sara kissed Jack once more. This kiss replaced urgency with a languid sweetness. His mouth felt like velvet—warm and smooth. She sighed and wrapped her leg up over him in a familiar movement.

From his pad in the corner, Fergus watched them balefully and growled softly from deep in his throat.

"Let's go to bed," Jack said, eyeing Fergus. And they did, climbing into the big bed they had bought together many years before.

They made love much of the night, and it was just as it had been at its best. The ache and emptiness inside her that had never really completely healed finally soothed and filled. And he was right; he knew just how to love her. He was skilled and sure of himself to the point of arrogance. Her body shamelessly responded to both qualities, as it always had.

So, just like that, Jack laid claim to her once more. *He might as well have branded me*, she thought. He was also, at least partially, right about Sam and sex. Sam was giving and attentive, but there was something tentative about his love-making, almost like he was a little afraid of her.

Later that night, Sara and Jack lay in bed together. She played with his silky chest hair, petting and combing it with her slim fingers. It was very blond, and now, she noticed, also interspersed generously with strands of gleaming white. He was still well-muscled, but a layer of soft padding now overlaid his abs. Mentally, she compared Jack's body with Sam's. Sam was long-muscled and lean, his chest a sleek, smooth brown.

"I'm your creature, Jack. At least sexually," she amended.

"Huh?" he said drowsily, his eyes closed.

"My sexuality was—hell, *is*—all bound up with you. After you left, I realized I couldn't even get myself off without thinking about us together. So, I stopped altogether, pleasuring myself, that is. It just made things worse. I needed to get you out of my head, out of my body. That really pissed me off."

"Poor baby," he murmured, obviously pleased with this revelation. "You're imprinted on me," he laughed. "All those *looove* hormones." He stretched out the word, trying to make her laugh. "Let me take care of you," he said as he rolled her over and made love to her once again. She sighed with a deep sense of relief and pleasure. Love hormones, indeed.

Afterwards, again laying in Jack's arms, she felt like he'd never left. She was lulled into a mindless bliss she hadn't felt for months.

"Sometimes I think that all the women I've had are really just the same woman," Jack said.

Sara bolted upright, once again surging with fiery anger.

"Jack, have you sunk so far into your narcissism, you can't even see people anymore? How can an otherwise intelligent man be so clueless? So dense? So deluded?" Her whole body shook with her rage. She wrapped the surrounding sheet around herself protectively, feeling exposed and foolish.

"Sara, jeez, calm down. I'm sorry. It was a stupid thing to say. I know who you are. You're my Sara."

She sank back down in bed, slightly mollified, but still upset. Then, he wrapped himself around her and she felt the bliss of it again. Once more he reeled her back in, and they fell asleep in each other's arms.

The next morning, very early, Jack got slowly and carefully out of bed. He jerked back when he looked at her face and saw Sara's wide-open eyes watching his every move.

"Oh, you're awake. I have to leave right now. Jazz is going to be furious."

"You're going back to Jazmin," she stated flatly. "Like nothing happened."

"Yeah." He looked sheepish, but said nothing to explain.

"You know you love me," she said desperately. "You know you do. Why are you doing this?"

"My feelings for you have nothing to do with my feelings for Jazz," he said. "I love you. Maybe we can see each other sometimes," he said hopefully.

At this, she buried her head in her pillow and moaned.

"Oh, my god. No. No, no, no, no. Can't you see how... You're *my husband*, Jack. *My* husband. Are you really that... that... callous?"

She searched his face, looking for something... something that wasn't there. And it hit her like a blow. She finally realized—really understood—it had never really been there at all.

"Well, of course you are. What am I saying? I put up with the others—so many others," she said. "As long as I was the one who was most important, the one you came home to, it seemed... possible, bearable. But this... this is..." The last word came out with a strangled sound as she started crying.

"Sara, you really don't need me anymore. Jazz needs me. She *needs* me." he repeated. "You know I need to be needed.  I need to take the lead. I need to be admired," he said in a flash of unusual self-awareness. "Shit, you even make more money than I do." Like that should be an obvious reason to walk away from their relationship. "I'm Jazz's mentor."

One harsh laugh burst from Sara's mouth.

"Oh, I bet you are! Is that what you call it? Mentoring? Were you mentoring me last night? Or was I mentoring you?"

Then another thought struck her, and she sat straight up in bed, the sheet again clutched around her body.

"It has never really been about my age or my body, has it? Not really. As soon as I outgrew being your... your... acolyte, that was the beginning of the end. Wasn't it? And the money thing. That was just evidence, a symbol, of me outgrowing my... my... cupcake-hood."

When her counseling practice had really taken off about five years before, she *had* made more money than Jack—a lot more money. She hadn't really taken much notice of it then. It didn't matter to her. She liked it that she was successful, and she liked the money, but what did it matter if she made more than he did?

But, surely, that was the point when he started getting more bitingly critical of her, and looking back, she was pretty sure that was also when his dalliances—his flirtations—had become more intense. Maybe that had also been when he had begun full blown affairs.

Jack didn't answer her question. He walked to the door and pulled it open, but before he walked out, he stopped and looked back.

"Is he bigger than me?" he asked.

She stared at him blankly. "What?"

"Sam. Is he bigger than I am?"

It was clear what he meant. Jack was a good two inches taller and thirty pounds heavier than Sam.

Sara shook her head in disbelief. But then smiled meanly.

"Yes, Jack. He is."

He grimaced, shrugged, and only then left, closing the bedroom door behind him. Sara sat dazed for a few minutes, staring at the closed door. She heard Fergus growl as Jack walked through the house. Her dog had made his disapproval obvious earlier in the evening, ending in banishment from the bedroom. He adored Sam and apparently had the excellent sense to a hate Jack.

Mechanically, Sara got to her feet and walked slowly—naked and numb—into the bathroom. Reaching into the shower, she cranked on the water, frantic to wash Jack off her. As she waited for the water to heat, she turned around to the vanity. The mirror had steamed up already, so she wiped an oval off of it and stared herself in the eyes.

"What have you done?" she asked the crazy-eyed woman looking back at her. "What have you done, you ridiculous fool?" The mirror steamed back up before the image in the mirror could give her an answer.

She stepped into the shower, turned the water as hot as she could tolerate, poured shower gel onto the rough washcloth she used to exfoliate her elbows and heels, and scrubbed her skin until it was raw.

She concentrated on the areas that Jack had touched, trying to purge him from her—from her skin, from her body, and from her brain. There was one patch on the tender skin between her upper thighs she scrubbed so roughly that it bled. She sobbed as she did this and the punishing water cascading from the showerhead washed her tears down her face and body, mixed with the blood from her scraped skin, and finally circled and disappeared down the drain.

# CHAPTER 17

## *A Veritable Quandary*

*Matthew*

Matthew and Aspasia's life together had settled into what seemed a contented rhythm. During the day, and especially when they made love, he would sink into the seductive mirage of having Lily back. When unwanted thoughts of guilt or betrayal entered his consciousness, he'd shake them off with little trouble.

*What's so wrong with being happy? Why shouldn't I have some joy?* It had been a very long time.

However, the doubt and uneasiness Matthew shook off during the day wouldn't leave his dreams alone. Even after Aspasia, he continued to dream of Lily—the real Lily—almost every night. The night before was no different. In this dream they had been lying in bed and talking and laughing together. He had stroked the skin on the underside of her arm and said, "It's so soft and lovely—your skin."

"My skin?" she said. She turned her arm to look at the smooth whiteness Matthew had been touching. "It looks like the underbelly of a fish, or maybe a frog," she said and laughed, making a face like a fish, sucking in her cheeks hard.

"No," he cooed, suppressing a smile. "It's like gleaming smooth alabaster—beautiful."

"Alabaster. Hmm," she said and sighed. "I'd give anything to tan."

She looked at him and, becoming mock serious, took his warm, olive-skinned hand and put her pale one next to it. "I'm afraid you're the really beautiful one in this relationship," she said as she lay her head on his chest, nestled into him and sighed a deep contented sigh.

It was at this point in the dream when it diverged from actual memory. It had been right before their world cracked apart and when they had still been obliviously unaware of the cancer growing in Lily's body. But this time, in dream time, as they laughed and held each other, Lily started fading. As Matthew watched in horror, Lily got paler and paler and then faded into an amorphous transparency in his arms. He tried frantically to hold on to her, to keep her with him, but soon his arms were empty and he was alone. Still in the dream, he howled in soundless pain.

He woke from the nightmare with a jerk, tears on his face, Lily's name in his mouth. Before he woke entirely, while he was still halfway in the dream, he looked over and there was Lily, right beside him in his bed again. Relief briefly flooded him... until he remembered—

*Not Lily.*

She was gone forever. A red-hot fury flared in his brain. *Imposter,* he thought, *god-damned imposter*. But just as quickly as it had arisen, the unreasonable anger faded. And as he stared at the ceiling, dread and a bleak loneliness descended, replacing the anger, and filled his every cell.

### Aspasia

Matthew didn't know that Aspasia was also awake, quietly lying beside him. First the burst of anger and then the fog of hopeless loneliness seeped from Matthew and into her as well. And even though his howl of pain was only in his dream, she had heard it... had felt it... deep, deep within her body and her soul. She knew she was failing... failing to give Matthew what he most desired... failing at being Lily. And there was nothing she could do about it. Wisps of panic twisted and wound themselves into her brain.

### Matthew

In the past, Matthew and Lily had occasionally socialized with people from Geneti-Search. But since she had gotten sick and then died, he hadn't been out with anyone... not for a very long time. More recently, since he had been Paired with Aspasia, he had been reluctant to leave her alone for too long. But he had now, somewhat reluctantly, decided with Aspasia's encouragement, that it was time to get back to a more normal life. That's how Matthew came to be sitting at a table in a darkened brew pub with his legal assistant and two lab techs from work.

He would probably never feel comfortable taking Aspasia out with him—especially not with these friends. Every one of them knew he had an Alpha Morfph, but they had never seen her and never would, if he had any say in it. Despite his obvious reluctance to talk about her, they persistently peppered him with questions. He, however, had *no* desire to explain or defend the "return" of Lily. So he sat, uncomfortable and silent, sullenly drinking one beer after another until they finally gave up and stopped asking.

He was working on his third pint, blearily staring at the dance floor, when an amazingly beautiful red-head transfixed him. Her hair, much redder than Lily's, was a wavy, aureole of fire around her head and face as she danced and laughed with her friends. He felt a surge of pleasure and desire. In the past, he'd have gone home and forgotten about her. Maybe, at most, briefly but guiltily picturing her the next time he made love to Lily.

Unfortunately, his friends noticed his gaze before he had stopped watching her.

"What's your problem, Matthew?" Sean said, his voice petulant. "You can just have her tonight at home—or anyone else you spot here." He waved around at all the women in the place. Everyone but Matthew and Alicia, the lone woman in the group, laughed.

Matthew physically recoiled, appalled at what Sean had suggested. He meant his Morfph. He meant that he, Matthew, could have Aspasia morph into the exact image of the woman on the dance floor. His friends, not understanding he had morphed Aspasia into Lily, also couldn't know how appalling Sean's suggestion would be to Matthew.

Lily had been well-liked by everyone sitting at the table tonight, and she had been especially close with his legal assistant, Alicia. Agitated, he brushed off the suggestion and quickly changed the topic. That would never happen. He would not turn Aspasia into his personal sex toy. That would be so many levels of wrong. Even more wrong than what he had already done.

Undeterred, Sean persisted for a while, riffing on the possibilities of having a Morfph.

"Leave him alone, Sean. Not everyone is as big an ass-hole as you," Alicia said, disgusted.

But later, as they walked out of the brew pub to go home, Sean sidled up to Matthew.

"Damn, Matthew, you could think her sixteen or seventeen years old," he said, low, so no one else could hear. "Shit. Go for the gold, bro... you could think her into a fourteen-year-old nymphet—your own real-life Lolita." He laughed an ugly laugh and winked.

Matthew recoiled, disgusted at what this situation had revealed about his friend.

"That's... disgusting, and... Jesus, Sean, what is wrong with you?" He shook his head. "Never mind, I guess that's pretty clear."

"You've always been a self-righteous prick, Matthew. Such a fucking boy scout. Get off your high horse. I think you've lost your moral high ground with this whole Morfph situation," Sean threw back, his voice dripping with derision. "Who would know? She—I assume it's a she—won't tell on you. We all know that."

"I would, Sean. I would know." Matthew stalked out of the pub, offended, sickened by his friend, but also sickened by himself. And what he had put into motion in his life. Sean was right about his slip from the moral high ground. He was down in the mud with the likes of Sean now.

He hadn't stopped thinking about the beautiful red-head at the bar.

———————————

When Matthew got home, Aspasia happily jumped up from a pile of pillows she had heaped in front of the blazing gas fireplace and met him at the door as soon as he walked in. He wrapped his arms around her and kissed her deeply. She returned the kiss with an equal passion.

Before he even knew what was happening, Aspasia started shape shifting into the exact image of the young woman at the pub. While he watched transfixed, her hair grew, became thicker, and darkened to a deeper, flaming red. Lily's wide, round eyes became almond shaped—sensuous, darkly outlined, and cat-like. Her lips plumped and reddened with the ruby-red lipstick the other woman had worn. Astonished and drunkenly excited, Matthew's body responded to Aspasia's passionate metamorphosis into the woman he had lusted after earlier in the evening.

She walked towards him and in a slow-motion, sinuous strip tease, she pulled her dress off over her head. She was naked underneath, and the fireplace illuminated her beautiful body. The fake flames put off a flickering light that sparked off her bright hair. When she was right in front of him, he pulled her to him and ran his fevered hands greedily over her smooth, unblemished, gleaming skin.

Her breasts were large, her ass perfect twin orbs. She looked exactly as he had imagined she would—like gravity didn't exist. Smooth and succulent as a ripe peach. She pulled him by his belt down to the cushions on the floor. She was slick with desire for him when he entered her and they made love on the pillows—fast, almost violently.

After an ecstatic release, and while still breathing hard, Matthew abruptly pulled away from her. Sitting on the floor, his knees bent, he buried his head in his hands in confusion and despair. With the broken emotional and physical connection from Matthew, Aspasia's form flickered and became unclear—as unformed as she had been when they had first met. She was no longer the Redhead, but she wasn't Lily either. She was as unclear as Matthew's idea of what he wanted from her.

"Matthew, I got it right. I know I did. That's what you desired. I know I got her right," Aspasia moaned. She was right, of course. It was *exactly* what he had wanted... had imagined... had fantasized... into existence.

"I'm sorry," he said. "I'm so sorry. You got it right. It's not your fault. Not at all."

But by the time Matthew looked back up, Aspasia's form had changed back into Lily.

Aspasia crawled on her hands and knees to get closer to him.

"Matthew, it's okay. It's me again. It's me. I love you so much."

Of course, Aspasia would know exactly what he wanted now—what he needed. And that was forgiveness—Lily's forgiveness.

"It's okay, Matthew. It's okay." She took him into her arms and stroked his hair and whispered into his ear. "You can't control who you're attracted to, who you desire. You're just being human. I know you love me. I know that."

She continued to talk soothingly into his ear.

"I'm so sorry I died and left you alone. I'm so sorry." Then she took his face in her hands and smiled into his eyes with Lily's smile and speaking in her gentlest voice.

He relaxed into her arms, sighed and smiled back; relieved. Everything seemed good again—so good—until he closed his eyes. As his head spun with the alcohol, the reality of the situation washed over him and finally sank all the way in. This person—Aspasia—would *never be* his Lily. And the grief came crashing back, even worse than before Aspasia had come into his life.

### Aspasia

Aspasia's form once again lost its sharpness, its outline, and became unclear. Almost as if she consisted of softened wax. She looked... melted. Vaguely, she heard Matthew's voice. It sounded far, far away, like it might if she were at the bottom of a deep well.

"Oh Lily, I'm so sorry," he was saying. "What have I done? Oh, Lily, what have I done?"

But Matthew wasn't talking to her, to Aspasia. He was looking up at the ceiling beseechingly, desperately, as he drunkenly babbled. He was talking to the real Lily—the dead Lily. And as much as Aspasia wanted to be her for him, she wasn't. She just wasn't and could never be.

She started crying. And it was not because Matthew wanted her to, she realized. It came from deep inside of her. It was *her* crying. It was Aspasia, whoever she was. And just as she was designed to be, this small emergence of her real self, of her own feelings—along with the failure to meet Matthew's desires—set off excruciating panic and terror. The feelings were so overwhelming. She fell away from Matthew, curled into a fetal position, clutched her sides, and rocked back and forth, trying to relieve the unremitting pain.

### *Matthew*

After Matthew's desperate drunken apology to the dead Lily, he rolled to his side and passed out in an oblivious heap—completely unaware of the crisis he had set off in Aspasia. Aspasia eventually fell asleep, also still on the floor and not far away from Matthew.

She woke a couple of hours later and hauled herself and a staggering Matthew to bed. He snored noisily next to her as she lay sleepless until morning. The morning brought apologies and then an uneasy status quo. They went on in the days after as if nothing had happened, because that was what Matthew desired. Aspasia, of course, could only want what Matthew wanted.

As the days went on, Matthew became increasingly restive and unsettled. The more time that passed, the more his dreams seeped into his waking misgivings and uneasiness. His Morfph was almost perfect—almost Lily, but not quite... ever so slightly off.... not exactly right. And the more time went on, the more it disturbed him. The guiltier it made him feel, the sadder and more irritated he became. As Aspasia had pointed out in the very beginning, she could only be as real as his perceptions and his memory of Lily were.

But the real crux of the problem, Matthew knew, came down to one thing: freewill. Specifically, Aspasia's lack of it. This should have come as no surprise. It was the very thing that had alarmed him when he'd first heard of the project. It was the very thing he'd argued with Alix about. The very thing that had made him know in his bones that the project was wrong. But he had overridden what he knew because of his own weakness, his own greed to have his happiness back and to have his soulmate back.

Finally, it was Aspasia who broke the uneasy truce.

"We need to talk about it, Matthew."

Matthew didn't need to ask what she meant, he knew.

"I know, Aspasia. I know. You have done nothing wrong. It's me."

Aspasia nodded encouragement.

"It's just that this situation, your need to please me, is making me feel not only guilty but lonely... and sometimes angry, which is completely unfair. I feel like I'm just talking to myself and making love to myself... like I'm masturbating. Like I'm really just by myself."

"Matthew, you're not by yourself. I'm with you. I'm a real person and I love you with all my heart."

"But it's not real," Matthew said.

"You're saying I'm not real? I'm real. Real feelings, real flesh and blood. I'm just as real as you are."

"But you only feel what I want you to feel. You only want what I want you to want. You have no choice."

"But that's why you Patroned me, isn't it? That's what you signed up for. And that's the one thing I can't do for you. You want the only thing I can't give you." Aspasia's tears spilled heavily down her face. "I *need* to please you, but the very thing I am, the very reason for my existence, is the thing you don't want."

"I'm so sorry, Aspasia. I know this is hurting you, and I know it is all my fault. I just don't know what to do. I don't seem to have any more control of my desires than you do."

Aspasia stared at him. Her hands clenched into tight fists, and her shoulders tensed up around her ears. Tears continued to drip down her face.

"Let's go to bed. We'll work it out... together. Don't cry."

Matthew opened his arms to her, and she walked into them gratefully. He kissed her wet eyelids and murmured more apologies in her ear.

As they lay in bed, Matthew held her to him tightly.

"Now all I desire is for you to be happy."

"Yes, I can feel that. And I am."

But a persistent anxiety remained, lurking... in both of them.

---

And it wasn't that Aspasia lacked in her efforts. She argued brilliantly, had "her own" opinions, and brought up ideas he'd never thought about. She had an incredibly sharp intellect, sharper than Lily's and much sharper than his. But in his heart, he knew it was all staged. Her independence of thought and her apparent trueness to herself weren't real. Everything was to please him. But she couldn't please him... precisely *because* that was what she wanted so badly to do.

## Aspasia

As for Aspasia, she was in continual and sustained mental turmoil. Like Matthew, she deeply knew the situation was impossible to resolve. But she could not stop trying. It wasn't in her to stop. Matthew wanted her to have freewill, and he wanted Lily back—the real Lily.

Aspasia's gene-level need was to meet Matthew's needs, his desires. The more disturbed he became, and the longer she couldn't satisfy his desires, the more agitated she became. All she could do was try even harder and a profound dissonance set in. Her body, too, was in continual physical flux as Matthew's desires changed and his confusion increased. The conflict and anxiety within her surged to an unbearable level.

She lay awake at night, ruminating and surreptitiously watching Matthew. Aspasia ate very little, and her head ached much of the time. She needed to solve this problem, but it always came back to one thing. What Matthew needed and desired, she was completely incapable of giving.

# CHAPTER 18

## *What's Wrong with You?*

*Sara*

Confused and filled with rage and self-loathing, Sara avoided Sam for several days after her ill-conceived night with Jack. She used various unconvincing excuses, but Sam was clearly picking up that something was wrong. His messages and texts were getting more frequent, anxious—and increasingly insistent.

Sara couldn't quite believe she had let Jack back in like that, couldn't believe she had let it happen. She finally came to the tortured conclusion that she had to tell Sam about Jack, about what had happened between them. She had no idea what would happen when she did, but they had agreed to be completely honest with each other, and she was determined to honor it. Even if she had honored nothing else in their relationship.

She was terrified.

Finally, Sam stayed late at their shared office building and waited for Sara after her last therapy session. He sat patiently in one of the cloth upholstered chairs in the waiting room until her client left. When the door opened, and a young woman exited, he ducked in and sat across from Sara in the lavender leather chair the client had just vacated.

Startled, Sara visibly flinched slightly away from Sam.

"I saw that. Okay, what gives? Why have you been avoiding me?"

"I haven't. I've just been…"

"Sara. C'mon. Don't."

Cornered, she finally told him. He was angrier than she had ever seen him—his pain palpable. She realized then that she'd never heard him yell before. There were tears in his eyes that he wiped away angrily. She had never seen that either.

"What's wrong with you? Why did you do such a stupid thing? Why?"

"I don't know. I really don't know," was all she could say. She stared down at her boots as tears filled her eyes, too. She could not bear to look at him.

"That's all you can say? You don't know? You really value what we have... had... so little?"

He shook his head, stood up, and walked out the door. He didn't really slam it, but closed it hard enough to make Sara jump.

*Had. Past tense*, she thought. *What we had.* With that one word, she knew it was over. And not just their love affair, but also their friendship. The pain of this loss doubled her over, punching her in the gut. Panic surged and flooded her mind and body. It was worse than when Jack had left... both times. This time, she knew she deserved it.

But exactly twenty-one agonizing days later, to her profound surprise and relief, Sam called—a reprieve she didn't deserve but grabbed with both hands. He knew how often this stuff happened, he said. Had seen it many times with his clients. Even had thought he had been prepared for it.

"I get it," he said. "I hate it, but I get it. Maybe more than anyone else, I know what kind of hold that jerk has on you. But I need to know—is this the end of it? I can't do this again. I just can't. It's too painful. Will you commit to making us work? Can you give me that assurance?"

"Yes," she said into the phone. "Yes, yes, I can. I do." And she meant it. Knew in her heart she could and would.

"So, let's see if we can get past this," he said.

But she hadn't told him everything. Maybe she should have, but she never told him she would've gone back to Jack that night. There were limits to how forgiving Sam could be. He wasn't a saint, after all.

*And I'm not that honest or that stupid*, she thought. She did not want to lose Sam. Not just because Jack rejected her once again. Sam was the first person she wanted to talk to when she was in pain or when she had good news. He had been that to her for a long while now. She trusted him and valued him. And really wanted him in her life. She would not blow that again.

She depended on, needed, and yes, loved him with all her heart. But even that didn't mean that she had stopped cycling between obsessing about and internally raging at Jack.

*This addiction needs to be rooted out and purged.*

Jack was right about one thing though; she didn't need him anymore. With these thoughts, she jumped up, ran to the bathroom, and hugging the toilet bowl, vomited until it turned to dry heaves.

*Maybe this is purging my anger,* she thought. *How did Alix describe it? Green and black and bilious. Please let this drain out of me now, from my body and my mind.*

---

So, Sam and Sara went back to seeing each other. They were both wary and raw and were being very careful with each other. But they had been friends for years and the easiness of their relationship reemerged, maybe even stronger. They knew what they had was breakable, and they both wanted it badly. They reaffirmed they would be totally honest with each other and that no topic would be off limits. They had both been in marriages where more and more topics had become off-limits. Neither wanted that this time around.

So they talked about Jack when they needed to, even though it made them both squirm with discomfort. Actually, they talked and talked and talked—about everything. They talked about books they read. They talked about movies they went to. They talked when they worked together in the garden. They talked every day, even if they didn't see each other. They talked at dinner and in bed on the three or four nights each week Sam slept over. They said goodnight and talked to each other on the phone every night Sam wasn't sleeping over. And they were both happy that sex was becoming *much* better as Sara steadily exorcised Jack from her brain and body.

Being with Sam was so different from being with Jack—easier, more relaxed. From the beginning, she had gotten comfortable being herself and had stopped worrying about staying whippet thin.

When with Jack, her rigid control had become fraught and obsessive. In the back of her mind lurked the suspicion that maybe her enforced leanness had caused her inability to get pregnant. After the initial ingrained fear subsided, she liked her body with a little more roundness. She even decided she looked better—softer, less severe. Sam said she was even more beautiful, and he meant every word.

"With Jack," Sara said to Sam one night as they lay in bed together, "every time I saw a beautiful young girl walk down the street or, worse, at Jack's department parties, I thought, of course he would rather have them in his bed than me. And they so often wanted him too, regardless of the age difference. How could he resist that, especially since he needs adulation so badly? I don't know. Maybe he did the best he could."

Sara saw Sam's face crease and quickly continued.

"Sam, I want you to know, I need you, but I also really *love* you—more than I ever did Jack. My feelings for Jack were closer to obsession than actual love."

"I wish you didn't feel the need to be fair to that guy. It's okay to get angry. He abused you. He was a bastard to you."

"I don't *completely* disagree with that," she said, "but I'm so tired of being angry and I wasn't the total innocent victim that you seem to think." Or maybe that was just what he really wanted to think.

"Listen, I loved Jack," Sara said. "Maybe I still do… a little… a very little. He listened to me and encouraged me for many years, but he also liked to keep the upper hand. And I obliged by trying to be what he wanted me to be. His little chameleon. I need something different now. I need to be whole and to be myself—authentic—whatever that is."

Sam took her head in both his hands and gently kissed her on both her closed eyes, and finally on her mouth.

"Yourself is a wonderful thing to be. No one else can do it nearly as well," he said, and then leaned over and turned off the lamp.

# CHAPTER 19

## *Who in the World Am I?*

*"Let me think: was I the same when I got up this morning?
I almost think I can remember feeling a little different. But
if I'm not the same the next question is 'Who in the world
am I?' Ah, that's the great puzzle."*

—Alice from <u>Alice's Adventures in Wonderland</u> by Lewis Carrol

### *Aspasia*

In the middle of the night, two weeks and one day after the evening Matthew had come home drunk, Aspasia changed—not morph as she did before—but changed deep down in her very soul.

It happened after Aspasia and Matthew had both finally fallen into their separate, but equally troubled, sleep. While Matthew dreamed and stewed in his perfect trifecta of guilt, shame, and sorrow, the unbearable stress he'd created in Aspasia caused a surge of neurochemicals and hormones. Building and snowballing, they set off a profound transformation within her.

Unused genes switched on, while others switched off, altering her very DNA. And so overnight, the Morfph's neural configuration changed—one synapse at a time. Technically termed an epigenetic switch, poets would more likely have rhapsodized about it as a Sea Change.

Her creators evidently had either not completely understood or perhaps had just not taken the great elasticity of the human brain into full consideration. Because Morfphs, regardless of their seemingly miraculous enhancements, were simply human beings.

When Aspasia woke up the next morning, she knew she was a completely different person than the one she had been when she had gone to sleep the night before. Much like Kafka's Gregor Samsa, she had gone through a metamorphosis—in her body and in her mind—as she slept. Something had snapped, and she felt a molten eruption rise inside her.

Feelings bombarded her—confusing, disorienting, and terrifying feelings. They were new, not just in their intensity, but also in their quality. And they were not feelings as she normally experienced them. They were *her own* feelings—generated from within herself.

Her head felt as if it were going to explode. She thrashed and yelled incoherently.

Matthew startled awake.

Aspasia's frenzied thrashing of arms and legs had twisted her bedcovers tightly around her body. She finally freed herself, threw them to the floor, and stumbled across the room to the full-length mirror on the door of the closet. She stood there, mesmerized, staring fixedly into her own eyes. Her moss-green eyes, Lily's eyes, were wide and fathomless. They pulled her deeper and deeper into herself, but at the same time, she felt as if she were floating and watching from above.

Matthew got out of bed and stood behind her as she stared into the mirror. He reached out for her shoulder, but she angrily wrenched away.

"Don't touch me," she screamed. "Get away from me. Just get away."

Matthew flinched back, wordless with shock.

As Matthew watched, open-jawed, eyes wide, Aspasia's physical form transformed. Her outlines grew fuzzy. She grew in height. Her hair darkened and became thick and wavy. Her eyes changed from green to brown—no... to hazel.

She reeled around, away from the mirror, her hands over her face. She collided with Matthew and shrieked at him again.

"You don't own me! You don't own me." Tears streamed out her changed eyes. Matthew stood frozen in place.

Aspasia turned back to the mirror and again peered at a face she had never really seen before. At Geneti-Search, before she was Paired, she had caught unclear or wavy glimpses of herself in glass, silverware and sometimes in water, but there were no mirrors at the facilities where she had been raised.

Her eyes were wide in crazed terror, but there was no doubt in her mind the image reflected was *her* face—her proper face. In a frenzy, she yanked at her hair, pulling out little tufts as she did. She stopped abruptly and looked down at her hands and arms—her shimmer was gone. Her skin had gone from Lily's pale white back to her own warm olive. She crackled with furious rage. Her feelings were drowning her.

*Too much. Too much. Too much.*

"Aspasia, Aspasia, please calm down." Matthew tried again to wrap his arms around her, to contain her.

She ripped free.

"Don't call me that. Don't call me that poor concubine's name. I'm not Lily and I'm not Aspasia," she spit. "I don't know who I am, but I'm not your creature—not anymore. I don't care how you feel. I don't care. My feelings are mine now, mine... not yours."

She sank to her knees on the floor and rocked back and forth, her arms wrapped around her legs, head down between her arms.

"Mine. Mine. Mine. Mine," she moaned. "Mine." She groaned loudly, a wrenching, painful sound, and then burst into violent tears.

### Matthew

Stunned and mute, Matthew stared down at Aspasia... and he knew. He had seen the shape-shifting before, but never this clearly. He knew immediately that she was different... and that this difference, this change, was profound and irrevocable.

She no longer looked anything like his wife, didn't even resemble her. Her Morfph shimmer had been flickering and dimming in the last couple of days, but he hadn't paid it much attention. Now she had lost it entirely.

He knew right then, without a doubt, that she was no longer his, or anyone else's, Morfph. This new person was young. Looked no older than twenty, maybe more like eighteen. She was lean, raw-boned and tall, much taller than she had ever appeared before. She was still definitely a "she," he thought, but much more androgynous in appearance and in her movements. Her dark hair and tawny skin, undoubtedly, now reflected her real genetic heritage.

She was shivering and shaking, still on the floor. Matthew grabbed a blanket and approached her cautiously, like she was a wounded, and quite wild, animal. As he stepped closer, she didn't protest, so he wrapped her in the blanket and sat next to her on the floor.

Encouraged, he tentatively rubbed her back in slow motion, put his arms around her. She let him and exhaled a wounded sounding puff of breath. She continued to quake and shiver in his arms for what seemed a very long time, and just when he thought she had stopped, she would jerk, and her spasms would start up again. Finally, she relaxed into his arms and lay her head on his chest. He caressed it and talked into her dark hair in a low, soothing voice.

"It's okay. It's okay," he whispered.

"I'm different," she said. Matthew could hear her teeth chattering. "Something has shifted in me. I can feel. Really feel... me. It's me. There's a Me there now... again. Before it was all you—but you're not in there anymore. My need to change to your desires is gone. I can't even sense what your desires are anymore."

She bowed her head into her hands, as if to block something out. Maybe everything.

"I'm so confused... so lost. It's total chaos in here." She pointed to her head. "So many feelings and... thoughts. It never stops. Constant chattering and noise... all from my own mind."

"Aspasia, it's good. Don't you see? It's so good. I'm glad you have your own feelings. It's a relief, you know. An enormous relief to me."

"Not Aspasia, please, don't call me that." She sniffed and shuddered. "I don't know who I am. It used to be so clear."

After a long silence, she spoke in a small voice.

"I'm scared." Her shaking had started again and, as Matthew readjusted her blanket, he could see goosebumps and accompanying raised fine hairs covering her bare arms and shoulders.

"I'm sorry, Asp... no, uh..." He shook his head and laughed, a little a shake in his voice. "Welcome to humanity, or maybe welcome back. We're all scared most of the time... but you know that."

"I just thought it was you," she sniffed.

He laughed again, amused this time.

"I don't think it's only me. Pretty sure its most people," he said ruefully.

"God, I remember. It really sucks," she said.

"Yeah. Sometimes it really does."

"There are memories... memories of before, but they are so fuzzy, more like a dream only half remembered."

Her head got heavy on his shoulder.

"So tired," she said, her eyes fluttering shut. "So tired."

"Let's get you back to bed then," he whispered, feeling an intense protectiveness wash over him.

After Matthew tucked her into their bed and thought she was asleep, her eyes popped wide open.

"Ruby. I'm Ruby," she said, as if the name had just bubbled up in her mind. "Ruby," she said again, then she closed her eyes again and fell into what turned out to be a deep twenty-hour sleep.

———————————

After Matthew put Ruby into bed and as she lay asleep, he thought and worried. He knew the dangers of this shift. She was now a "Defective Morfph" and they expected him—contractually required him—to report her defect.

The irony of this was the change, the transition, must have come from his desire, his need, for her to have free-will. So, if it was his desire that caused her to become "defective," then she was not defective at all. Just the opposite. She was merely performing her genetic imperative—her very reason for being—which was to please him, her Patron.

He had heard about other so-called defective Morfphs. As a Patron, he was told that when they reported defective Morfphs, Geneti-Search *adjusted* the Morfphs. He didn't know what they really did with defective Morfphs, but he knew that there was no "tuning up" a defective Morfph. He also knew there was no way he was going to report her. But the real danger lay in the strict and stringently enforced requirement that all Morfphs be monitored monthly.

Now he was the one who was terrified. Aspasia... *no, Ruby, I must remember that...* had no idea about the consequences of what had just happened. *Focus,* he said to himself, *focus!* Luckily, they had just been in for her last check-up two days before. He had twenty-eight days to figure out what they were going to do.

# CHAPTER 20

## *Ruby Becomes... Herself*

*"I celebrate and sing myself"*

—Walt Whitman

### Matthew

After her transition, Ruby no longer slept in Matthew's bed at night. By unspoken and, Matthew thought, mutual agreement, they had also decided to not talk about the future... for now. It would have to wait until Ruby became used to her re-discovered Self.

Ruby's transition seemed to Matthew to be very like the passage in adolescence, but instead of happening over years, it was magnified and condensed into a matter of days. All the irrational behavior, pain, and confusion boiled down and condensed into a sticky syrup of turmoil.

He watched her, trying—with mixed results—to be unobtrusive. She was so very young. *Newly hatched*, he thought. Her eyes shone with curiosity and a blazing intelligence. And she was still changing every time he saw her. Becoming more herself. It was fascinating—and utterly unnerving.

*A cross between a hummingbird and a young horse*, he thought—all angles and legs, with a raw, humming energy. Her skin was a smooth, tawny golden-brown and her dark auburn hair gleamed like a new chestnut, fresh from its spiny case. She had taken scissors and chopped her long hair off and now it stuck up in spikes formed from her hands being run through it over and over in agitation and excitement.

Her eyes were a startling hazel, sometimes dark brown flecked and rimmed with bluish-green, sometimes more of an all-over golden brown... depending mostly on the light and colors she wore. Her angular facial features were not really pretty, certainly not cute, but she was striking, and maybe even beautiful.

In an interesting coincidental twist, she looked a lot like him now—the hair and skin color so similar to the coloring from his Indian heritage. Now she could easily be mistaken for his daughter. She certainly wasn't his lovely Lily anymore. Lily had been outspoken and passionate, yes—but warm, full of compassion, and rounded and lush in her body and heart. There was a raw fierceness to this new person who had been his Morfph. *Ruby*, he reminded himself mentally, *Ruby*. He really had to stop thinking of her as Aspasia.

Matthew felt his heart swelling painfully—with both a renewed grief for the final and complete loss of Lily, but also with to an intense fear and protectiveness for this fierce, but vulnerable, young woman.

In the beginning, he had thought he was getting a Morfph to assuage his grief… and then he realized he had been trying to resurrect his wife. Now he had both his grief for Lily and this new terror for Ruby's fate. Once again, his heart was in hostage to his love, this time for Ruby. The human dilemma: to not love is to despair, and to love is despair in the making.

### *Ruby*

Transitioning from Aspasia back to Ruby had abruptly hurled her face to face with herself. Biological drives bombarded with a confusing cacophony of emotional needs.

As an un-Transitioned Morfph, her need to please and become what her Patron wanted her to be and do determined who she was. The biological imperative to become what her Patron wanted her to be overrode her temperament, the inherited characteristics that determined how she responded to the world, her body makeup, and her appearance.

With her Transition, the personality she was born with burst forth. But at the same time, she became hardened into a more rigid sense of self—the sense of being an individual with choices.

---

Two days after her abrupt change, Ruby woke up in the middle of the night with a dull pain and cramps in her abdomen. She got up to walk to the bathroom, hoping it would relieve the cramps. As she pulled back the covers, she saw a dark spot on the sheets where she had been lying. With the switching on of the bedside lamp, the dark spot became bright red in the light. And there on her night gown was another vivid splotch of blood.

After a sharp intake of breath, she calmed herself. She knew what this was even though she, or any of her Podmates, had ever had one before. This was part of the female monthly reproductive cycle. But Morfphs were sterile.

Geneti-Search wanted complete control over the production of new Morfphs, and who knew what characteristics a Morfph offspring might carry? But she still wasn't completely sure what it meant. Was she still sterile?

*No one must know. Not yet. Not even Matthew.*

She stripped the sheets off the bed and shoved them, along with her night-gown, into the hamper in the bathroom. She then found tampons in the bath-room—left over from Lily. Putting one in was a tricky procedure. She imagined it would get easier.

*Will they leave us alone, me and Matthew, if they find out? No, they definitely won't. And what will happen if one of us—a Morfph—gets pregnant?*

She could imagine the uproar. The headlines. "First Morfph Baby." It would no doubt happen to someone—and probably soon.

The next day, Ruby washed the sheets and nightgown while Matthew was at work.

She would handle this. Just like everything else, she'd have to figure it out by herself.

## Matthew

The days that followed were sometimes tense, sometimes sweet, but real this time. He and Ruby were adjusting to the new situation, but trepidation and dread filled Matthew. The specter of the next monthly check-up loomed. It was now in exactly twenty-five days, the third Tuesday of the month. Matthew hadn't talked to Ruby of his fears, but he was certain she also must feel the sense of impending doom hanging over them.

The monitoring appointments consisted of thorough medical and mental health examinations. Every month Ruby... Aspasia then... went through a battery of tests and scans to monitor physical, cognitive, and emotional functioning and health.

The first thing the lab tech did each time, as soon as she walked in the door, was to scan the surgically implanted chip in her forearm. The chip identified who she was, who her Patron was, and found her location at all times. All Morfphs were chipped. They also had a barcode tattooed along the hairlines at the nape of their necks.

The barcode identified the date they were engineered, the date they were implanted, and the group of other Morfphs with whom they were raised. It hid under their hair and remained on their skin, whatever shape or form they might take.

The tests given during this monthly check-up were grueling and took a full day. The checkup was officially said to be a protection for Morfphs, to monitor their health and well-being and also to monitor them for abuse. The first stipulation on the contract that Patroni signed included an agreement that there could be *no* physical damage to a Morfph.

This had proven problematic, as Morfphs could and would, erase any bruises, contusions, or other damage done them if their Patron desired it. They would not report abuse against their Patron's wishes. Patroni were, of course, not told this specifically, but if they were so disposed, they figured it out quickly.

So mostly the exam served as a protection for Geneti-Search and its huge monetary investment. Matthew knew they were primarily monitoring the functioning of the Morfph and testing for defects. This human genotype was completely new. Geneti-Search had no idea what mental or physical health issues these Morfphs might be prone to develop. Even their average expected lifespan was a mystery. Would they burn out faster than the average human, since every aspect of their development and mental functioning was intense and rapid?

Should read: What Matthew knew, and that neither Ruby nor any of the other Patroni or Morfphs knew, was that if they found a Morfph to be a Defective, they would be Culled—removed and replaced... every time. These Cullings would be rare and would not be disclosed to the Patron, unless that was what they had requested.

Patroni had three options if their Morfph was defective. They could have their original Morfph corrected or adjusted and returned to them, they could opt for replacement with another Morfph, or a return with complete remuneration. But Matthew knew Morfphs could not be corrected or adjusted. All defectives were Culled... no exception.

But it was crucial that Geneti-Search kept the Cullings secret. Besides being bad for their corporate image and their bottom line, some Patroni would inevitably get sentimentally attached to an individual Morfph. Who knew what kind of trouble these spoiled rich clients might make if they knew an exchange had been made?

They would simply be told that they needed to be re-Paired with their Morfph to correct discovered glitches. They would then be promptly Paired with another Morfph. It would never be detected because the new Morfph would easily read all the memories and feelings of the Patron. They would know what had been shared with the other Morfph and they would easily fit into the Patron's life and become the embodiment of their Patron's desires, just as the original Morfph had been.

*Easy-peasy*, Matthew thought, and then shuddered. He had no idea what would then become of the Culled Morfphs or what would become of Ruby, if... when?... she was discovered. Was there any way to hide her change? What in the world were they going to do?

# CHAPTER 21

## Mania

*"You can do nothing worse in your life... than to force the body into servitude... To eat with someone else's mouth, to sleep with the eyes of others, to move as someone else desires, and to risk the shipwreck of your faculties and your life-what fate could be worse?"*

—Mid-1600th century Venetian courtesan, Veronica Franco

## Matthew

Ruby seemed to be in the throes of a sort of mania. As with all Morfphs, her mind was analytical, razor sharp... and wildfire quick. That part of her genetic engineering hadn't changed. She asked Matthew endless questions and often acted impatient with the answers or lack of answers. She didn't say it outright, but she seemed to find him slow-witted and he was—compared to her.

Also, with the Transition, came a seemingly insatiable hunger to fill all her senses—with music, images, tastes and smells and an equally burning need to fill her mind with knowledge and ideas—"the whole human experience," she said.

"That's a pretty big area," Matthew had said when Ruby told him this.

As she sat curled up in a chair in Lily's book-lined office, she rapidly read—devoured—volume after volume. She sped through all the books in the house and easily retained everything she read. She pored over books on neurology, religion, philosophy, sociology and psychology—books that explored human behavior and the concept of freewill and the illusion of the Self.

She read fiction, both great literature (as Matthew called it) and less than great literature, as well. She read Spinoza, Rumi, Socrates, Khayyam and Confucius. She read books on Buddhism, several versions of the Tao Te Ching, The Bhagavad Gita, The Torah, The Koran, The Avesta, and The Bible. She read books on history and was especially interested in Lily's Women's History books. There were ones on women in Ancient Greece and Rome and others on the "Witch" hunts—the mass murder of tens of thousands of mostly women in Europe and early America.

She read books about, and by, Freud and Jung and early Psychology. She read books by Oats, Joyce, Walker, Kesey, Vonnegut, Whitman, Nin, Atwood and both Shelleys—Frankenstein's monster fascinated her for obvious reasons. She read Angelou, Mead, Ghandi, Mandela, Coates, Lahiri, and Steinbeck.

The books about Geishas, courtesans, and Hetaera, and others who had to seduce and sexually please others for their livelihood especially caught her interest. She found a section about the historical Aspasia in a book about women in ancient Greece. She'd shouted for Matthew, apparently appalled and indignant for how women were treated. She'd glared accusingly at him like it was all his fault.

"Morfphs," she said, "are the modern, new and improved, courtesans. That's why we were made, isn't it? That's our function."

As uncomfortable as it made him, Matthew had to agree.

She found it all fascinating, but it just left her with more questions to be answered. She'd often be reading, then break out in excited, sometimes worried, questions, burning to understand, to figure it all out. Her intellect was sharp, but in this, she was also like a teenager just out of adolescence, just becoming an adult, asking all the questions people that age find so perplexing and amazing.

"Listen to this," she said. "Eleanor Roosevelt said that adopting or surrendering to other people's values makes a person less of a human being. A Morfph's surrender to their Patron's values, is total. Does that make us—them—less human, do you think?"

Before he could answer, she'd ask another question.

"Here's another thing. This says the Self is an illusion," she said, looking up from her book, her eyes wild. "What does that mean? How can that be? I can feel that I'm a Self now. Really feel it now." This concept particularly bothered her, probably since her sense of self was so new.

When she ran out of the books in his and Lily's large personal library, which she did quickly, Matthew took her to the one remaining public library in the whole northern part of the state. It had been a huge, abandoned warehouse before being converted to take millions of books collected from all the closed libraries in the region or books discarded from people's personal libraries.

They shelved books from floor to ceiling with old-fashioned rolling ladders to reach them. The facility was almost empty of people but had a few attendants, all volunteers, to help find and reach books.

Ruby's ebullience delighted the helpers whenever she and Matthew visited, and they hurried to get her whatever she wanted. Excited and exclaiming, she flitted from aisle to aisle, ran up and down ladders, pulled out scores of books, read them at an amazing speed, and then moved on to the next.

In this and in all that she did, her movements were exuberant—quick and awkward—and sometimes heartbreakingly graceful, like the young animal she was. She reminded him of a fawn or a colt, kicking up their legs, happy to be alive. They would walk out with their arms full of as many books as the library would lend at one time.

---

Ruby spent her time reading, asking questions, debating philosophy, listening to music, and watching movies. She played Matthew's music collection—jazz and bluegrass, classic rock-and-roll—everything he had. She had moved on from actual books from the library to books she downloaded.

She had also read all of Lily's personal journals and was re-reading them now. She had skimmed through some of them before her Transition, but now she seemed particularly fascinated and obsessed with the written thoughts of the woman she had been Morfphing since their Pairing... before she had changed.

"I feel curiously close to her... like I was her in a previous life... or maybe like she was my mother or something." Ruby's forehead creased. "I've never really had an actual mother... not one I remember, anyway. We had our Caretakers but..."

Matthew reached for her hand.

"So many things to feel," she said.

After a pause, she shrugged, as if shaking off a mood.

"I really like her—your Lily," she said.

"Yes," he'd replied, "She was wonderful. I liked her, too. "

"I can see why you miss her." She looked over at him and smiled a sympathetic, sad smile. "But you didn't get her quite right, you know. She wasn't everything you thought... and also more than you thought."

Matthew looked at Ruby with his head tilted to one side, his eyebrows raised questioningly. Ruby, when she was Aspasia, knew exactly how Matthew saw Lily... how he experienced her... even more than he did.

She continued, trying to explain. "She wasn't quite as.... well... perfect. She was funnier and sometimes kind of cynical..."

Matthew had never read Lily's journals, had felt like it would be an invasion... still did. He wasn't surprised that Lily had protected him from a lot of her thoughts and her feelings and didn't resent it. He didn't want to know what she had kept private. He knew who Lily was with him. That was enough.

"I guess we can never really completely know another person," he said.

"Morfphs can," she said, and he looked at her sharply, discomfited, as he realized again that she, in fact, knew all his secrets up until the Transformation.

"Maybe we shouldn't try," he said. "Maybe that would be a terrible invasion."

"Yes," she agreed, "it is."

---

Matthew had wanted to keep Ruby off the internet for as long as possible, but he had finally introduced it to her. Just as he had been afraid, she was now obsessed and was on his laptop for hours a day. He had especially wanted to keep her from hearing the ongoing news about Morfphs that was getting media attention. He didn't know for sure how many Morfphs had been Paired so far, but he knew after the Alpha and Beta batches, production had increased. There could be a thousand by now, maybe more.

As the story of Morfphs had leaked out, Geneti-Search tried to keep it—not exactly a secret, but—under the radar. But people do talk and what a juicy story it was. It was, of course, all very disturbing to Ruby. There were some reports of abused, mutilated, and abandoned Morfphs coming out. Just hints of it so far. But Matthew was sure there would be more of that coming to light. These were just the tip of the iceberg.

He'd heard a rumor at work that a recent suicide of a young woman found alone in a wealthy man's house had been what was being called an "orphaned" Morfph. They'd warned Patroni against extended separations from their Morfph. If a separation was too long, they were told, the Morfph could decline, possibly go into a deep depression, and the stress would likely affect their functioning and maybe shorten their lifespan. It seemed maybe it was even worse than expected, as other rumors said that some Orphaned Morfphs had actually gone mad with the loss of their Patron, eventually lapsing into comas.

Morfphs were so vulnerable, Matthew thought... at the mercy and under the control of their Patroni—like children and animals. Of course, Geneti-Search and everyone else making money off Morfphs refuted this. But now there was an increasing number of critics taking up the call. Right now, it was just a little snowball, but it was gathering speed and headed downhill. It was part of his job as the corporation's lawyer to defend the ethics of this project. How could he possibly continue to do that now?

———————

At night Ruby would almost collapse in fatigue. She slept very little, maybe four hours a night, still in the grips of her mania. She would suddenly be fast asleep in her chair, books strewn all around her, and Matthew would pick her up and take her to her bed. She was heavy, even though lean, all legs and arms and completely dead to the world. He'd look at her with tenderness, but she was no longer his lover. That had ended when she had gone through "The Change," as Ruby now jokingly called her transition. He couldn't even imagine making love to this young, whirling force of nature, and she showed no interest either.

When Matthew watched Ruby as she read, he thought again about the loss of her unearthly glow, her Morfph glimmer. She looked more substantial now. Firmer. In place of the idealized form of his wife that was previously imposed on her, was an ordinary young human, though a pretty disheveled one.

He insisted she brush her teeth and her hair and that she bathe, but other than that, he didn't impose his will on her, and her appearance was seemingly of no concern to her or to him, either.

She seemed to be completely over her initial anger at him and was affectionate, like the daughter or younger sister she resembled. She'd hug him often and kiss him on the cheek. And he felt great affection for her as well. Though his affection seemed fiercer to him. She was his responsibility, and he would do anything he had to do to protect her.

---

After she'd read everything in the house and all the books of interest at the public library, had watched all the documentaries she could find, had tired of Googling everything under the sun and had listened to all his music over and over, she was ready for "field trips," as Matthew called their outings.

First, he took her to the Silver Bridge Park in the heart of the city. Armed guards patrolled everywhere and checked their IDs at various checkpoints along the way, but even that couldn't spoil their fun. At the Arboretum, they exclaimed over the exotically beautiful and sometimes huge orchids.

"That one looks like it could ingest a small dog," she said and shivered.

He laughed. It did. Then they ventured to the science museum, where they stayed in the area with the multicolored butterflies fluttering around them for a long, long time. One butterfly lit on Ruby's hand and she stared in open-mouthed in delight and amazement. It was an iridescent blue and green and shimmered much as she used to.

They went all over the city riding in armored drone taxis and peered down the streets at the beautiful neighborhoods with their big colorfully painted old houses. They were looking worse for wear these days. Just a handful of years previously, they would have hopped on and off the streetcars to walk by those houses on the steep, twisty streets, Matthew thought, briefly mourning the changes to his beautiful city.

They went down to the heavily patrolled waterfront and ate clam chowder out of sourdough bread bowls and then to the Museum of Modern Art. There, Ruby marveled over the art.

"All the amazing creations!" she exclaimed breathlessly. "These are in the books! But they're so different here. Look at the thick paint, the colors, the patterns. Oh my, so alive. Pulsing. I couldn't see that in the books."

# CHAPTER 22

## *The Adam of Her Labors*

Anonymous reviews by female Mor∫ph Patroni* used in a marketing campaign by Geneti-Search, specifically targeting women:

*"(Freeborn) men are such a disappointment."*

*"[Freeborn] Men bully me, patronize me, mansplain to me, try to control me, and hurt me. Men expect to be taken care of, waited on, catered to, and have sex on demand. Men don't satisfy me sexually… don't do what I like in bed...don't even try. Men get fat and old. I'm tired of these whiney baby men. I'm tired of men who expect me to be perfect physically but don't even cut their toe nails… who are always talking about women like they are pieces of meat… or pieces of ass… who think women are just here to serve them and their all-important needs. I'm tired of men who really hate women. I'm tired of men, period. What do I want? I want my Morfph."*

*"My Morfph lets me be myself. He supports my autonomy, and my ambitions, and my interests. He lets me be me; he celebrates it. No nagging or complaining that I don't spend enough time with him; no complaints that I don't have dinner ready for him or that we don't have enough sex. In fact, sex is great! I want it all the time with him. That's new. He never tells me*

*I'm getting fat. He never compares me to other women. My Morfph adores everything about me. And I adore everything about him."*

\* *Note: I believe all the reviews attributed to female Patroni were written by Alix Edison herself. At the time of this writing, almost all Morfphs have been Paired with men. After the campaign to target more marketing to women, there was a measurable upward tick in female Patroni.*

*D.M. Lawrence*

### Alix

When Alix had first started the Morfph project, she had had no intention of taking a Morfph for herself. Her ambitions were much grander than that. She saw it not only as a way of making her mark in her company but also in the world. She wanted to change—to improve—the course of the whole human race. That is what she had told herself, anyway.

Then two things happened: her daughter cut her out of her life entirely and her most recent boyfriend—*what a ridiculous thing to call a forty-nine-year-old man*—had left her for a much younger woman and her thirteen-year-old daughter. *A two-fer,* Alix thought darkly.

After Alix had been Paired with a Morfph—her Adam–it had been perfect. At least it had in the beginning. *Isn't that always the way? It seems there's a honeymoon period, even with Morfphs. Who would have thought?* But things were not so perfect now. It was aggravating—even worrisome.

During a therapy session, when Sara had asked her about her newest relationship, Alix talked about Adam—not revealing that she had been Paired with a Morfph, of course. She wasn't ready to tell Sara that… not yet. Maybe never.

"Well, he adores me, that's for sure… does anything to please me… *anything…*"

Alix saw Sara's face change. She looked puzzled, then recognition and maybe even alarm replaced the puzzlement. *You get it, Doc, whether or not you'll admit it*, Alix thought.

"But by the sound of your voice, it sounds like that's a... uh, a problem?" Sara said.

"He changes with my every whim. He's everything I want him to be all the time... It's all about me... pleasing *me*. I thought that was what I wanted... but..."

"But?... So that's *not* what you want...?

"I mean... there's just no there, there."

"No there, there...?

"I can't lean on him... there's nothing to come up against... just... no one there. And it's aggravating, I guess. It infuriates me."

"Uh, huh, yes. I think I understand," Sara said, and Alix could tell she did. "Have you talked to him about it... let him know how you feel? Communication is very imp..."

"Oh, he knows exactly how I feel. Lack of communication is definitely *not* the problem. Quite the opposite."

"Really? Hmm. Maybe you need to accept him the way he is. Take the good... and it sounds like there's a lot... with the bad."

Alix shook her head in answer to Sara. *No, I shouldn't have to compromise or accept anything. If I wanted that, I would have just gotten another normal man... a Freeborn. He needs to be perfect. That was the whole point...*

"Well, you might not be able to change him, really. Sometimes we just need to either..."

"No, you're right about that. There will be no changing him... not in that way."

"Alix, what *do* you want from a relationship? What would make you happy, do you think?"

Alix thought back to the night before when Adam had so enraged her. She couldn't even remember why... couldn't remember what he did or didn't do. Alix had turned bright red, her face contorted with frustration and fury.

"You're not getting it right," she had shrieked at her Morfph. "You're not getting anything right at all. What's the good of you? Do I seem happy to you? Do I sound pleased?" she screamed. "Get out of here. I can hardly stand the sight of you."

*What do I want from him?* she wondered now.

After a long silence, Alix finally responded to Sara. Softly, but loud enough for her to hear, "He's my last chance."

"Well, I doubt that, Alix."

"No, he is. He definitely is." *And maybe, just maybe, the fault isn't with Adam at all,* Alix thought. *Maybe it's I who has gotten it all wrong.*

### Adam

The previous night, Alix had come home from work late. She walked in, stepped out of her high heels, and flopped onto the big white sectional and exhaled a deep sigh. Adam had been waiting all day, and all evening, for this moment—the moment she came home and joined him. He walked to the liquor cabinet and poured her two fingers of expensive whiskey... some special reserve stuff she liked so much. Then he joined her on the couch and handed her the crystal glass.

She took it, drank a big swallow, winced slightly.

"Exactly what I needed. How did you know?" They both laughed at that.

"You look so hot when you're knackered," Adam said as he moved closer to her and slipped his hand up her skirt.

"Knackered? You've been watching too much British TV," Alix said, and then moaned as his hand reached its desired destination.

Suddenly Alix roughly pushed him away, stood up out of his reach, and walked around the room.

"So, Adam, what did *you* do today?" Her voice dripped sarcasm. They both knew what he had done—he'd waited. Waited for her to come home.

"Do you really want to know, Alix?"

"Of course, I don't. You know that. Why even say it?" she snapped.

Adam took another tack. "You've had a hard day, babe. Why don't you tell me about it?"

"I'm too tired."

"Come on down here with me," he said, as he patted the couch next to him. "I'll rub your feet."

She slowly walked back over and lay down, putting her stockinged feet in his lap.

As he expertly rubbed and massaged, she sighed again.

"That's lovely," she said. But after a few minutes, she jerked upright and pulled her feet away.

"I've changed my mind."

"Yes, I can tell."

"Well, of course you can. What else is new?"

Adam's facial expression wavered as he sensed her next mood swing. He knew what he needed to do.

"You're a real bitch tonight, Alix. But as you say, 'what else is new?'"

Alix gasped. *He could still surprise her*, he thought. *Good.*

"And I lied. You don't look hot, you just look old. Old and dried up."

At this, Alix started crying.

"And you think you're a genius? You're a moron, Alix. All Freeborns are morons. Freakin' wastes of DNA."

"Stop. Please stop," Alix said. Her eyes squeezed shut and her face seemed to collapse and crumple before his eyes.

Adam continued to stare her down, his face hard. "Oh Alix, you love it... to be abused. You know you do."

But soon, at just the right time, he softened, walked over, wrapped her in his arms and whispered in her ear.

"It's okay Alix, I'm here, my dearest. I'm here."

"Promise me," she demanded.

He knew what she needed to hear. "I'll never leave you, Alix.

"Say it."

"I promise. I'll never leave you, my love. I never could."

Adam felt her melt and relax into his arms, but it was only a few minutes before she pushed him away once more. And that's when she started screaming at him and telling him he wasn't getting it right. Adam recoiled at Alix's words and at the feelings emanating from her like heat waves. There was more than just anger pulsing off her, though. There was also a palpable, dark terror. He could feel it pulling at him, threatening to take him down as well.

Being Adam—being Alix's Morfph—had never been easy, and it was getting harder. Alix's mind was a twisty, brambly path studded with hidden landmines and tripwires that could explode at any time.

He accurately read Alix's longing to be loved, agreed with, adored, and catered to. And he did all those things... perfectly. But instead of making her happy, it often triggered her rage. For, coexisting with her need to be adored was the opposite and equally strong need to be punished for her flaws.

She had no tolerance for flaws, hers or anyone else's. He knew Alix's inner voice told her she was irreparably flawed and not just undeserving of anyone's love, but also completely unlovable. Instead of being pleased, Alix reviled Adam for his adoration. So, just as she desired, Adam punished her as well as adored her. He'd often treat her very like all her abusive and arrogant boyfriends had.

So, Adam yo-yoed back and forth, bouncing from one of Alix's needs or desires to another. When she tired of his adoration and praise, he would sense it and become abusive and rejecting—harshly belittling her. She would work to regain his approval and love. He'd eventually smooth her down and seduce her back with more sweet talk. It was becoming a familiar, ever-repeating dance—back and forth, back and forth.

It reminded Adam of an old cartoon he had watched with Alix. In the cartoon there was a cat chasing a mouse, and then the mouse would pivot and start chasing the cat, only to be chased by the cat once more—over and over again. He wasn't sure if he was the cat or the mouse. They were both the same in the end, anyway.

Even with all Adam's skillful Morfphing gymnastics, Alix became more dissatisfied and angrier with every passing day. Nothing was enough. Nothing was right. And one thing was becoming increasingly and disturbingly clear to him. Alix was almost certainly incapable of being pleased. Despite this realization, Adam's overriding need, the need that Alix had inserted into his very DNA, remained unchanged. He *needed*, he *must*, above all else, please Alix.

Every time he couldn't make Alix happy, every time Alix see-sawed into dissatisfaction and rage with him, the other trait that she had purposely engineered into his emotional matrix kicked in, triggering extreme panic. And unlike any of his other feelings, this state of panic was completely independent of what his Patron—what Alix—desired for him to feel. Adam was often dizzy and confused with the emotional roller-coaster that was Alix's inner life.

As disturbing and as panic-inducing as this was for Adam, there was something further, something even more alarming, lurking in the depths of Alix's mind. Sometimes he felt he could reach it—the very dark thing flickering there—but just as he went to grab it, off it would skitter back into the far reaches of her mind.

But he was sure that sometimes—just sometimes—and thankfully, briefly, Alix wanted to die, and she wanted *him* to make it happen. With this epiphany, Adam's anxiety, which was already sky high, would peak and crackle over him like an electrical storm. The abyss loomed. He must do better. He must redouble his efforts. For fulfilling that particular desire would surely destroy them both.

# CHAPTER 23

## *Ruby Remembers*

*"We must believe in freewill—we have no choice."*

—*Isaac Bashevis Singer*

### *Ruby*

Ruby was disoriented and agitated when she opened her eyes after a night of vivid and unsettling dreams. The liquid morning sun lit up the walls of a room that was both familiar *and* pleasant, but was not *her* room. It was filled up with someone else—someone else's clothes, someone else's things, someone else's very essence. Then she re-remembered.

*Of course, Lily's room, Lily's things.* It was odd, since she had never met Lily, but she missed her with an odd sense of hollow longing.

Since Ruby's change, images and fragments of memories flashed through her mind and her dreams. She had visions of a big, light-filled room with tall ceilings. And in the room were girls—*friends? sisters? No, Podmates. Yes, that's right, Podmates*—talking, laughing, dancing and playing games.

Beloved faces, especially one, swam before her mind. Each time she saw this particular face, her heart felt like it was being squeezed in her chest. The face—the one that hurt her heart to think about—was round, with soft tawny skin, big, deep-set brown eyes, tumbled dark hair... and dimples.

She remembered kissing those sweet dimples. Snippets of conversation also came back. She was warning this person about something—something bad that was about to happen. And they were both afraid.

Then a name popped into her mind. *Pearl*, she whispered, then repeated more loudly—*Pearl*.

After Pearl's name came to her, a dam seemed to break and the memories and images that had been slowly seeping into her dreams and her daytime memories started flooding back, washing over her in waves.

At first, she did not share these feelings or memories with Matthew. They felt too tender, too personal, and she needed to process them. By the end of the day, however, they came tumbling out of her mouth, along with all the rest of the feelings and ideas that were bombarding her.

Matthew listened intently. Sometimes it was with avid, or perhaps amused, interest, sometimes with alarm, but always with patience.

## Matthew

A few days after her memory dam broke, Ruby walked into the kitchen where Matthew sat eating breakfast at the table in the kitchen. The morning sun that had filled Ruby's room earlier in the week shone again today and streamed through the window, illuminating Ruby's dark hair. Matthew absently noticed that the light picked up glints of gleaming auburn, giving it a burnished glow. He was drinking a big mug of steaming coffee and was enjoying a precious and quiet rare moment. Since the droughts, coffee cost a small fortune... but was worth every penny. Unfortunately, he was almost out of it now, and he wondered when he might find more. Probably not for a while.

With no preamble, her eyes focused on Matthew's face, Ruby launched back into the middle of a conversation they had been having the night before. It was as if there had been no time in between. Since full memory had returned, her mania had peaked.

"You know, Matthew, Morfphs have the ultimate fluidity of body and mind. That's what I've lost—that fluidity—but I think I'm still a bit of a Morfph inside," she said.

"Whoa, Ruby, I'm still waking up. I need to drink my coffee before we start this conversation again."

Ignoring him, she paced across the kitchen.

"But I must have more freewill now than I did before, don't you think? I mean, it sure feels like it... I *feel* freed. I'm just like the rest of you now, I guess—living an illusion of freewill. That's what Spinoza would say, anyway... and Buddhists, and neurologists too. But I like the illusion. I guess I am truly a Freeborn now."

Ruby only stopped talking to take a deep breath and then she laughed, obviously amused at herself. Being with Ruby now was like riding a roller coaster. Sometimes she was giddy, sometimes morose and crying. She laughed a lot, talked incessantly, yelled, and sometimes muttered to herself.

Matthew remembered the first time she had laughed at something as herself, as Ruby, after her Transition. She couldn't seem to stop, or maybe she didn't want to. Tears had streamed down her face, and she folded at the waist, her hands wrapped tightly around her sides.

She had been watching an old Charlie Chaplin movie. She especially loved the slapstick, physical humor. Matthew smiled at the memory and at her current musings, but he just nodded—bemused, amused. This was the conversation they had most every day now.

"Sit down, Ruby. I'll get you some breakfast. Eggs and toast?"

"Sure. Whatever," Ruby answered. "No coffee." She sat down at the table but was still shaking her leg up and down.

"No, you certainly don't need any coffee. But about the Morfph thing, maybe we all are," Matthew said. "A bit of a Morfph inside, I mean."

"Hmm. I suppose you're right." With that, Ruby jumped up, grabbed a piece of toast from Matthew's plate, and walked rapidly out of the room.

Matthew didn't know how she had so much energy when she ate so little. If today was anything like the last few days, she'd probably flit in and out several times before Matthew had finished his coffee and breakfast. And their conversation would likely continue in fits and starts, taking up where they left off earlier or starting a new topic altogether.

---

Prior to the Transition, Matthew had talked very little to Ruby about her life before they were Paired. He hadn't wanted to dwell on it or to even think about it. He knew the official Morfph background story put out by Geneti-Search given to all Patroni, but he was not involved in the rearing of Morfphs, nor did he have any inside information on the nitty-gritty everyday lives of their education or their development.

He knew that all Morfphs were born sterile girls. No male embryos seemed to survive long enough even to implant in the surrogates. He knew Morfphs looked like their biological parents, as most children do, until they were mature enough to be Paired. He also knew they grew up all together, were educated, and had caretakers. That's all he knew. That's all he had wanted to know.

But now, as Ruby's memories resurfaced, Matthew learned more and more about her life before he had become her Patron. In great detail, she described everything she could remember of her brief childhood and adolescence. She described her eleven Morfph sisters and their Caretakers. She described her favorite place in the Natural Area, and she told him about getting ready to be Paired.

"Did you have to grow up with veils on? How would that work?"

"Oh, no," she said impatiently, "the veils were only necessary at the very end when we were almost to full maturation, I guess." By this time, she had other things on her mind and was tired of answering his questions.

She looked away from him.

"I miss them now. I miss them all. How could I have forgotten? Even Pearl. I even forgot about Pearl. How could I?"

"Pearl? Pearl was special?"

"Yeah, Pearl *is* special."

"I don't know, Ruby. I guess that's just how it works. It's not your fault."

"Of course, it's not my fault. It's hers. It's her fault."

"Who... Pearl's?"

"No, not Pearl's, *hers*." Disgust dripped off every word.

"I still don't understand. Whose?"

She ignored the last question.

"I need to see her. I have to see Pearl," she said as she grabbed Matthew, her fingers digging painfully into his arm. "Can I see her? Please," she said, "I need to see Pearl. I must see Pearl."

Matthew pulled his arm away carefully and rubbed it.

"I don't know, Ruby. Who exactly *is* Pearl?"

"Pearl is my sister."

"A Morfph? Part of your Pod?"

"Yes, of course. Alpha One. The first Alpha. The first Morfph. She's my sister," she said between clenched teeth. "My sister!"

"I just don't think that would be possible..."

"Not possible? You could do it. I know you can."

"No, no. I really can't."

"I *have* to find Pearl. I need to know where she is. She was Paired to a woman they called the Mother of Morfphs. You must know who that is."

"The Mother of Morfphs? I'm sorry, I don't."

But even though he continued to hedge, being vague and obviously evasive, he suspected who it was. Who else could it be?

Ruby pressed on as her eyes drilled into him.

"She was also called the Creator. Tall, skinny, pale, white hair—no, white-blonde. Old. Older than you, even."

"That old?" he said, trying to divert her by making her laugh.

He got a glare instead.

Matthew finally broke down.

"You must mean Alix. Your friend was probably Paired with Alix Edison. You saw her?... you saw Alix?"

"Yeah. She came to assess us. To check out her inventory, I guess. She didn't seem too impressed with us."

"Matthew, I need to see her, and you need to arrange it," she repeated stubbornly.

"I really do not see how, Ruby. Alix has told no one she's been bonded to a Morfph. She'll flip if I ask. She will never admit it, and she certainly won't let you see Pearl. And you must know Pearl won't be Pearl anymore. Who knows who she is now? She could be anyone. She probably won't even want to see you. Would you have wanted to see her before you... well, before?"

Ruby didn't answer, her glare deepening.

"Besides, we can't tell Alix that you've... changed. We can't let anyone know that. It's dangerous. You don't know how dangerous."

"But..."

"No, Ruby. It's impossible."

Ruby became completely silent, her face a mask of angry disappointment. Then she strode on her long legs into her room and firmly closed her door behind her.

A few minutes later she reemerged, an envelope in her hand.

"Will you at least get this to her?" she said tightly. "Matthew, I'm begging you and I *really hate* to beg."

"I'll try, Ruby. I'll try."

———————————

Later, Matthew opened the unsealed envelope and read the note. It was quite short.

Written in Ruby's distinctive hand-writing, it read:

*My very dearest Pearl,*

*I'll reach you somehow. I'll never stop trying. Watch for me. I now look just as I did when you left us. But how will*

180

*I recognize you? Who are you now, my sweet Pearl? I hope this letter gets to you. There's so much to tell you.*

*Your Ruby*

Matthew guiltily returned it to the envelope and stuffed it into his pocket. He *would* try, he thought, but not without feeling a chill of trepidation go down his spine. But the note was just a small part of the ice that went down his spine. It all hit him at once, square on. There was no way they were going to hide this from *anyone,* let alone the inspectors who were trained to note any aberrations in Morfph behavior. She was so much an individual now. Because of his position in the company, he had managed to put off the impending check-up by a couple of weeks. If he tried another delay, suspicions would be raised and that was the last thing they wanted. Time was running out fast.

### Ruby

A week later, Ruby approached Matthew.

"Did you get my note to Pearl yet?" She, too, knew time was rapidly running out.

"Not yet. But I'll figure out something."

"It's important, Matthew. Really important."

"I know, Ruby. I told you I'd figure something out... soon. Soon."

She frowned. She wanted to push, but held herself back. Instead, she rapidly switched gears to something even more pressing.

"I want my own tablet, Matthew. I need to go on-line. Get me one. Today. Now."

"What's wrong with mine? You use it all the time. Isn't it working for you?"

"No, no. I need my own."

He hesitated.

"I don't know if that's wise, Ruby."

"Today, Matthew. Today. You owe me. Get me one. *Please*."

The "*please*" was strained, as was her smile after she said it.

Matthew sighed. It sounded both despairing and resigned.

"I'll make you a deal. If you'll actually sit down for a few minutes and let me take some pictures of you, I'll get you one… today… or the latest, by tomorrow."

"Why," she said suspiciously, squinting her eyes at him. "Why do you need pictures of me so badly?"

"I want to frame one… like the one I have of Lily… the one in the bedroom. I'll put them side by side. My two girls."

Ruby grimaced. "I'm not a girl. Neither was Lily."

"I know, I know… it's just an expression. My two women sounds worse."

"True." It was a lame excuse and Ruby didn't believe him, but she trusted him and she needed the laptop too much to argue.

"Okay, whatever."

"Good. Let's do it in my bedroom. You can sit on the bed."

He snapped pictures with the white wall behind her until she squirmed with impatience.

"Are you done? I have things I want to do."

"Okay, all done."

Ruby returned to her bedroom with Matthew's laptop and, through her wall, she heard him rummaging around his office in the room next to hers. She vaguely and briefly wondered what he was doing in there. It had something to do with the pictures he had taken, and she did not for a minute believe he suddenly wanted a framed picture of her on the dresser next to Lily.

# CHAPTER 24

## *Passport Outa Here*

*Matthew*

Matthew watched as the little portable printer quickly spit out several two-by-two-inch pictures of Ruby and one additional five by seven from the phone he had set on top of it. To keep up the pretense, at least for a while, he put the larger print in an emptied frame that had contained a picture of his parents and placed it on the dresser.

Matthew had another use for the smaller pictures. But first there was a phone call he needed to make, and he did not want Ruby to overhear. He grabbed his phone, his car fob, and a light jacket and called to Ruby through her door.

"Going out for a little while."

She jumped up and stuck her head out her door.

"Where are you going? To get my laptop?"

He shook his head. "Not now. Later."

"When? You promised."

"Yeah, yeah. How could I possibly forget? I'll get it."

Ruby frowned and stared at him.

"By tomorrow, Ruby. Promise. Gotta go. See you later."

She grunted and slammed her door shut.

Matthew got into his car, drove it around the corner, and parked. Then he fished his phone from his pocket, pulled up his contact list, and scrolled to the name he wanted.

"C'mon Sy, answer, answer, answer."

It had been a long time since he had seen or talked to his best buddy from law school—actually, since Lily's memorial service. He didn't even know if his old friend would answer his call. After Lily had died, he had shut down and stopped returning texts, calls, and emails from all his friends, including Syrus Lee.

After three rings, he heard a familiar voice and almost cried in relief.

"Matty, Matt. My god. Is that you, my friend?"

"Hi Sy. Yeah, it's me." His voice became gravelly, and he cleared his throat.

Syrus had called and texted him many times after Lily had died, but after multiple months of no response, he had finally stopped. Matthew had met Lily through him and they had all been good friends, both while in law school and for years after. But when Lily died, Matthew had disintegrated into a million painful pieces, and when he finally felt whole enough to make contact again, it had just been too long. The longer he put it off, the harder it became.

"It's great to hear your voice, Matt. I didn't think I ever would again."

"I'm sorry, Sy. It... uh... I... was just too..."

"Don't worry about it, Matt. I'm just so glad to hear from you, man." He sounded like he had tears in his voice, too.

With Sy's easy forgiveness, Matthew felt an even sharper stab of guilt. He had obviously hurt his friend and most likely many others, and he had only called now because he needed a favor. Girding himself with thoughts of Ruby, he pushed on. Syrus was the only person he knew who might help him now. He was a defense attorney in the city and had many contacts—both prominent, upstanding citizens and, hopefully, many not-so-upstanding ones. A person who worked in the shadows was who he was interested in today.

"Sy, I'm so sorry. This is going to seem terrible after so long, but I need your help."

Matthew almost cried again when Sy answered with no hesitation.

"Anything, man. You got me through so much. I would feel honored to finally be able to return the favor."

Sy's brother and mother had died in a car accident while they were in law school and he had almost dropped out. Matthew was the one person who helped him through it.

"Just tell me what you need."

"Fake passports. Two. Mine and someone else's. The other one may be more difficult."

Matthew waited through an impenetrable pause. And then Sy cleared his throat.

"Let me think." Another pause. "I might know someone. Or he might know someone. It'll be expensive, though. And it absolutely cannot come back to me."

"No problem. I expected that. But I need to tell you more," Matthew said.

"Okay, okay," Sy said. "You've got my full attention. Spill."

"Have you ever heard of Morfphs?" Matthew asked.

––––––––––––––––––––

Keeping his word, that evening, after he had finished the phone call with Sy, Matthew went online and bought Ruby her tablet. It was delivered to their doorstep the following day. He almost tripped over the package as he was leaving.

"Something for you on the porch," he yelled into the condo.

Ruby ran out, grabbed the package with a squeal, and scurried back toward her room.

"I'll help you set it up when I get home," he yelled after her.

"That's hilarious, Matthew," she yelled back at him over her shoulder. "I don't need your help. See ya."

"Okay," he said to the air with an amused shrug.

Matthew had gotten the address for his destination from Sy that morning. It turned out to be in a rundown, mostly deserted, part of town. At one time, it had been a rather chic area with lots of interesting little boutique-type shops, but almost all of them had gone out of business and the others held on by a shabby thread.

He pulled into a parking space in front of one of the thread-hangers. There was only one old car parked on the entire block. His made two. The sputtering neon sign outside said "Photography."

Holding a file folder, he walked into the shop and a real, old-fashioned bell attached to the door rang, alerting anyone inside that he had arrived. The dusty shelves held very little merchandise—mostly old-school photography equipment: darkroom enlargers, papers, reagents, tongs, photo trays, red lights, and old film-type cameras. The walls were lined with large, well-lit, framed, black and white "artsy" prints. On closer inspection, they seemed to be close-ups of various body parts: butts, breasts, noses, toes—mood lighting on the subjects produced intriguing shadows and lit areas. In the rear of the store, there was a counter, but no one was behind it.

Suddenly, a tall, lean woman, maybe fifty or fifty-five, burst through the door behind the counter. Her skin was the color of brewed Earl Grey tea, and her hair was pure-white dreads tipped with purple. She held a shotgun aimed at Matthew's head.

She wore a black, short- sleeved t-shirt with a logo of a large red spider on it. Her sinewy, tattooed arms rippled with the weight of the gun and her effort to hold it steady. The tattoos were serpents that wrapped around her arms and whose heads ended right above her elbows. Her finger was on the trigger of the gun, prepared to fire.

"Name and business," she said in a low, husky voice.

"Matthew. Silas Lee sent me."

She lowered the gun, smiled, flicked the safety, and leaned it against the counter, but left it close to her hand.

"Did you bring the money?"

Matthew handed her a roll of large bills.

"Photos?"

Matthew pulled the small printed photos out of the file folder and also retrieved a thumb drive from his pocket.

"I didn't know how you wanted them, so I brought both."

She took the printed photos. "I prefer these."

She studied the pictures, especially Ruby's.

"Morfph?" she asked.

He inhaled sharply. "Yes. How did you…"

"I've seen a few come through here. I have just one question for you."

"Okay."

"Are you a good guy or a bad guy?"

"Good," he blurted, then faltered. "I guess… I don't know. Yeah, good. At least I try. In this case, good."

"Okay. I'll accept that. Especially since it was Sy who sent you. He's one of the good guys. Not many of those anymore, as far as I can tell. Come on back. Let's take your picture. Then you'll have to wait for me to finish them up."

She pulled out two blank passports from a drawer and set up the photo equipment. All the equipment in the back room looked new and state-of-the-art. No dust here.

He nodded.

"Sit over there and say *cheese*."

After they took the picture, he looked around and saw more old cameras and dark room paraphernalia stacked around the room. He nodded at the stacks.

"Does anyone really do this anymore?"

"Not many. Luddites, purists… me."

"Are those yours? The pictures on the wall." he said, pointing in the direction of the front room.

She shrugged and nodded. "Now be quiet and let me work. I don't have all day."

———————————

Finally, only four days before the impending monitoring check-up, Matthew was ready. He walked to Ruby's room and stood outside it, listening. He could hear her rapidly tapping on the keys of her laptop through the partially opened door. When he knocked lightly on the door frame, he saw her head jerk up and she quickly closed the laptop with a snap.

*What's she up to?* he wondered with a twitch of foreboding. *None of my business*, he answered himself. But the uneasy feeling didn't subside.

"Yes?" she said. "Do you need something, Matthew?"

"Ruby, we need to talk... to make plans. We're running out of time."

"Uh huh," she said, watching his face warily.

"I've decided we need to leave here—soon—and we have to do it so we can't be traced. I have been taking money out for a while now. I haven't spent very much in the last year. It's just been building up in my accounts. I have quite a bit of savings. It's enough to keep us for quite a while. I had fake passports made up for both of us. That wasn't easy, but I did it. Pulled in some favors."

"What? No." Ruby looked at him. "Do you really think we need to do all that? Can't we just tell them we're both good with the way it is. Maybe they'll just leave us alone."

"No, we really have to go," he said urgently. "We can leave in two days. We need to get everything ready by then. And we still need to get your chip out. Geez, and there's that damned tattoo, too," he said, frowning. "I forgot about that..."

"You've certainly been very busy," Ruby said. "You should have consulted me... at least told me about it, you know. I'm not a child." She paused.

"Matthew, this plan will ruin your life. There must be another way. Maybe we just stay and tell the truth... they should know. There must be others."

"No," he yelled. "I told you that won't work." Then, with great effort, he calmed himself. "There're things I *haven't* told you."

"What things?" Her voice had pitched up, constricted and tight.

Matthew told her everything he knew about the Cullings.

She didn't seem surprised.

"Matthew, what do they do to the Culled Morfphs?"

"I have no idea. Do you really want to find out?" he asked.

"No... yes," she said. "Yes, yes, I do. Do you think they kill them—us? Would they really kill me?"

"No, no. Alix isn't that evil... I don't think. But they do disappear."

Ruby stared off into space.

"Okay, Okay. We'll talk. But not now. I have to think. Tomorrow. Let's do it tomorrow."

"Okay," Matthew said, frustrated but agreeing. "I'll give it until tomorrow."

# CHAPTER 25

## *Gone*

### *Ruby*

After much discussion and loud disagreement, they made a plan the next day. The plan—Matthew's plan—was to leave early the following morning. They took all day to get ready, but still hadn't decided what to do about the chip in Ruby's arm or the bar-code tattoo on the nape of her neck under her hair.

"I'll just cut them out," Ruby said. "Get me the alcohol, gauze, and some of those butterfly bandages. And your knife, I guess. The one in your dresser."

"You can't do it by yourself."

"Sure, I can. Never mind. I know where everything is," she said as she stood and walked into the bathroom. She rummaged around in the cabinet, found what she was looking for, and came out with a handful of first aid supplies.

"No, no, leave them. We can do it together... later. Maybe I can find something at the store to numb the skin. Lidocaine or something. Even so, that tattoo is going to be really painful. I'm not sure if we'll be able... maybe we should just... I don't know. I have some oxy stashed somewhere. I wish we had figured this out before."

Ruby nodded, not really listening. "It'll be fine. Just go get the skin stuff."

———

When Matthew returned from the store, lidocaine spray in hand. Ruby was in her bedroom, intently focused on her laptop, and she again snapped it shut as Matthew stood at her door.

"Found everything we need. Do you want to do it now?" Matthew asked.

"No, let's do it tomorrow morning. I'm not up to it right now."

"Ruby, we should do it now. The chip anyway."

"I said no," Ruby said and glared. "No."

"Okay, okay. Whatever you decide. But we need to do it before we leave. I'm going to bed now. We still have a lot to do tomorrow before we leave."

Ruby nodded and opened her laptop as he walked away. She paused midway. "Matthew?"

He stopped, turned back, and looked at her. After putting the laptop down, she stood and stepped toward him. In a gesture very like the one at their first meeting, she extended her hand and took his. And just as she had done then, she looked directly into his eyes.

"I know I've been hard on you, but I thank you. With all *my* heart, I thank you."

"It's fine, Ruby. Everything will be fine."

She nodded, and he continued to walk out of her room.

––––––––––––––––

Late that night, Ruby, barefoot, padded softly into Matthew's room. She stood next to the bed and stared down, intently studying his face for a long while. He twitched and grimaced and mumbled in his sleep.

Poor Matthew. This was so hard for him. She'd had a clear window into his mind for months before she had Transitioned so she knew intimately how he struggled. A wave of tenderness for him washed over her. She loved him, she realized, and her body responded to that feeling in a way she had never really felt before.

She kept staring down at him for several minutes and after a while all his body movements stopped—everything but his eyes. They were darting back and forth behind his lids. Interesting, she thought. She'd never seen that before, but she knew it meant he was dreaming.

Was he dreaming of Lily again? Not long ago, she would have known exactly what he was dreaming about. Maybe he was having anxious dreams about their escape. She, very briefly, thought about slipping into bed with him like she used to when she was Lily. She didn't think the seduction would be difficult, especially since he would be half asleep. She quickly dismissed the idea. It would be hard enough for him tomorrow without adding that to the mix.

Using her new tablet, she had made her own contacts and her own plans. The time had come and her plans must be carried out now. She walked back to her own room and prepared for the next day.

*To hell with it,* she thought, as she was throwing her clothes—Lily's clothes, really—into the big backpack she had found in the closet. They were all inches too short for her and too tight in some places and too loose in others, but they were all she owned.

Before she could talk herself out of it, she stole quietly back into Matthew's room, stripped off all of Lily's clothes and slipped her body between the sheets and slid up against him. And she had been right. The seduction was easy.

*They're so needy and weak,* she thought with a twinge of contempt, *even the very best of them.*

But when his arms went around her, he breathed her name—*her* name.

"Ruby," he sighed. Not Lily this time. With the sound of her name, she gasped in surprise at the pleasure it gave her. And she realized then that he wasn't the only needy human being in the bed.

## Matthew

Matthew came quickly awake with a jerk of his body. The sheets had been crumpled into a twisted pile at the end of the bed. He knew even before he opened his eyes that Ruby was gone. And not just gone from the bed. He lurched to his feet, jerked open the top drawer of his dresser where he had put the passports and emptied it, flinging everything to the floor.

Gone... his was there, but not hers. He searched the rest of the drawers, desperately knowing it wouldn't be there but throwing all his clothes on the floor, anyway. Then he went from room to room, frantically hoping against hope that she wasn't really gone.

In her room, she'd neatly made her bed. The large suitcase he had pulled out for her was still there, sitting on the floor where he had put it. He threw open the closet. Lily's backpack was gone. Her clothes, too. He realized, with an additional guilty twinge, that all those clothes had been Lily's. They had never gotten around to shopping for new clothes for Ruby. She had said she liked Lily's clothes. He wondered if she still felt that way. Maybe it just didn't matter anymore.

In her bathroom, a soggy pile of partially rinsed out towels had been heaped in the bathtub. They were still pink with the blood they had been used to clean up. A hand mirror smeared with more blood was on the counter. It looked as if she had tried to wipe the blood away, but some still spotted the counter, the sink, and the floor.

The small chip from her arm lay near the sink in a pool of congealed blood. Bandage wrappings littered the wastebasket, and the large first aid kit he had put together was missing.

She had managed, probably painfully, to remove the chip in her forearm by herself... but had she done anything with the barcode tattoo? Probably not. Even though it was only about a centimeter, it would be harder to reach and much harder to gouge out. But it was well-covered, hidden under her hair.

How could he have slept through all this? he wondered.

The big packet of money he had put together was also missing. That relieved him. But damn, she had left about half of the cash on the top of the dresser. She should have taken it all, he thought. He had so much more he hadn't been able to make liquid with brief notice.

Finally, he ran to the garage. The old Silver Prius was also gone. He had taught her to drive it. It had taken her less than a day to learn. She was a better driver than he by the end of that day.

He plodded back into the house and spotted the note that lay on her carefully made bed. How had he missed it before? Faint bloody fingerprints dotted the corners of it.

*Dearest Matthew,*

*Please don't come looking for me. I know where I'm going. I'll be OK. There's more of us than you know. I've been* in contact. I've found my people— other freed Morfphs. As you know by now, we are genetically superior to normal Freeborns. I need to be with my kind. Who knows what we can be and what we can do. We will find out together. Thank you for setting me free. Thank you for loving me.

I have discovered that Freeborns tenaciously cling to an illusionary sense of themselves— of their Self— as being consistent and static. But even biologically, most cells in our bodies completely renew every seven years. I bet in Morfphs, even that is sped up. But Freeborns— now me— are more similar to Morfphs than they admit to themselves. They are different people at different times, at different ages, under different circumstances, with different people and when in different roles. None of those selves are any less real or genuine than the other.

I'm on my way to a brand-new Self today. I haven't even lived six years yet. I know a normal six-year-old Freeborn is barely past babyhood. I'm so jealous of that innocence... of that leisurely time to be young. They stole it from me. I feel a thousand years old.

Another Interesting thought... your previous desire for me to stay looking like Lily at the age she was when she died will no longer keep me looking one age. I assume my looks will now change as I grow older. I will now visibly age, like everyone else. You may not even know me when... if... we see each other again.

Matthew, you MUST report that I have run away. But wait as long as you safely can. I know you don't want to, but *you MUST. I can guarantee they will not find me. Neither will you. I've got this covered. Please trust me on this.*

*Take care of yourself, Matthew. Maybe after all this is over, we will see each other again... I hope so. You're a good man. A good person.*

*I love you,*

*Ruby*

*P.S Sorry about the money and the car. I'll pay you back some day, I promise. Forgive me.*

After reading Ruby's letter, Matthew sat heavily in the big cushioned chair in the corner of her room, his head in his hands. He sat and thought—agonized—for a very long time, but in the end, he decided he must honor her choice. He didn't go after her. He waited until the day of the re-scheduled monitoring appointment and only then did he report to Geneti-Search that she had run.

"An investigation will promptly start," was their reply.

And, even though it was probably too late, he *would* get that letter to Pearl... just as he had promised.

### *Ruby*

Matthew was not aware of it, but several days earlier, Ruby had found Alix Edison's address in his laptop and she was now waiting outside Alix's condo, desperately hoping for a glimpse of Pearl.

She crouched behind a tree in a grassy area about fifty yards away and to the side of the entrance. She focused her acute hearing and sight on the place Alix and, hopefully, Pearl would appear if they left the building. A dozen burley men armed with automatic weapons and draped with extra ammunition paced, eagle-eyed, guarding the building.

She couldn't figure out how to get inside, as it appeared to be heavily patrolled twenty-four hours a day. She wished she could still shape shift... but at her own desire, not someone else's. If she could, she would turn herself into Alix and go right past them to rescue Pearl. *Maybe if I concentrate hard enough...* she thought.

For a while, it seemed like she could feel her molecules tingle with the effort, but she had definitely hardened into one form. So, she had to just watch and wait instead.

Matthew was right; She had no idea what Pearl looked like now, but she knew she would recognize her. She just knew. She didn't know how, but she had decided she would get Pearl to come with her. She had to. She couldn't leave her as that horrible woman's slave—not one more day.

Finally, after hours of agonized waiting, Ruby saw Alix emerge from the building. With her was a tall, muscular, improbably handsome, dark-haired man. *Probably another of her bodyguards,* Ruby thought.

Before she even knew what she was doing, she ran towards them and yelled at Alix.

"Where's Pearl? Where is she? Alpha One... I need to see her. Please just let me talk to her."

Neither Alix nor the guards had yet heard or taken notice of Ruby. She was still too far away. But the man with Alix had. He flinched, dropped the keys in his hand, and stared at her, his mouth gaping open.

Ruby looked closer, and she noticed his glimmer. *He's a Morfph,* she thought... *and he's with Alix.* And he was *exactly* what Alix would want from a Morfph.

"Pearl," she screamed. "Pearl, is that you? *Pearrrl!*"

Adam's form wavered slightly, losing its clear outlines. When their eyes met, Ruby clearly saw a shocked recognition and then a yearning sadness. With the momentary blurring of his features, she was sure she glimpsed a brief, but definite, image of Pearl's face within his and maybe... Was he silently mouthing Ruby's name?

"Adam, what are you doing?" Alix said shrilly. With that, his face snapped back into vivid focus and was, again, Adam's face. He shook his head, looking as if he was trying to clear away a distressing thought.

All these reactions happened so quickly, anyone else would have wondered if they had imagined it, but Ruby knew. This tall man was Pearl. She had no doubt.

Alix looked at Ruby as she came closer, still running. Confusion and then hatred flashed across Alix's face. She possessively took Adam's arm and said something even Ruby could not hear, and then he turned back to Alix with a smile.

Without a backward glance, he walked on, even as Ruby screamed Pearl's name again and again. They got into Alix's car, Adam at the wheel, and then they drove away. By the time the guards ran over to grab Ruby, she, too, was gone.

Winded and heartbroken, Ruby finally stopped running. The last she had seen of Pearl, she—he—was laughing and solicitously helping Alix into the car. Ruby knew then that whatever was left of Pearl was lost to her—probably forever.

# CHAPTER 26

## *A Sick feeling*

*Sara*

Several weeks after Sam forgave her, Sara woke, groaned, and sat up in bed. She pulled her knees to her chest and wrapped her arms around them to relieve a sudden wave of nausea.

Next to her, Sam opened one eye and said, drowsily, "What's wrong, babe? You okay?" She scrunched up closer to him and lay her head in the hollow between his shoulder and his chest. He shifted and put his arm around her comfortably.

"I've been feeling so sick recently."

"Uh oh. Sick how? Do you need to go in?"

"No, no. Just sick to my stomach, but it usually goes away if I eat something. The only thing that makes me feel better is eating. I've gained about five pounds… five *more* pounds. I feel so bloated and yucky."

"Fergus, move over." The dog was on the bed and trying to worm himself between them.

Sam looked at her more closely.

"Sara, when was the last time you had your period? I don't remember you complaining about it at all for a while."

"Hey, I don't complain about it all the time." But she thought about it. "Let's see. It's been a couple of months, I guess, but it's perimenopause. I'm just getting old."

"Your breasts have been pretty tender, recently haven't they?"

"Sam, it's not what you're thinking. I can't get pregnant. I told you that," she said, irritably.

He looked skeptical.

"Sara, I'd get a pregnancy test if I were you." He sounded excited, happy. But she knew he was wrong.

"You're wrong, you know. I *can't* get pregnant." And she abruptly dismissed the topic. She'd been through this before. How many times had she thought she was pregnant and never been? She was just too old for it now.

Sam still didn't look convinced, but he dropped the subject. To her renewed irritation, he bought her a pregnancy test kit the next day and left it on her nightstand in a prominent place. He had drawn a smiley face on it.

She wasn't amused. Well, maybe a little. But not enough to pee on some stupid stick. She knew what it would say. And she would not do that again. This time, she wasn't even sure what she would want it to say.

She impatiently picked up the pregnancy kit and started to throw it in the trash can. Just as she was going to drop it in, she stopped, scowled and threw it in the drawer of her nightstand instead.

———————————

A few weeks later, Sam and Sara again lay in bed, wound around each other, talking. It was one of their great pleasures, but they could usually only indulge on weekends. It was on one of these lazy Sunday mornings when Sam said, sounding like he was trying hard to be casual, "Your breasts are getting even bigger, Sara. Mind you, I'm not complaining—just sayin'."

"I know. They're still tender, too. Maybe I'm finally going to have my period."

"You still haven't had one? It's been a very long time, huh? How long, now?"

"I dunno. I've lost track. Maybe three months, I guess. Give or take." She yawned.

"Maybe it's time. What do you think?"

"Time? For what?"

"Time to take the test."

"Oh gawd," she said, and buried her head under the pillow.

"Sara, I know you really don't want to be pregnant. But you haven't been using birth control. You should take the test. You really should."

She pulled her head out from under the pillow.

"No, you're wrong about that," she said.

"You *have* been using birth control?" he said.

"No, no birth control. I've never been able to get pregnant. I've told you that over and over."

"Then what...?"

"I'm scared," she said loudly. "I'm just scared."

"I can understand that. Having a baby is a pretty scary business but..."

"No, you don't get it. I'm not just scared that I'm pregnant. I'm also scared I'm not. I've gotten my hopes up many times. So many times."

"Do it now. I'll be here with you. Whatever happens is fine. We'll do it together."

"No way. I'm definitely not peeing on a stick with you watching."

"Sara, come on, I didn't mean I'd watch."

"Not now. Not now. Later. I want to be by myself. Later. Soon. I promise."

"Okay," he said and sighed, obviously trying to hide his disappointment. She could read him like a book.

"Later," he said. "But soon. You'll tell me though?"

"You'll be the first to know. Promise," she said.

---

Sara perched on the toilet seat, her pants down around her ankles, and peed on the wand from the box. She swore as some pee missed its intended mark and sprayed onto her hand. Holding the box in her other hand, she read the directions: a single blue line is negative, a blue cross is positive. As she stared at the plastic stick, she could see the blue cross form.

Positive. It was positive.

"Now?" she felt a wildness grow in her, threatening to erupt.

"Are you kidding me?" she wailed.

"What *are* you doing in there?" Sam yelled from living room.

"None of your business," she yelled back. She heard him laugh.

She pulled up her pants, ran into the hall, and grabbed her coat. She needed to drive to the store. Just as she'd seen in all those movies and TV shows, she needed to buy more tests—just to make sure. Maybe three more would do it.

As she ran out, Sam yelled after her, "Hey where are you going? I thought we were going to make dinner?"

"I'll be right back," she said over her shoulder as she went out the door.

When she got home again, she went directly into the bathroom and shut and locked the door. She could hear Sam saying something outside the door. Asking if she was okay, probably.

"Yeah, yeah," she said. "I just need some privacy. Everything is fine. Geez, *do not* stand outside that door!"

Another muffled response, but he wasn't laughing now.

One... positive. Two... positive! Three... POSITIVE!!! They all said the same thing. She was pregnant. SHE WAS PREGNANT!

"Oh shit," she moaned. She didn't even know whose baby it was.

---

Finally, Sara came out of the bathroom.

"Move over, Fergus. I need to sit down." She pushed him off the couch so she could sit next to Sam. Fergus groaned. He enjoyed sitting between them so he could get petted from both sides.

Sam looked at her closely. "You finally took the test, didn't you?" he said.

"Sam, we need to talk." She had barely absorbed the reality of it all.

"Tell me."

She swallowed hard but didn't answer.

"You're pregnant. Aren't you? I knew it. I knew it. You're pregnant! Oh, Sara. Tell me you are."

She nodded bleakly.

"But that's amazing. Are you sure?"

She nodded and held up three fingers.

"Three tests."

"I'm... I'm..." He choked a little on the next word and her stomach clutched.

"... so happy. I'm ecstatic." He took her hands in his, but she wouldn't look at him.

Fergus was staring at her, too. He looked concerned.

"Be happy, Sara," Sam said. It sounded more like a command than a plea. "This is outstanding."

"But is it? Is it really? What if its Jack's?"

Sam went silent and his face pinched into an angry scowl at the mention of Jack's name.

"It's mine," he said, sounding stubborn and grim.

"I'll get a paternity test."

"No. No test. Absolutely not. The baby will be mine no matter what that test says. You're mine. I'm yours. We'll be a family."

"I don't know, Sam. Maybe I'm too old. Just think how old I will be when the baby is ten or fifteen, or twenty. And that's not even thinking about the problems the baby might have because of my age."

"But what do *you* want, Sara? I know what I want. I want our baby." A slightly peevish note had crept into his voice. It felt like he was accusing her of something.

He looked over at her, and his tone softened a little. "But... it's your decision... your choice. I won't stop you."

Sara looked at him balefully.

"Really?" she said sarcastically. "My choice. That's rich. What choices do I have, exactly?

Abortion was illegal. Had been for several years, punishable by death now. She remembered when she was young and this pregnancy could have ended... but not now. Not for any reason. Not even if the baby had only a brain stem or some other terrible condition... not that they even did those types of prenatal tests anymore.

How could she have been so cavalier about not using birth control? But after all those years not being able to get pregnant, she had been so certain she was barren. Such a laden, old-fashioned word: barren. Sterile? Not much better. Infertile? Ugh.

"You can still get them... abortions. Not here, but we could go to Canada or somewhere. I would completely support you with that decision. I'd help you every step of the way." His voice cracked when he said it.

"No. It's too risky, you know that. I had to give my ID to even buy the tests. They have put it all in the registry. They'll be tracking me. I won't even be able to leave the country for any reason... for a year or maybe more now."

"We can figure this out," Sam said, again sounding stubborn.

"The thing is," Sara said, "I *do* want this baby. I really do. I want it so badly. But it terrifies me... and enrages me, too. I mean, god, I *have* no choice. No control. I can't even see if the fetus is okay. And it also terrifies me to bring an innocent baby into this screwed up world. What are things even going to be like when he or she is grown up?"

"I know, Sara, but this baby will be will be so loved... our joy. Let's grab that joy. We'll get through it together, all of us. Let's get married."

She looked at her hands, so he couldn't see the pained expression that was surely written on her face.

He took her head between his hands and tilted it up so he could peer into her face. He gently smoothed the tangle of wild dark hair, now shot with pure white, that her fingers had raked into chaos. His hands calmed her as he petted.

"God, you're gorgeous... and your breasts have gotten.... my, my."

"It's just fat," she said in a low voice.

He shook his head, ignoring the comment.

"And lest you think I'm completely hormone driven, I also love your wonderful mind... and you're funny and kind. The full package. You must know I'm completely love struck. Have been for... well, forever.

"And I hate your horrible husband, who shakes your confidence every chance he gets. I really don't understand what he gets out of it, making you feel less than you are. I'm done holding my tongue about Jack. I did in the past because of how you adored him. For the life of me, I still cannot figure out why.

"And my girls love you, too," he continued. "You will be such a wonderful mother to our child, too. So, marry me."

"How do I know you're not just asking because I'm pregnant? I don't want..."

"God, Sara, what do I have to do to convince you? I am not just asking because you're pregnant. And I know it could be Jack's... biologically. I'd prefer it if it were mine, but it *really* doesn't matter. I want us to be a family."

"Just so you know, I will not name this baby Joy," she said. "I hate the name Joy. And what a burden to put on a child," she kidded. "And listen to you. You are the most careful, methodical person I know. 'Grab the joy,'" she mimicked and laughed.

"So, you'll marry me? "

"I still need to think about it. I need some time. And there's still the little detail of divorcing Jack."

"Okay, okay, whatever. I've been patient until now. I can be patient a little longer, I guess."

"Thank you. I do love you, Sam. You know that, don't you?"

"Yeah, I do."

"It won't be long. I'll decide soon."

"Okay. Fair enough. Think about it. Then say you'll marry me."

Sara smiled tightly, acknowledging his attempt at humor.

"Hey, how about we skip making dinner here tonight? Let's take Fergus for a walk. We could get some takeout from that new little brew pub down the street."

The pub was within their patrolled area. She remembered a time, with a brief hit of nostalgic melancholy, when they could have sat down in the restaurant, surrounded by a happy din of people laughing and talking, dishes clattering and steamed milk machines hissing.

"Yeah, okay. That sounds good. Walking would be nice."

———

They were only five minutes into the walk when Sara decided. They were both wearing masks over their mouths and noses; the fires were raging again. There had hardly been a break from them this year. Between the fires and the pandemics, everyone wore masks in public most of the time now, even the homeless. They even had a special one for Fergus' doggy snout. You could never see other people's expressions anymore. She missed seeing acquaintances and even strangers smile and nod in passing. That never happened now.

She took her mask off.

"Okay, Sam. Let's do it. Let's get married. And make a family. And I *am* happy… terrified, but happy."

"You're sure?"

She nodded.

"Really sure?"

"Yes, really sure." And she was sure, wasn't she?

"Really, really sure?"

"Yes, Sam. I'm really, really, really, really sure!"

He whooped like a kid that had finally gotten his own way. Catching his giddy excitement, Fergus barked and danced around them in a circle, wrapping them up in his leash as they held each other in the middle of the sidewalk.

# CHAPTER 27

## *His Creature No More*

*Sara*

Sara knew she must get up the nerve to talk to Jack. She was dreading the meeting, but she had already put it off too long. After their unfortunate incident, she had stopped replying to his texts and, mercifully, they had dwindled and then stopped altogether.

But they hadn't even started the divorce process yet—a minor detail that needed addressing before she could marry Sam. Plus, of course, there was the pregnancy. Sam had stayed rigidly adamant about not getting a paternity test—he didn't even want Sara to tell Jack she was pregnant. Reluctantly, she went along with the first demand... but the second? She was still unsure about that.

Sam and Sara discussed it and decided she would invite Jack over to the house to talk and Sam would vacate the premises for the evening. If he worried about Sara meeting with Jack again, he said nothing.

"It'll be fine. Believe me."

He nodded. Recently, he had become harder for her to read.

Sara texted Jack an invitation. It simply said they needed to talk. He texted right back with a winky smile emoji which made her cringe uneasily, but she dismissed her unease and arranged a date and time two days away.

---

When Jack arrived, Sara, as before, jerked her head away from his kiss. He shrugged and headed to the living room, but she waved him to the kitchen table. She didn't want him to get the wrong idea or to get too comfortable.

Agreeing with another shrug, he walked towards the kitchen and looked around warily.

"Where's that flea-bitten mutt?"

"Fergus? I put him away. Why? Do you want me to get him so you two can snuggle? I know how much you like dogs," she said and snorted.

Jack grunted his response.

Sara got the distinct feeling he thought this was going to be a repeat performance of last time. Like, maybe she was taking him up on the offer to be his new "bit on the side." The irony of that wasn't lost on her. A prickly irritation was growing, and she took a deep breath to shake it off.

"I've really missed you, Sara," he said, right on cue. "I assume, with this invitation, you've missed me, too."

"You assume wrong, Jack. We've got business to discuss."

"So formal," he said, and laughed. "Hey, you're looking a little, uh... let's say filled out? Better not let yourself go too far. Sammy might lose interest."

Sara rolled her eyes, not taking the bait.

"How's Jazmin?" she asked.

It was Jack's turn to roll his eyes.

"The bloom has come off the rose, I'm afraid," he said.

"Do tell."

"You know how I am—how I get. You understand me. I hadn't felt so alive in years. I thought I was in love. But now..." He shook his head. "Now she's just a... well, I can't talk to her like I can with you. And she doesn't laugh at my jokes," he said, seemingly outraged and amazed at the idea.

"Imagine that," she said, her tone sarcastic. "So, what's really going on? Are you two still together, or what?"

After a lot of hemming and hawing, she deciphered that Jazmin had stopped putting up with his shit. In fact, she was so fed up, she had kicked him out. Sara couldn't figure out the entire problem. Another woman? Jack trying to control her? Who knew? Who cared?

"And I don't think she's very smart either," Jack said.

*Oh, did those grapes turn out to be sour?* she wondered.

"Well, she's smart enough to kick you out. Evidently smarter than I was."

Ignoring her, he pushed on.

"I miss what we had, Sara. I miss *you*." And he tried to kiss her again. But this time she pushed him away, disgusted.

"C'mon Sara. You haven't started the divorce for a reason. I'll eat crow for a while. I'll admit I was wrong, and you were right. Let's start again. Let me move back in. I'll get you back into fighting weight in no time."

"Not this time. Not ever," she said. "I was going to say I'm sorry you're unhappy, but I'm not. I just don't care."

Jack's mouth gaped opened like a fish, but before he could say anything, she started talking again.

"And just shut up about my body. I'm fine and its none of your damn business... it never was."

This was clearly not what he expected to hear when he asked to come back. He had undoubtedly thought she would jump at the chance. She continued, aware of his surprise and enjoying it. She'd just gotten warmed up.

"I don't want you back, Jack. I'm just done with how you make me feel. Like I'm not good enough and need to keep working to be better—but your version of better, not mine. I was always a project to you, wasn't I? Someone you could mold, prod, control, criticize—for my own good, of course."

"Sara, that's not how it was. C'mon."

"You know, honestly, you sleeping with other people was the least of it," she continued. "That I might actually have understood. But you made me feel like it was my failings that made you want someone else. You even made it seem like it was my fault I was aging. You were always looking over my shoulder to see if there might be someone better. I've finally realized just how shitty you make me feel about myself. I'm so over it... over us.

"And," she blurted, looking straight at him, "I do not want my child to be around it either."

His head jerked around and he stared at her.

"Child? What child?"

"My child. I'm pregnant."

"You're having a baby? Whoa," he said. "Kind of long in the tooth for that, aren't you, babe?"

"Do not call me babe," she said between her teeth.

Suddenly, like a flip of a switch, Jack's entire demeanor changed. Catching Sara off guard, eyes bulging, he lurched toward her and shoved his flushed face into hers.

"Whose is it?" he yelled.

Alarmed, she flinched back from his looming face.

"How do you know it's not yours?" she shrieked in return.

The comment about her age had hit a nerve, and it had briefly stung her, but his anger was unexpected; something beyond his normal acerbic insults. But with her question, his mien abruptly changed once more. He became still and the strangest look came over his face; like he'd been caught or outed.

Sara was shaken, but determined to press on. Instead of stopping to puzzle out Jack's odd behavior, she said, "I'm really embarrassed, but I don't know who the *biological* father is. I mean, it's either yours or Sam's... but all that really matters to me is, it's mine. And unless you force my hand, I will not get a test to find out."

Jack stared at Sara, still silent.

"Sam is going to be the only father that really matters... we're getting married. Just as soon as our divorce is final."

That broke Jack's silence.

"Sam? Sam Hamada?" he said, shouting again. "What the hell? Sam? You always said you were just friends. Were you lying to me? Sam? Christ!"

210

Fergus had heard the shouting and was barking loudly from the back room.

"Oh, come on, give me a break. You knew about Sam. But that's rich… you outraged about the possibility of me lying to *you*. How terrible! What a whore! How could I do that?"

Sara broke away from him and paced the room, panting. Her hands were on her hips and her was head down. Jack watched her, glaring.

"We *were* just friends, Jack. Now we're not—*just* friends, I mean. He makes me feel good about myself. Actually likes me—loves me—and tells me I'm beautiful, and he means it. It's nice. Really nice, you asshole. It's nice. He's nice."

"Oh, he's 'nice' is he?" he mocked. "So, you don't love him. I know you. You hate nice. That do-gooder social worker. That wimpy pussy. He'll bore the shit out of you and you know it. I never liked that guy," he said, still openly outraged, still shouting with anger.

"So, what else is new? You never liked any of my friends. Always ridiculing them, calling them names. Making fun of them."

She hated what Jack was saying, but he had hit a sensitive spot. She got impatient with Sam's niceness sometimes, and with his total devotion to her. It didn't make logical sense. She knew that. But there it was. And she did have a problem with boredom when things were too easy.

"You don't know me anymore. Maybe you never did," she said hotly. "I've changed."

But he had gotten another part of it right, too. She didn't love Sam in the same way she had loved Jack—desperately, madly… *obsessively*—but look how that had worked out. Maybe she *needed* to love Sam differently. Maybe she needed to find a different way of living and loving.

She was so tired of obsession and a self-destructive love. And she was definitely not going back to Jack. She owed that to her baby, and she owed it to herself. He wasn't what anyone would call good "daddy" material. He had already proven that with Seth.

"You're wrong," she said, "Now go. Go see if your girlfriend will take you back because I won't."

But he wasn't done. If he'd been smarter, he would have gone then. But he didn't.

"Get an abortion," he said. "You're too old to have a baby. It will be a defective. I have connections, you know. I can get you out of the country. I've done it before... simple and easy. I'll do that for you. You love me, you know you do. Get rid of it and we can have our life back. Just you and me. We're meant to be together. What happened to us being soul-mates like you always said?"

She stopped, stunned. He could get her an abortion. It was her way out of this. She believed him, too. He had friends everywhere. He was that kind of guy. Probably knew someone high in the government.

But she shook her head.

"Just you and me? It was never just you and me. For a while, I felt I was the most important one. You came back to *me* every night. I put up with your flirtations *and* your dalliances for years—resigned to them. Even felt like maybe they helped our life together work. But then you left me... for *Jazmin*."

"I know. That was my bad," he said. She cringed at that stupid old phrase.

"Now it will just be you and me. I promise."

"Why in god's name would I believe that? I've grown up, Jack. You should try it."

And she didn't believe him—not at all. But she felt herself once more being pulled to him... and to his offer of a reprieve. She could feel the tug of his narcissistic orbit.

Panicked, she felt the possibility of her resolve weakening. She understood Jack. She had loved him, body and soul, for years. He had made her feel vibrantly alive. And she understood his demons. He couldn't stand anyone having any power over him emotionally or in any other way. He had kept her unbalanced to keep her from getting any sort of hold on him, especially when it seemed like she was feeling especially good about herself. But he had also been her great love.

Then something suddenly struck her as odd. Something was a bit off. What was it? *Oh yeah,* she thought. It was his reaction when she had said she was pregnant. He had assumed it wasn't his. And it definitely could have been. Couldn't it? The timing was right, and they'd had sex—baby-making kind of sex—more than once that night.

She gave him a piercing look.

"Jack, why didn't you ask me if the baby was yours?" she said in a calm, steely voice.

Again, that odd, furtive look came over his face. He shifted from foot to foot.

"I don't know. I was surprised, that's all. I mean, we tried for years and you never got pregnant, did you?" He said it defensively, not looking at her.

It still didn't sit right with her. She persisted.

"You always said it was me. It was my fault because you were obviously not shooting blanks. There was Seth to prove that, right? But you weren't surprised I was pregnant. You were angry that I had been with someone else. Why's that? Do you know something I don't? Tell me, damn it. Tell me. I know you. I know your looks. I know how you react. Tell me." *She* was furious now, her voice still low and ice cold.

"Okay," he yelled. "Okay, I had a vasectomy after Seth was a year old. I didn't want any more kids. I don't like kids. They're so needy." His face had a look of disgust on it.

"And then they grow up and hate you. And you pay for them for years. Now Sally's pressuring me to pay for Seth's college. Says I owe it to him for disappearing from his life. Isn't he a little old for college? He's in his twenties. It just keeps on and on."

Seth had been having a lot of problems, some with the law, and she knew Sally had been terrified for a long time. Evidently, Seth now wanted to go back to college, which should have been good news. But that was the last thing she wanted to talk about now.

Fergus's barking got louder and more frantic.

"I wanted it to be just us. What's so terrible about that?"

"All those years," she said. "All those years. And you let me think it was me. You knew I wanted a baby... desperately... and you said nothing." She was shaking with emotion; rage, sadness, and a feeling of profound betrayal. She didn't know whether to cry or scream or kill this man she had trusted and loved so much. He had moved past the line of mere selfishness into cruelty.

"You would have pressured me to have it reversed. You know you would have. And I didn't want to. I didn't want any more kids. What else could I have done?" He was almost whining.

As white-hot rage exploded in her brain, Sara lunged at Jack's chest and shoved him hard with both hands.

"Get out, get out," she screamed over and over. The shove propelled him to the front door and, as he turned to open it, she shoved him again. He tripped over the sill and fell out onto the front porch, his head grazing the railing on the way down.

Luckily for him, his outstretched hands broke most of the fall. Quickly rolling over to sit on his butt, he looked up, shocked and speechless. There was a little rivulet of blood dripping down his face. After a stunned second, Jack shook his head and scrambled to his feet.

Right before Sara slammed the door, she regained enough control to say one last thing.

"Don't pout, Jack. It's so irritating." A small, tight smile briefly twisted up the corners of her mouth and then faded as fast as it had appeared.

The last look on his face before the door slammed in it was disbelief, but also bewilderment. And she had thought there was nothing left that could surprise her.

She leaned her back against the closed door, her entire body shaking. She willed herself calm—breathing in, breathing out, deep and slow. She could vaguely hear Fergus whining from the bedroom, but couldn't bring herself to let him out yet. Then suddenly, she realized she had stopped shaking and a deep calmness had descended in its place. It was a new feeling for her, or at least a forgotten one. It was as if an enchantment broke.

"It's over," she breathed out loud. "I think it's finally and truly over."

Slowly, she slid down the wall and onto her bottom. She sat like that for a full half hour more, head in hands, breathing deeply the whole time.

Groaning, she finally heaved herself up off the floor and walked to the bedroom to let Fergus out. As she squatted down to him, he jumped and wriggled all over her, ecstatically licking her face. She was glad the anger had dissipated. It wasn't good for the sprout.

She'd finally exorcised Jack, and she was ready to make a life and a family with Sam and her baby... *their* baby. Their beautiful little baby.

And there'd also be every other week with Sam's two little girls, her sprout's half-sisters. *If* she got bored or restless, she would just do more yoga or run or... But she doubted she would have the time for boredom and that was just fine.

She picked up her phone and dialed Sam's number. When he answered the phone, she smiled into it.

"Hi, Sam. I just changed Jack's diagnosis from Narcissist to Sociopath."

Sam laughed. "What took you so long?"

# CHAPTER 28

## *In Therapy... Just Once More*

*Alix*

Although Sara Wilde had tried to delve more deeply into Morfphs in the months following Alix's disclosures during therapy, her client had doggedly resisted the topic. It had become just another topic Alix would not discuss. They would sometimes sit for much of the fifty minutes, almost silent after Sara's initial questions.

Alix deeply resented Sara's reaction to her "creations" and had decided silence was the best punishment. And she had divulged too much. She had decided that today would be her last day here. Maybe she would find another therapist. Maybe not. But today, one last time, she would talk about it again. Confess all. Good for the soul and all that. She felt high, manic, really. Charged with energy. On a roll.

"Remember our discussion of Morfphs, Doc?"

"You know I do, Alix. And you know I find it troublesome. Have you really thought this through—all the ramifications? The cruelty of it?"

"Cruelty?" Alix visibly bristled, then laughed. "That's harsh, don't you think? But we're at a point of no return now, Doc. It's a thing. It's done. No going back. No putting the genie back in the bottle." Alix smoothed her hair, twisted in her chair, and laughed. She was laughing lot today.

"But I haven't told you everything. I have one now," Alix said, barely contained glee in her voice.

"What?" Sara said anxiously. "You have one what?"

"A Morfph. I have my own Morfph. Do you want one? I could fix you up."

Alix could see Sara physically recoil. *Bitch*, she thought.

"Jesus, Alix. What are you talking about?"

216

"I'm sorry," Sara said, visibly struggling to regain her professional demeanor. "I shouldn't have reacted like that. It's just hard to take in, hard to process. Please continue. And no, I don't want a Morfph. Thank you."

"I think you knew that already, Doc. Why so shocked?"

"I may have had my suspicions... but no, I didn't *know*."

"Should I continue, then?"

———————

Alix told her everything she had left out before, especially about her Pairing and relationship with Adam.

After a long time, Sara finally spoke. What she said surprised and, frankly, disappointed Alix.

"But what about real love, Alix?"

"This *is* real love. We've been through this before. Morfphs truly love their Patroni. They are fully human. They, of course, *must* love their Patron. They have no choice—no freewill—in the matter, but Morfphs also have no illusions. Unlike the rest of us, they are totally aware of why they do what they do."

Alix stopped, having run out of energy and breath. Her manic anger seemed to dissipate, like air out of a tire. She felt wrung out, worn down. And not nearly as sure of herself as she had just claimed to be.

She put her hand over her eyes and tried to regain her equilibrium, breathing rapidly. *How many times have I repeated all this?* she wondered. It was wearing thin, even with her. Not that it was incorrect or wrong, just that, maybe, it wasn't good enough. Maybe it was just more of the same. What had Matthew said about two wrongs?

But no. That wasn't it. *What is really wrong with me?* she wondered. She was not the type to have a crisis of conscience. She'd always scoffed at others for their weak self-reflection and constant rumination about ethics and the right and wrong of things. So tedious—all that bellybutton gazing.

No, guilt was not the problem. But her doubts were building. And just as her dissatisfaction with Adam was worsening, the number of defective Morfphs being collected was increasing. Patroni had been contacting Geneti-search in increasing numbers to report that their Morfphs were having some sort of breakdown.

In addition, information about the project was getting out and the criticisms and outrage were picking up steam. She was feeling a growing sense of unease, even dread. And then, that disturbing encounter with Adam and that girl outside her condo....

"I sense that you may have some doubts about this project, Alix. Do you want to talk about it? Explore what you're feeling, and why?"

*Geez, can this bitch read my mind?*

"No," Alix snapped, coldly. "No, I do not. I've already told you way too much... about everything."

"We've talked about this before. I'm bound by our confidentiality. You don't need to worry about that. You can trust me, you know. We've been together for a long time now. I'm on your side. I know, in your life, few people have been."

"Trust you? I suppose I do trust you as much as I ever have anybody." She looked away, her face grim.

"Exactly. But that's not much... is it?"

"I have seen little evidence that it's a good idea. Did I ever tell you she used to call me Piglet? Sometimes she pretended it was supposed to be humorous, or affectionate, like a pet name... a joke we shared. But it wasn't."

"What? Who called you Piglet?"

"Mother, of course. Mother called me Piglet."

"Why Piglet? Why did she call you that?"

"Because I was fat, like a little pig, obviously."

"That must have been very painful and confusing. And were you? That's hard to imagine."

"Was I what?"

"Chubby... fat?"

"Uh... yes. I mean... I certainly thought I was."

"But were you, Alix?"

Alix looked momentarily confused. "Yes... no... god, I don't know."

"I bet you were darling. You didn't deserve that treatment... even if you had been... chubby—for want of a better word."

"I stopped eating then. To take control. Not entirely, of course... but..." Her voice faded off, her eyes drifting to the side of the room.

She was silent for a while before she started again.

"I wonder why she didn't love me." Alix's voice was as devoid of emotion as her face.

"It was her, not you, Alix. She must have been damaged—broken inside."

"Like me, huh, Doc? Just like me. Like mother, like daughter." She shrugged indifferently. "Whatever."

Alix paused.

"Well, it's all evened up now. She's been taken care of. Right now, she's probably sitting in her diapers, marinating in her own piss and shit, too, I would imagine."

"What? I thought she was deceased? You told me she was dead."

"What? Oh, no, no. I guess I did tell you that, didn't I?" Alix laughed. "Only metaphorically, Doc. Dead to me. She's in one of those warehousing facilities. Not a very good one, either." Alix smiled.

"That was another thing my daughter was mad at me about. Said I could afford a better one for her. But it's plenty good enough for her."

Alix looked up, and her face refocused. As she often did at the end of the session, she stood up abruptly.

"This will be our last session. I'm done. I'm feeling so much better now. You've been great, Doc... really. Thanks for all the help. Just send my bill. My secretary will take care of it."

Alix noticed, slightly miffed, that Dr. Wilde looked a bit relieved.

She also noticed something else. For the first time that day, Alix looked carefully at Sara. *Slender frame thickened, face filled out, breasts larger. She's plump— yeah, that's the word—all plumped up.* Alix could see it even through Sara's loose, layered clothing. And then there was her glowing skin and thick, shining hair. She'd seen that look enough times.

"Why, Dr Wilde, I do believe you are pregnant, aren't you?" She laughed an unpleasant laugh. "Good luck with that."

Before Sara could answer, Alix swept out the door. She was going home to Adam now. He'd be missing her.

# III

# INTO THE
# FIRE

# RAWBEAT

## *Mutilated body of second young woman with barcode tattoo on neck and microchip in arm found in shallow grave*

By Glory Rubins                    July 5, 20**, posted 1 day ago

Yesterday, the shallow grave of a young woman was discovered by a hiker and her dog in a wooded area near a suburban area in Loma Cynda County. On autopsy, the victim was found to have a barcode tattoo on her neck under the hairline, and a micro-chip implanted in her left inner forearm. This body, and a previous murder victim found last September in very similar circumstances, both showed signs of repeated, long-term torture and sexual abuse. The previous victim also reportedly had a similar barcode and micro-chip. Cause of death in both instances was manual strangulation.

An anonymous source links these two deaths to Geneti-Search Laboratories and their, until recently, top-secret program called the Morfph Project. This program has been dogged with scandal in the last few months, and these are just the latest of suspected abuses and suspicious deaths.

Earlier this year, another young woman was found dead in the mansion of the infamous billionaire, Grant Stewart, heir to the Grant fortune. The death was judged to be a suicide. Our anonymous source tells us the dead woman was what Geneti-Search calls an abandoned or

*Orphaned Morfph.* Mr. Stewart was reported to be her *Patron.*

Evidently, the young woman became despondent and took her own life after Mr. Stewart left for what was to be a year-long trip to Europe. Servants in the house said they heard but never saw her, as she didn't leave her suite and refused most food after their employer's departure. Cause of death was an overdose of opioids. Mr. Grant was contacted but would not comment.

Geneti-Search has also refused to comment on these unsubstantiated reports.

# CHAPTER 29

## *Objects of Desire*

*Matthew*

After Ruby left, Matthew started obsessively researching and documenting everything about the Morfph situation he could unearth. He *needed* to know their fates. He needed to know everything that was happening to the vulnerable young people who had gone out into the world and were now at the mercy of their wealthy Patroni.

This knowledge was necessary, not only to figure out the best way to protect Ruby but also because it was part of his ethical duty as the attorney for Geneti-Search. And last, he needed to know so he could assess and own his personal culpability.

He interviewed lab techs, geneticists, Caretakers, Patroni, office staff, even Culled Morfphs being kept at Geneti-Search. All was done in the guise of protecting the company from legal liability.

During one of these interviews, a recently Culled Morfph fidgeted and nervously twisted a strand of her hair around her finger. She had been found to be Defective during her last check-up and was promptly replaced with another Morfph. Her Patron had no idea of the replacement, but he was now happy with his newly "adjusted" Morfph.

"I'm not sure what they're going to do with me," she said, her voice tight. "I think I'll be alright... if I don't make any trouble. Can you really guarantee me this will remain anonymous? I'm a little scared... more than a little, really. Some of us have disappeared... like, for good. Mostly abandoned and Orphaned Morfphs, though, and honestly, they're bad off. They go crazy, you know. I mean, bat shit crazy. Sometimes they sit for hours, just rocking back and forth... moaning the whole time. It's awful. I'm glad I'm a Defective... and not one of those."

"I won't name names, I guarantee it," Matthew answered. "And you will never be asked to testify or anything. I'm on your side... I am."

"Yeah, I trust you. I'm pretty good at reading people even if I have lost my so-called empathic abilities." She leaned closer to him. "I've heard and seen some weird shit. You sure you want to hear it?" she said in a low voice.

Matthew nodded.

"You ever heard of *Objects of Desire*? They're shows or contests... auctions... whatever."

"No." Matthew shook his head. *Objects of Desire?*

"Yeah. My Patron called himself Rossetti, a Romantic artist. It wasn't so bad for me. Usually, the men who bought me for a night were romantics themselves... and so was my Patron. Treated me well. Nothing too rapey or sadistic. But other girls... they told me some terrible things... I don't even want to think about them. I can give you some names of Patroni who take part, but you can't tell them I told you and you have to pretend you're into it. It won't be any problem. You're one of them. You'll be 'In like Flynn.' Can't remember where I heard that." She laughed, but it sounded strained.

"In like Flynn," she repeated.

"I don't understand. Rosetti? Artists? Rape? What's... what do I have to pretend I'm into?"

"Another thing you need to know... a lot of the Patroni *want* their Morfphs to feel pain, you know. To suffer... to feel fear and anguish... so they do... every day. I know they say Morfphs don't suffer... but we do. We do. It's weird because it's all overlaid with needing to please and getting satisfaction and pleasure from it, but we suffer, too. It's twisted, ya know? Fucked up shit, for sure."

"But what is this? I still don't..."

"You just have to go see for yourself. Go and see."

After that interview, Matthew contacted the Patron the Culled Morfph had identified. And, as she said, it was no problem to convince him Matthew wanted to attend an event. She'd filled him in enough to know what to say. He used the story of his runaway Morfph for sympathy and the Patron got Matthew all set up.

*In like Flynn*, Matthew thought.

Following the Patron's instructions, he found the run-down warehouse in a deserted part of town even the homeless avoided. Garbage and other things best not examined were heaped and strewn around the building and its surrounding parking lot.

Matthew found the door on the alley and descended the clanking metal stairs into the dark bowels of the building. At the end of a long, sweating concrete hallway was another door. This one needed a face scan to get through, and being a Certified Patron was all he needed for that.

After a buzz and a loud click, he walked through into another hall, this one shorter than the first. At the end of this hall, two large, dead-faced men with automatic weapons met him, examined his ID, scanned his E-vite and frisked him. As the last door swung open, he stepped into a dazzling cavernous room, hung with hundreds of chandeliers whose light glittered off the mirrored walls.

Temporarily blinded, he put his hand over his eyes, blinked several times, and finally opened them slowly. The central feature and focus of the room was a long, elevated runway with a stage in the round at the end. It ran through the center of the large room, dividing it in two. On the floor, a large audience sat in red velvet upholstered chairs that lined the runway on all sides.

A frisson of anticipation crackled in the air as they talked to each other in animated but slightly lowered voices. The audience was mostly made up of men dressed in black tuxes, but there were a handful of women, and some men, dressed in bright jewel-like satins, silks, and velvets.

The audience hushed further as a man in a long black buttoned-up smock walked up on the round stage, opened a stool and sat down without saying anything. The lights in the large room dimmed and several spotlights focused on one circle in the center of the stage. Everyone sat forward in their seats, hardly containing their excitement.

A man Matthew hadn't noticed before, and who stood at a dais to the side of the runway, started to speak.

"Welcome to *Objects of Desire*. Our first artist tonight is Botticelli Secundo. As always, the canvas is his Morfph, and the medium is the power of his mind. Gentlemen, ladies, the sublime beauty of The Birth of Venus–always a great favorite—will be *thought* to life tonight before your eyes. By special request, tonight the bidding for this Venus will begin right after the artwork is completed. So be prepared."

Matthew slipped into a chair in the back row. The two men seated in chairs in front of him were speaking loudly enough to overhear.

"Oh my fucking god. The Birth of Venus again? It's been done to death. How many Botticellis are there now anyway, six... seven?"

The other man laughed. "Didn't you know? The first five tonight are all Birth of Venus."

"Oh, for Christ's sake."

"I know, I know. I'm getting really bored with this whole Classics category. Their tits are never big enough for me. But the Picasso section later should be a gas. And then there's a children's category. I'm definitely sticking around for that. I might bid."

"You swing that way?" the other man said, his voice disapproving.

"Sometimes. For kicks. They're not really kids, you know."

"Oh, I know..."

"Don't get judgey with me, Judge. You got no room. Besides, you have your own Morfph you can do anything you want with. I'm not so..."

"Yeah, yeah. Shhh... he's starting. The Morfph is out."

Theatrical music—lutes and maybe a flute?—swelled as a naked young female figure walked down the runway and stood in the middle of the circle of light on the stage.

Her outline was blurry, but as Matthew watched, she firmed up. She was looking intently at her Patron, the artist in black on the stage with her. Continuing to concentrate on his face, as if looking for cues, she gradually got taller and her hair turned blond, growing longer and longer in cascading waves until it was long enough for her to hold it in her hand in front of her.

Her face and body became clearer, too. They both elongated and smoothed into the visage of an ethereally lovely young woman. Her other hand was now open and placed over her right breast in a modest gesture. As she shifted her gaze out into the audience, her head slightly tipped to the side.

Matthew had seen the original painting of "The Birth of Venus," and this young woman was now, as the moderator had said, art come to life. Matthew sucked in his breath, dazzled despite himself and in his revulsion at what was happening here tonight. The woman on the stage *was* glowingly, breathtakingly beautiful.

The audience oohed in appreciation of the artist, as this version of the Venus was an especially good one.

"We will now begin the bidding," the moderator said. "For one night of ecstasy with this very special Venus, Gentlemen... let's start the bidding at $10,000?"

With the loud crack of the gavel, the flesh and blood woman on the stage jerked like a puppet on a string and, except for the very brief flash of abject animal terror in her eyes, her expression seemed to remain unchanged.

Matthew lurched to his feet. He had seen enough. Everything the Transitioned Morfph at Geneti-Search had told him was true. Completely, horrifyingly, true.

# CHAPTER 30

### *The Truth Must Out*

*"... but now that I had finished, the dream vanished and breathless horror and disgust filled my heart."*

—*Victor Frankenstein from* Frankenstein: Or, The Modern Prometheus *by Mary Shelley*

### *Matthew*

By getting into the system and burying the investigation into Ruby's departure, he had kept the knowledge of it from Alix and the powers-that-be for over two months. He had needed that time to conduct his investigation and to decide what he was going to do. But the time had come to make a move. He now stood in Alix's office, watching her as she exercised.

Alix ran on a treadmill facing large windows. Her feet beat a rapid tattoo on the fast-moving belt, and sweat gleamed on her forehead and dripped down the side of her face.

She wore skin-tight, iridescent leggings and a sleeveless top that revealed her emaciation. Bones jutted and protruded through the shiny fabric: hips, scapula, shoulder blades, and clearly visible vertebrae. If he chose, he could probably count every one of them running down her backbone. Matthew looked away and winced inwardly.

"Hey, Matt. What's up? Don't have much time right now, but we can talk while I'm working out."

Without preamble, Matthew spoke loudly over the treadmill.

"My Morfph left, Alix. She's gone."

"What?" Her running slowed as she adjusted the speed and looked at him.

"My Morfph. She ran away."

Now Alix stopped the treadmill and stared.

232

"She what? Why? What did you do?"

"I was going to call the police..."

"The police? You idiot," she screamed.

"... but I didn't," he finished and looked at Alix coldly. "The neighbors saw her after she... well, I'll get to that. They might report her missing. It's possible."

Alix stepped off the treadmill, picked up a fluffy turquoise towel from a table at the side of the room, and wiped her face and neck.

"We'll deal with that if we need to. I doubt it will be a problem. Right now, let's figure this whole thing out," she said carefully.

Throwing the towel around her neck, she walked to her big glass desk and leaned against it, crossing her ankles over each other.

"I thought you were happy with Alpha Two, Matthew. Did you tire of her? What went wrong? Why did you want her to leave?"

"I didn't. She left because *she* wanted to. I begged her to stay with me. I was arranging for us to run away... together. But she left alone... of her own free-will."

"Free will? What are you talking about? That's simply not possible. Besides, why would you both run away? It doesn't make any sense." Her short-lived calm seemed to be wearing thin.

"Evidently it *is* possible, Alix. Since she did." Matthew answered. "Surely you're aware of the problems. She's not the only one. You must know what's been happening."

"Yeah, yeah, I'm aware of a few Morfphs running away. But their Patroni must not have wanted them anymore. I thought that might be an issue. A small one, I hoped."

Now it was Matthew's turn to shake his head.

"Maybe some of them. But not all, Alix. You really don't know what's happening? They have a name for them. They call them Defectives."

"Wait." She waved away his words like flies. "Okay, Matthew, just tell me *exactly* what happened. Exactly. Start to finish."

"You must have been told about everything… not just defective Morfphs but about Morfphs being abandoned and abused… about all of it, Alix. This surely can't be news to you."

"Please, Matthew. Enough with the histrionics and outrage. I just need for you to tell me *exactly* what happened with you and your Morfph."

So he did. From start to finish.

Alix seemed to have been struck dumb by what Matthew said. She sat silent and motionless for a long time.

"You say that she lost her empathic *and* her shape-shifting-abilities… *completely*. So, she is no longer a Morfph—just a girl? She was functioning fine, and then she lost it? How could that happen? How?"

"You're the scientist, Alix. You tell me. But my theory is simple. It happened because I wanted it to. That's probably the essence of it. I wanted—*desired*—for her to have freewill. And that desire must have caused a… uh… I don't know… a dissonance, maybe? Something deep inside of her just snapped."

"Shit, shit, shit, shit. What happened? What in the hell happened? How many? And how many more?" Alix murmured to herself.

For some reason he couldn't really identify, something in this recent information seemed to flick up alarm and even panic in her. But he ignored her mutterings.

"And yeah, she can't morph at all… doesn't want to. She lost her glimmer first and then she had a total… I can only describe it as a total breakdown. She's still incredibly brilliant, though. Still learns new things at a phenomenal rate," shaking his head, apparently still amazed. "I would never call Ruby 'just a girl' though."

"Ruby? Oh, the Morfph. Yeah, great, just great, I'm so relieved. That will be easy to market. 'Come get 'um… smart girls!' Always been a hot item. Christ! How could I not know this? They've been keeping it from me. Bastards!"

"They're terrified of you, Alix. And besides, you have seemed pretty distracted lately. Not really on your game. But you must know about the Cullings at the monitoring appointments. They couldn't have hidden that entirely from you. Even I had heard about those. It horrified Ruby... and me too."

"I knew very little. They told me a few Morfphs were 'malfunctioning' and were being replaced. And that some had apparently run off. I wasn't really surprised that there were some defectives. But Jesus, to be fine and then lose their abilities..."

Alix had been staring at the floor, and then she looked up.

"And she's gone? Where the hell did she go?" she demanded.

Matthew just shook his head.

"She said she was going to other Morfphs like her. Other changed Morfphs. She called it Going Through The Change. Thought it was funny."

"Wait a minute. When did she leave? I think I saw her. It had to be her. She was outside my condo yelling at Ad... uh, yelling something. Tall, nineteen, maybe twenty, rangy, dark hair?"

"You saw Ruby? My god. What was she doing? And stop the charade, I know you have a Morfph, too."

"Yeah, well. It didn't take a genius to figure that out, I guess. Yeah, I saw her. She was screaming for someone named Pearl. Adam, *my Morfph*, was really agitated at first. He was unsettled afterwards, too. Took a while to settle him down."

"Oh my god," Matthew said again. "Is she okay? Where is she now?"

"I don't know." Alix said dismissively. "Gone. My guards couldn't catch her. That bitch can run, I'll give her that."

"How could I have been so stupid?" she said two times. It then turned into a one word, repeated over and over again. "Stupid, stupid, stupid..."

Impatiently interrupting her mantra, Matthew got louder.

"There's more... so much more. And it all has to be answered for."

"I'm sure you'll enlighten me, won't you? You're enjoying this. But you're waist deep in the shit, too. You know."

"Believe me, Alix, I'm aware. What I'd really like to know is how many Morfphs have committed suicide or gone insane or just died of grief from abandonment or rejection?"

"Not that many, Matthew. They have assured me," Alix said absent-mindedly.

"So, you know more than you're letting on. Christ, Alix," Matthew said, acid in his voice. "Not that many! Is that really your answer? How many is not that many? Any is too many. *Any* is your... no, *our*... responsibility. I guess the ones who Transitioned are the lucky ones..."

"Stop talking. Just shut up. I have to think."

## *Alix*

The fact was, Alix knew more, much more, than she was letting on to Matthew, and the truth was even more complicated than he suspected. There hadn't been many of what they now were calling Orphaned Morfphs... just a handful. But she knew a Morfph's... a *functioning* Morfph's... whole existence and meaning, their very I-ness, was based on a connection with their Patron.

When Morfphs lost that connection, through death of their Patron or abandonment, the result was extreme. They emotionally and then physically fell apart. They went mad with loneliness.

First, they'd become frantic, followed by despondency and terrifying hallucinations. If they had access to them, they rapidly fell into drug and alcohol addiction. Eventually, if they hadn't committed suicide, they totally shut down. They became mute, finally curling up in a fetal position and lapsing into a coma.

All outcomes rapidly ended in death for these Orphaned Morfphs. So far, there had been only a couple of documented suicides and a few more who had died after a month-long coma. But there would be more. She knew there would be more.

But what Alix hadn't known about—hadn't known anything about at all—was this change, *this transition,* that Matthew was talking about now. She really needed to be alone to think this through. She wanted Matthew gone and this conversation over.

"Matthew, get out. I'll let you know when I've decided what needs to be done." She walked around her desk, sat in the swiveling chair, and started tapping on her computer keys.

"There's a lot more to talk about," Matthew said, undeterred. "I'm not going anywhere yet. Have you heard of the *Objects of Desire* beauty contests?"

Alix still didn't respond, just continued typing, so a revved-up Matthew kept talking.

"These things are unbelievable. Totally dehumanizing. Treating people like commodities—*things* to be bought and sold, and used and abused for their entertainment. I guess wealthy people are used to being allowed to do that.

"It's all done in secret, totally under the radar. Get this, Patroni are having beauty contests using their Morfphs... calling them Living Art. Their canvas, or maybe their clay, is their Morfph—the body of a real, flesh and blood human being. There are different categories: men, women, everything in between... fantasy figures, teens, even young children..."

Alix finally looked up.

"Oh Matthew," she interrupted, "that's ridiculous. That whole thing is just made up. Someone's vivid imagination or just one of those anti-technology freaks or maybe someone who has a hard-on for me... and not in a good way." She laughed mirthlessly.

"No, it's real, Alix. I... I've seen it."

"What? You've seen what?" Alix said, disbelief in her voice.

"And then there's the pedophile orgies... Patroni stage orgies with Morfphs they have shape shifted into children."

"Well, I mean, that's repugnant, no doubt, but it's not even illegal. They're not really children…"

Matthew ignored that with a grimace. "But even worse, at least two known Morfphs have been found dead… murdered. Cut up. Tortured."

"They were ones who ran away," Alix said. "Their Patroni didn't have anything to do with those, and neither did we. Why would a Patron kill a Morfph? They pay a fortune for them."

"I don't know. Torture gone too far?" Matthew said. "Of course they'd say they ran away. And you are just taking their words for it. They are both wealthy as God, after all. We don't really have any idea how many have been physically abused, do we?"

"We check for physical abuse and interview them monthly."

"Don't be disingenuous, Alix. If their Patron doesn't want us to know, they won't—they *can't*—report it. Not unless their Patron wants them to. They can't even get mad about it. Or sad. They just have to take it and like it, for god's sake. And that's not even including the abandoned Morfphs and all they suffer."

But there was something else Alix knew about, something further regarding Morfphs' fates… and this *must never* come out. There were a few… a very few… of the Morfphs who had been… dealt with. Some unruly Culled Morfphs had been euthanized.

What else could they have done?

They were a danger… to everything. Orphaned Morfphs were easier. They quickly slipped into a comatose state and, after that, they simply didn't last long. She didn't want to think about it. She didn't feel guilt easily, but this penetrated enough to prick her conscience. She was, however, in too deep at this point to change the course now.

But, really, her pricked conscience was the least of her agitation by this point in the conversation. All she could focus on now was what all this meant to her… and to her program.

The real problem wasn't the abuse of Morfphs... or even the problem of dealing with Orphaned Morfphs. Much of this was inevitable. Anyone who knew anything about human beings knew that. It was manageable. But this was much more than just a few casualties.

This transitioning that Matthew was talking about meant Morfphs could and were losing the very abilities that made them Morfphs. *No, no, no. This simply can't be true.* She had anticipated almost everything he had mentioned. Factored it all in. But not this, never this. She felt numb. She knew this was quite likely the end of her project.

The end of her career, too? Probably.

But surely this transition, this change, couldn't—wouldn't—happen very often. Alix knew some Patroni might say, or even think, they wanted their Morfphs to have free thought. But in reality, the Patroni who claimed they wanted their Morfphs' "real" opinions, or wanted them to have their own mind, were deceiving themselves. What they truly desired was for their Morfph to be and act exactly as they, the Patron, wanted them to, but also to "freely" want it themselves as well.

So, in this type of case, the Morfph would continue to be exactly what the Patron wanted them to be, meanwhile reassuring them, correctly, that it was exactly who they wanted to be.

"I *am* being myself," they would say, "and it's exactly who I want to be."

This would pacify the Patron and life would go on.

Jerked abruptly back from her musings, Alix heard Matthew say it out loud.

"Pull the plug, Alix. You need to shut it all down. Now."

"What? No, no. I can fix it," Alix said, staring blindly out the glass wall to the side of her. Her voice was low as she talked. "I'll fix it. It won't be that bad."

"It's not fixable, Alix. You must know that. There's no fixing this. It's gone too far. There's too many of them now. How many Morfphs are out there? Hundreds? Thousands? And how many have had the switch to freewill? How many will? Five percent… ten… more? It needs to be shut down. I'll help you. I'll support you. We can do it together."

Alix shook her head slowly back and forth.

"No, no. I can't do that. I'll never do that."

"If you don't, I will. I'll do by myself."

"Matthew, Matthew, wait." She reached across the desk toward him. He leaned away.

"You really don't want to do that," she said. "I realize what a shock this is for you. You must be reeling with this new loss. First your wife, now your Morfph. Look. I'm, seeing a great therapist. Let me give you her name. It's Sara Wilde. You'll love her…"

Alix rifled through her drawer and found Sara's card. She stuffed it in Matthew's shirt pocket.

Matthew jerked back in the chair.

"Alix, I don't need a therapist."

Alix towered over Matthew, and her veins turned to ice.

"Matthew, you don't want to take me on. I'll ruin you. We have attorney-client privilege. You can't say anything… to anybody."

"I'm not your personal attorney, Alix. No attorney-client privilege exists between us."

"Don't forget you signed a non-disclosure agreement." Alix said, desperate now.

"I don't care, Alix. I just don't care. Don't you see? If I don't right this, I *will* be ruined. But not the way you mean. I'll be beyond redemption. At some point, you just have to save your own soul. Lily and then Ruby taught me that. Think of your soul, Alix."

"Souls again, huh? Christ, I don't have the luxury of worrying about my freakin' soul." She felt both frantic and angry.

"Remember our conversation in the bar after the meeting? I asked you if you'd read Frankenstein. I never finished my point that night. His own hubris destroyed Frankenstein, Dr. Frankenstein, not the monster... by playing God. There are lessons in there, Alix. I highly recommend you heed them before it's too late."

But instead of responding or reacting, Alix, having lost the thread once more, just looked blankly at Matthew. *Ah, there it is,* she thought. The reason for her niggling panic had hit her square in the gut.

What she suddenly realized, really understood for the first time, was that Adam *could* stop loving her. Not only that, he could leave her. Just like the rest. Just like everyone else. Anger and anxiety turned to ice cold panic.

And with total amazement and complete disgust, she realized that for the first time in perhaps forty years, there were tears running down her face.

# CHAPTER 31
## *You've Lost Control of Your Creatures*

*Alix*

Alix had no doubt that Matthew meant every word he had said. He would blow the story wide open, bringing the whole world shrieking down on them... on *her*. The media, and so the unwashed hoards, had gotten glimmerings of what was happening and the outraged screeching had already begun. Much of the fury, Alix thought cynically, seemed to center on the leaking of the cost of Morfphs, and with that, the realization that they, the plebes, could never have one for themselves.

After their initial devastating conversation, Alix had worked at Matthew and had finally convinced him to come to a meeting with her and their boss, Arthur Riche, at the latter's palatial office at the top of the Geneti-Search building. The reason given was: "to find an agreeable solution to the Morfph problem."

The real reason, of course, was damage control. Alix, however, feared it was too late for that. She had desperately hoped to fix the problems quietly, notifying no one else at Geneti-Search, except a few handpicked geneticists and lab techs. That had been doomed to failure from the beginning, and she had known it before she even tried.

Now, sitting in the meeting she had arranged, they all eyed each other warily. They were in a brief lull after an initial hostile verbal battle. Just as she had expected, the meeting wasn't going well. Not well at all.

She could not bring herself to tell her boss all the damning details before the meeting. And since she had last talked to Matthew, she had collected even more detailed information and numbers concerning Morfph abuse, suicides and other suspicious deaths. She imagined he had done the same, as she knew he had been nosing around and asking many detailed questions. He had even visited the compounds where Culled Morfphs were being kept, awaiting who knew what—many against their newly found wills.

But the extent of the information Matthew seemed to know today, especially about the Morfph runaways, was odd and frankly suspicious. The rumor was—and now Matthew was corroborating it—the runaway Morfphs, the ones Matthew was calling Transitioned Morfphs, had formed their own compound in some secret location. How they could stay hidden with all the surveillance drones they had sent out, she simply couldn't figure out.

They must have some fancy advanced technology set up. But Alix was sure that Matthew was in contact with his Morfph, even as he vehemently continued to deny it. He remained unbendingly adamant that the whole Morfph program needed to be scrapped and reparations made.

"You know—of course you must know," Matthew said, "that they are vastly superior to us... in intelligence especially. They learn at a phenomenal rate. Their problem-solving ability, abstract thinking, spatial intelligence, strategic thinking... you name it... all enhanced. They also have enhanced strength, agility, and hand-eye coordination.

"And they're royally pissed at us, really at everyone—everyone we call Freeborns. They have other, less complimentary, names for us. 'The Dotards' is popular. There's also 'Normies' and 'Ordinaries' which seem less insulting but to them are scathing epithets." Matthew stopped talking abruptly, as if he realized he was saying too much.

"How do you know all this, Matthew? If you're in touch with Alpha Two, you have to tell us where she is. We need to find them. We have several teams out hunting them. We *will* find them."

"I'm not in touch with her or any of them," Matthew said, an edge in his voice. "I tested Aspas... *Ruby* before she left. She was incredible. And I have other sources. You don't need to know what they are."

Their boss finally spoke. His voice was low and his diction precise, but the acid-edged anger was clear.

"But we need to know, Matthew. We need to know *everything* you know. It's essential that we do."

"Well, *Arthur,* what are you going to do with them if you find them, huh? They won't just come along meekly. And they'll be a formidable force. There will be some terrible publicity. The sympathy will not be with you, that's for sure. Have you even looked at social media today? Or any of the media outlets? You won't be able to keep a lid on this. Not anymore. Besides, you *won't* find them. They're smarter than you. They're light years smarter than any of us."

"That won't matter. We have more resources at our disposal. You'd be surprised what we can keep quiet. We can handle this, believe me," Arthur Riche said darkly.

"Well, I don't, Arthur. I really don't believe you. Another thing you likely do not know is that the Morfph compound is being funded, sponsored... whatever... by at least one of their super-wealthy ex-Patroni. He, maybe others too, has been supplying them with weapons, shielding equipment, money, and supplies of all sorts. They are not without their own resources. And they are armed to the teeth."

Matthew gave them a steely look.

"Besides, even if you can bury all this, what I really don't believe is that you will right any of the wrongs that have been done to them. And as I've already told Alix, I *will* end this program myself and soon. I don't need your permission or your help. I was hoping we could all work together to make this right, but I see now that that will not happen." He stood up to leave.

Arthur also came to his feet, walked aggressively toward Mathew, grabbed his hand and shook it, his grip vice-like and painful.

"Well, Matthew, thank you for coming today. Alix and I will discuss how we will move forward and let you know ASAP. Please hold off on any action for a little while longer, at least. We would greatly appreciate *that* courtesy."

Even though Matthew had not gone to the police, the media had somehow gotten wind of the whole situation, anyway. Now they had their teeth deep into the neck of the story. Since then, Geneti-Search had been in full damage control.

Matthew must know he was putting himself in dire jeopardy, and not only about losing his job, if he didn't go along with whatever plan Arthur devised. Alix and Arthur had tried to reassure him, bribe him, then subtly, but clearly, to threaten him... all to no avail.

Matthew yanked his hand back.

"I'll give you five days... no four. By Friday. That's it. And that's too generous."

Matthew strode out of the meeting, dropping an envelope in Alix's lap. His back was ramrod straight; his defeated slump now completely gone. It looked as if he had finally thrown off the last of his depression and grief, and he was a sight to behold. He was quite beautiful in his rage and determination. Alix marveled at her newfound fear of him—and for him.

Before she could look at the envelope, The Big Guy—Arthur—turned slowly, deliberately, to her. The look on his face made the fine hairs stand up at the base of her neck. His demeanor with Matthew had been deliberate, even concerned, with only a glimpse of tamped down menace. His aspect now transformed; his fury on full display.

"You stupid, stupid bitch. This is one fucked up mess *you* created. Why wasn't I kept up to speed? Why did I have to learn it *today* from that... that... *disloyal piece of shit? That rat.* You kept telling me everything was going smoothly.

"I should have known I couldn't trust a fucking cunt with anything, let alone a multi-trillion-dollar project like this." His face puffed up bright red. Sweat dripped down his forehead and down the side of his face.

All the names Alix had been called over the years came rushing back as she looked into his rage-distorted face. Sometimes they were hurled by strangers as she drove by a homeless camp, sometimes, like today, by colleagues. And not infrequently she'd heard it from husbands and boyfriends. Cunt and bitch topped the list, of course. But there were many more: slut, whore, pussy, snatch, gash, slit, piece of ass, cow, pig, slag, split tail... the list seemed endless. And in the last few years, she started noticing the additional adjectives to accommodate her age.

"I thought it was going well—amazingly well," Alix stammered. "I really thought it was until..." She stopped. "They weren't telling me about all the problems." Her face fluctuated between whipped dog and defensive defiance.

"Weren't telling you? You lost control, Alix. You should have been on them like stink on shit. That was your job. Your damned job."

"I know. I know. But I can fix the glitch in future Morfph genes. I know I can. This can still go. It will blow over. We can control the fallout."

"You can fix it? Have you seen what's being reported? Maybe your Morfph fucked you stupid... or probably you just started out that way and got stupider. Why did I let a woman lead me down this shit hole? We'll be very lucky we still have a company when this is done."

"No, no. I can put it right. Please..."

"Get out, Alix. Just get the hell out of here. I'll take care of this. I'll take care of Matthew. I'll take care of that nest of traitor Morfphs. I'll take care of everything."

"What do you mean? What are you going to do?" Alix said, her voice a constricted squeak.

"Get out," he bellowed again. "Get out of here. *Now!*"

Alix reeled out the door and stumbled to her office. She stared out her window, far, far below her. *No windows open this high up. Is that good or bad?* she wondered numbly.

She didn't move until night descended on her. Finally, she looked around at the darkened office and stood up stiffly. She slowly collected everything that was hers from the office, which only consisted of two laptops, a smaller tablet, her cell, and the letter Matthew had given her. Stuffing the letter into the pocket of her suit coat, she walked out of her office and out of the building without a backward glance.

———————

Woodenly, Alix walked in the door of her condo and carefully placed her computers, the tablet, and her phone on the table. After pulling off her stilettos, she pitched them down the hall with a short, contained shriek.

Then, moving slowly and mechanically once more, she peeled off her suit jacket as she walked toward the living room. Matthew's letter fell out and hit the floor. When she bent down to retrieve it, she saw *Pearl* written in large letters across the outside of the envelope. With a scoffing grunt, she crammed the envelope back into the suit pocket and let the jacket fall to the plush, white carpet of the living room. She sat heavily on the deep sectional sofa.

Adam, who must have heard and *felt* her come home, walked tentatively into the room. He seemed to take one scan of Alix and then, to her relief, walked right back out again. Not knowing what else to do, Alix started swiping obsessively through her tablet.

Oh, here's something she hadn't known about. There was now an organization called The Association for the Protection of Morfphs and other Genetically Engineered Human Beings, or APM. She grimaced.

She scanned quickly through everything she brought up, sometimes reading whole Twitcher storms. Some phrases came up repeatedly: "monstrous embodiment of human pride," "... Alex Edison's exercise in extreme hubris," *(Couldn't even spell her name right.)* "This is no better than human trafficking... No. This *is* human trafficking... just a new form of slavery!... real human beings with no choice... no personal autonomy... no control of their own bodies... no rights... and of course, all women of color!"

On and on. Editorials, reports of campaigns, petitions, and protests swam before her eyes and reverberated in her now throbbing, aching head.

Alix flipped her tablet closed, picked up one of her laptops, and went into the dining room. She took one cut-crystal glass and a bottle of Laphroaig out of the cabinet and, arms full, walked slowly into her bedroom. Once there, she precisely placed her laptop, and the glass and bottle on the small bedside table, pulled off her clothes and crawled, naked, into the smooth sheets of her carefully made bed.

# CHAPTER 32

## *End of a (Fever) Dream*

*"... you, my creator, detest and spurn me, thy creature, to whom thou are bound by ties only dissoluble by the annihilation of one of us."*

—*the monster in* <u>*Frankenstein: Or, The Modern Prometheus*</u> *by Mary Shelley*

### *Adam*

Alix didn't leave her bedroom suite for three days except twice to fetch new, full bottles of whiskey from outside the door where Adam put them according to her desire. The door and the whiskey could not muffle or drown out their connection with each other. He had also put food—fruit and yogurt mostly—with the whiskey bottles because Adam could read her hunger. She ate nothing of his offerings, but the whiskey bottles were drained. He knew Matthew had given her four days before he would act. But what would Arthur Riche be doing in the meantime?

Adam had found the letter to Pearl from Ruby when he went to hang up Alix's jacket. He knew he had *been* Pearl at one time, but he wasn't her anymore, and so the letter meant very little to him. He also knew, in a previous time, he had felt love for this girl named Ruby, but now the letter was simply a curious artifact from that earlier time.

He smoothed it out and put it on the console in the dining room. He couldn't quite bring himself to throw it away. It seemed disrespectful somehow. It was obviously written with passion and hope.

But now all Adam could focus on was Alix. He could fully, viscerally, feel her despair, fear and anger... and a new feeling he had never read in her... guilt? But it was more nuanced than guilt... regret, maybe. His own personal panic was building, as well. He felt helpless, as he knew much of her turmoil was tied up in the innate, designed-in flaws of Morfphs. And that included him, maybe especially

248

in him. He could feel her turning away from him. So, the despair he felt was not just hers, it was his, too.

Alix finally emerged from her bedroom suite late in the afternoon of the third day. The sickly acrid smell of whisky and stress sweat emanated from her. Her silvery, white-blond hair, normally expertly twisted up in a chic knot on the back of her head, hung in snarled strands around her face. There were dark smudges of old mascara under her blood-shot eyes. She had pulled on some old sweats she must have found at the bottom of her drawer. Adam had never seen them before.

Alix took one look at Adam.

"Christ, you look worse than I do."

"I'm so glad you're feeling better, Alix," Adam said hopefully. He could feel her lift in mood but could not discern what she was thinking. *That's odd*, Adam thought. There was something, though, something important, but she was blocking it. She didn't want him to know. His brow creased, and he shivered as a jolt of foreboding ran down his spine.

### Alix

Alix darted a piercing look at her Adam and then just as quickly looked away again. Before she turned away, she saw his confusion and puzzlement, like he couldn't quite hear a broadcast that was usually crystal clear.

*I can hardly make myself look at him,* she thought with equal parts pity and disgust... *so flawed... so flawed. And when I do, he is languishing, sick, and so pale he is almost disappearing before my eyes. Because that's what I desire from him now—to disappear, to never have existed at all... not like this anyway.*

"There is one thing you can still do for me," Alix said. "One last thing."

Adam looked at her, despair written on his face.

*Ah,* Alix thought sadly, *he is finally reading what I'm planning.* She was no empath, but she knew him well enough to see that all the feelings and thoughts she had been blocking had broken through and were washing over him like a burst dam.

"I can't kill you," he whispered. "I can't."

"It's the only thing I desire of you now," Alix said. "There's nothing else."

Panic and horror suffused his face.

"Alix," Adam said desperately, "stop worrying about me leaving you or stopping loving you. I never could. No matter what, I'd never leave."

"I know you think that, Adam. I know you do. But you can't know that for sure. And there's so much more wrong here. This is the only way."

"I'll do what you want of me. You know I have to. But what about me, Alix? What about me?"

"I have pills for you if you can't endure living... after," she said and pointed to a pill bottle she had brought out of the bedroom that now sat on the table. A new, full whiskey bottle was next to it.

"Alix, no. Please, no. Change your mind, please. We can get through this together."

"No, Adam. The villagers are gathering. The digital mobs are forming. Maybe not with real pitchforks, but, come to think of it, maybe with real fire. I've had death threats and hate mail.

"Talk radio jocks, ministers, and politicians are calling me the devil or a witch... saying I should be purged from the earth. My company has made me the scapegoat and cut me loose. I have no friends or family who want anything to do with me. I *will* be killed sooner or later, probably sooner, and then what would become of you? That is, if they don't kill you, too. No, this is best. This way I can make sure the program is deep-sixed. No Alix Edison. No more Morfph program. We can go together, my Love."

Adam bowed his head, his hands covering his face.

"Oh, my poor Adam," Alix said gently, as he raised his head and looked miserably at her and then at the pills. Tears ran down his face and pooled in the depression above his beautiful lips. *What's that called?* Alix wondered. *Oh yes, the philtrum.*

*I must want him to be sad about all this.*

*But his pain is real. I made sure of that in his design.*

"I'm truly sorry, Adam, but I'm afraid we are both doomed now."

Adam gazed fixedly at his hands for several seconds, as if he'd never seen them before. He then looked at Alix in the same intense way.

Finally, his face a mask of defeated resignation, he walked slowly to her and wrapped those hands around her long, slim neck. They didn't feel weak now, the hands. They were warm, big, and quite powerful. He paused and loosened his hands briefly as a wave of fear washed over Alix.

But she remained determined, so he kissed her tenderly and did what she desired of him. His hands squeezed and tightened and then tightened even more.

*Did I wish for that kiss?* she wondered right before she lost consciousness.

"Yes, my dearest," he whispered softly into her ear. The last words she heard.

What she did not hear was the unearthly, keening howl that burst from Adam as he held her lifeless body in his arms.

### Adam/Pearl/Alpha One

The Morfph kneeled on the edge of the bed, staring at Alix's lifeless body. After his keening had quieted and finally ceased, he carefully washed her, dressed her in her best dress—the red silk one that set off Alix's icy beauty so well—smoothed her hair and perfectly made up her face.

Adam, now a *she* once more, just as her genetics dictated, had lost her shimmer, and had shrunk in on herself in despair.

*I'm nameless now,* she thought. *Not Adam anymore, but not really Pearl either. Not anymore. Once more, I'm reduced to Alpha One.* She sat despondent, glassy eyed, staring into space, filled with a terrifying, unbearable black hole of loneliness. The emptiness was complete, horrible, and total; an annihilation, devoid of hope or light.

"I've left the pills for you," Alix had said to Adam... when she had been a he. "I want you to kill me. I want *your* hands to do it." Adam understood then that Alix didn't want any chance that he would not kill himself, too.

"I want us to go together," she had said. Which was perplexing, since Alix most definitely did not believe in anything but science and, before this all happened, in herself.

The Morfph desperately wished she could remember the *feeling* of being Pearl. She knew she must have loved Ruby, and she remembered her life and things they had said and done, but she couldn't feel it anymore.

But before she could join Alix in death, she had one more thing she needed to do for her here—one last desire to fulfill. She took the manila envelope Alix had given her earlier in the day and propped it up on the dresser in clear view. Then she found Alix's mobile phone, searched her contacts and texted Matthew.

"Bring latex gloves. Alix has left two letters and a thumb-drive in a manilla envelope on the dresser in her bedroom—down the hall, third door on the right. One letter for you, one for the police. Use the gloves to open the manilla envelope. You mustn't leave prints on that or the letter to the police. Take only your letter and the thumb-drive away with you when you leave. The letter to the police makes it clear you are not involved."

Her last duty as a Morfph completed, she grabbed the bottle and poured out the contents into her hand. She swallowed every pill, one by one, and washed them down with the whiskey Alix had left for her for this purpose.

For what is a Morfph without her Patron?

# CHAPTER 33

## *The Queen is Dead*

*Matthew*

The Morfph had already notified the guards at Alix's building that Matthew was coming, so they escorted him up and let him into Alix's condo. They had been instructed not to enter themselves. Late-day sun bathed the walls and floors with gold and flashed in splinters of light from the glass chandelier hanging over the long dining table.

He gazed around in wonder at the opulence of the place. The ceilings were high and vaulted. Windows took up an entire wall, very like her office at Geneti-Search. Sliding glass doors opened onto a sweeping outside terrace with large potted trees, flowers, and cushioned teak furniture.

In the hall, he recognized the letter Ruby had written to Pearl laying on a console. It looked as if someone had crumpled it into a ball, then smoothed it out again. He pocketed it as he walked by.

Slowly, reluctantly, he walked past several rooms until he found the master bedroom. The scene that welcomed him was both macabre and heart-wrenchingly sad. It reminded him, somehow, of a painting he'd seen in the Louvre when he had been there many years before.. *The Death of Sardanapalus.*

*I*n the painting, the cruel and despotic king lay on his bed, surrounded by his dead and dying servants, concubines, and even his horse—all of which he had ordered to be killed as he awaited his own impending death.

A small, youthful woman with a cascade of curly, dark-brown hair lay on the bed nestled into Alix's side. She was dressed in men's clothes that were so large for her, they appeared to have swallowed her up. Her head rested on Alix's chest, with one of her legs wrapped up over her body and an arm draped loosely around her waist. Both women were clearly dead. And he knew: here, next to her beloved Patron, lay Ruby's Pearl.

Alix's lifeless body had been carefully laid out on her ice blue satin-covered bed. Dressed in bright-red, she was a splash of vivid scarlet against the smooth quilted duvet. Her blond hair fanned out in a bright halo around her head, and a silky square of gleaming white fabric covered her face.

He recognized that fabric. It was just like the face veil Ruby had been wearing at their Pairing. Matthew could see an angry red circle, almost the color of her dress, ringing Alix's neck. He did not pull off the white fabric, but knew the horror of what he would find if he did. It would reveal the illusion of a calm and graceful death.

He found the manilla envelope where Alix, or possibly her Morfph, had left it. "Police" was written on the outside in Alix's sweeping script. Putting on the latex gloves as instructed, he walked to the dresser and opened the envelope with shaking hands.

He pulled out the two letters. After returning the letter for the police back inside, he took the large envelope and his letter and sat heavily down in a brocade chair on the other side of the room. He unfolded his letter, leaving wet marks on the paper from his sweaty hands. It had been penned in obvious haste, and, he could only imagine, great agitation.

The ink used, like Alix's dress, was bright red and there were many scratch outs and splotches of ink from a leaking pen that looked disturbingly like drops of blood. Remembering the thumb-drive, he turned the envelope over, shook it, and it fell onto his lap. With it clasped in his hand, he read the letter.

*Matthew,*

*I have made many mistakes and I'm sure you will not be surprised that admitting that does not come easily to me. But I am writing this in a state of profound regret about what has come to be and the part my mistakes have had in it.*

*I especially regret Adam's fate. He was everything to me, and he deserved much better. What will become of them* now—my Morfphs? I saved Adam from his agony, but what of the others?

What, I wonder, will be the fate of old, worn out Morfphs? I believe they will, at some point in aging, stop being able to Morfph as quickly and smoothly. Eventually they will inevitably be stuck in one form, and when they can no longer Morfph themselves to appear forever young, they will come to look their true age. This failing, the wearing out and wearing down, may not be even be noticed for years. By that time, their warranty will have expired and they won't be able to be returned. Some lucky ones will, no doubt, be kept because Patroni will grow attached and will have pity... just as we grow attached to old dogs. But others will probably simply discard them. And then they'll, like other abandoned Morfphs, die of grief.

Ironically, in my quest to alleviate humankind's lone-liness, I have created the loneliest people on Earth; human beings who can't endure being separated from their Patron and who experience unendurable pain when abandoned. This profound loneliness can only be assuaged and held at bay by that one person... their Patron. With no autonomy, they are as vulnerable as a human being can be.

People will say, and they will not be entirely wrong, that I was driven by monstrous hubris, greed, selfishness, and entitlement. But like most things, it isn't that simple. My motives were many; some selfish, but others less so. I genuinely thought this project would improve the world. But as it turns out, I am to be the designated monster and my Morfphs may share my fate. The shrieking hordes that are about to descend on me are right about one thing—I got much wrong. I regret there is to be only one chance for me.

In my defense, my hubris was no different from the hubris of many… I'd say, most, great scientists. Who among us has stopped to question ourselves or the consequences of what we do? How many have unleashed unintended results? The suicides, the murders, the abuse, and the extreme vulnerability and suffering of Morfphs do haunt me even as I live.

And, in the spirit of full disclosure, despite Gensti-Search's continuing denials, we euthanized (murdered?) many of the Culled Morfphs. Abandoned and Orphaned Morfphs cannot be re-bonded and Defective Morfphs cannot be adjusted, or healed, or fixed.

I could rationalize the killing at first, as most were Orphaned or abandoned and wanted to die. But then things changed and the number of Culled Morfphs increased. The newer "defective" Morfphs were unlike the Orphaned Morfphs. I didn't realize at that point that these Morfphs had been fully functioning and then transitioned in some way. But they weren't choosing euthanasia. They wanted badly to live. I didn't let the murder continue much after the defective Morfphs starting arriving, but unfortunately, some killing of "defective" Morfphs occurred, anyway. Most were without my knowledge, but I knew enough—more than enough. I had lost control.

I know, especially after the nature of my death comes to light, that my experiment… my dream, is doomed. The Morfph Program will be dismantled now. It has been a long time coming, this death. As more and more problems were revealed, it was just a matter of time.

Matthew, you were, of course, right about much. This project needs to be terminated. I leave that to you. My death at the hands of my Morſph will ensure the program's demise. I played God, but not well enough, I fear.

One more request: I am leaving you my uncompleted Morſph Compendium. Matthew, please finish it for me. I won't be around to know how it all ends, and I know you will see it to completion.

I can just see the headlines now. "Alix Edison slain by her own Morſph, a fitting end for this malignant, narcissistic and arrogant woman." Harsh words, but essentially, I agree. Certainly, there's justice in it. I lost all control of my creatures. And they will have their revenge.

But please, do not misinterpret what I say. Despite everything, I'd do it again if given the chance.

I'd do it differently. I'd do it better. And this time, I'd have succeeded.

Alix Hoffman Edison, PhD

--------

After finishing the letter, Matthew unfolded his palm computer. His hands still shaking and wet with sweat, he fumbled and dropped the thumb-drive two times before he got it plugged in properly. Up popped *The Morſph's Compendium and Handbook* and he rapidly scanned it.

Suddenly, as if surfacing from a bad anxiety dream, he jerked up straight. He needed to call the police... immediately. He'd already been there too long. The guards would know how long. He folded his letter into a small square and put it, the gloves, and the thumb-drive into the inside zippered pocket of his coat.

Only then did he call the police. As he waited for them to arrive, still sitting in Alix's luxurious bedroom, he stared, transfixed, at the tableaux of Alix and Pearl on the sumptuous bed. He had no idea how this encounter with the police would go. When he called, he had identified himself as a co-worker who checked on Alix after she stopped showing up for work. He had no real plan. *Just play it by ear, Devansh,* he thought, surprised as his original given name popped into his mind.

Voices approached from the front room.

Two people dressed in black suits who were clearly used to be being in charge and obeyed, swept in, surveyed the room, walked to the side of the bed, and looked closely at the bodies. One was a fit man of about fifty with flint grey hair, the other was about ten years younger.

The older man glanced at Matthew.

"Did you touch anything while you were here?"

"Well, I mean, I let myself in and opened doors. But nothing else, I guess," he lied.

"I definitely didn't touch the bodies."

"Okay, okay. We'll need to question you. Possibly at the station. So, you said when you called 911, your name is Matthew Lawrence and that you knew the victims? I.D. please."

He pulled out his wallet, handed his chipped ID card to the younger detective, who had his hand outstretched.

"Victim, singular. Yes, I'm Matthew Lawrence and I was a co-worker of Dr. Edison." He pointed to Alix's body. "I did not know the young woman."

"What was her relationship to Dr. Edison?"

"I said I didn't know her, and I didn't know Dr. Edison well, either. We worked together."

"Why are you here?"

"My boss sent me to check on Alix. She hadn't come in to work for a few weeks."

"A few weeks. It took you long enough. Your boss? Who's your boss?"

"Arthur Riche at Geneti-Search. I'm the staff attorney." Matthew knew Arthur would be obliged to corroborate his story to save his own ass.

"Arthur Riche?" He sounded alarmed and looked pointedly at his partner. He had turned pale.

The older detective took the ID from his partner and quickly handed it back to Matthew. They hadn't scanned it.

"We've gotten enough information, sir. You can go now. We'll take care of this."

As Matthew left the bedroom, he glanced back and saw the detectives conferring in furtive whispers; their brows furrowed and intent.

Arthur's tentacles were evidently long and wide.

———————

When Matthew arrived home, he read Alix's compendium with rapt attention. He read it all—every word—and then read it again, and then a third time.

———————

# THE DAILYFEED

*Controversial multi-billion-dollar genetic
engineering program creating enhanced human
beings ends in tragedy, chaos and scandal*

*Morfph™ kills Patron and self in shocking murder/suicide*

Geneti-Search Corporation's "Morfph" project, long plagued with scandal, public outrage, and protests, ended today in a shocking finale. Dr. Alix Edison, the genetic scientist who conceived and lead the program, was found dead in her condominium bedroom. Found with her, also deceased, was a young woman, reported to be Ms. Edison's Morfph™ of three years. The Morfph™ apparently killed Ms. Edison before killing herself.

# THE BAY POST

August 6, 20**

## *Genetic engineer and creator of the infamous Morfph™ project slain by own "brainchild."*

### By Marsh Madison

Alix Hoffman Edison, 55, was found strangled by her own Morfph™, in what appears to be a murder/suicide.

Dr. Edison's body was discovered in her condominium by a co-worker from Geneti-Search Technologies and Laboratories. Dr. Edison had stopped coming into work or responding to outreach for several weeks. Found with her was a second body, a woman estimated to be in her late teens or early twenties. The young woman has unofficially been identified as Ms. Edison's Morfph™.

Geneti-Search's head CCO, Arthur Riche, confirmed that Ms. Edison had been Paired with the first mature experimental "Alpha" Morfph™. The discovery that a Morfph™ could kill her Patron has likely become the death knell of this controversial program.

For readers unfamiliar with the program, Morfphs™ are genetically engineered human beings with extraordinary capabilities. An unnamed spokesperson for the beleaguered Geneti-Search provided this reporter with the official definition of Morfphs:

"Morfphs™ are human beings who have been genetically designed, engineered and raised to have the enhanced characteristics of targeted perfect empathy i.e. the ability to read perfectly one individual's (their Patron's) emotions, wants and desires, and the extraordinary capacity to shape shift, and to behaviorally and emotionally 'morph' or transform into the embodiment of those desires. They have the desire and overriding need to meet their Paired Patron's desires."

Alix Edison, now often referred to as the "Mother of Morfphs," created and spearheaded the program. She, along with a handful of assistants, using the gene-splicing technology best known as Crispr, developed the genetic codes necessary to produce Morfphs™.

From the beginning, the program was fraught with turmoil and controversy. There was an attempt to keep it secret from the public. Non-Disclosure Agreements were signed by all. But when Morfphs™ became available to a select group of the wealthy individuals, rampant rumors spread like wildfire. Scandal, public outrage, reports of abuse, and protests followed rapidly.

Human Rights advocates posit that a tragic result was inevitable, and at least now this project will probably end. Many say it should

never have been allowed at all, as the project was a grotesque, immoral, and ethically
challenged experiment. It is variously being
called a crime against humanity, human trafficking, and slavery. According to Natalie Leong,
the spokesperson for the new organization,
*The Society for the Protection of Morfphs™
and Other Genetically Engineered Human Beings
(SPM)*, "It [the Morfph™ program] was spurred
by the dark motives of greed and profit over
the dignity and rights of humans and other
beings. Let us, also, not forget that most of
the exploited humans called Morfphs™ are people of color."

Other groups, especially those religious
groups identifying themselves with the Right
Thinkers, are less concerned with the rights
of the individuals called Morfphs™, but are
just as morally outraged. They prefer identifying Morfphs™ as Grifs, or more often,
Mogs. These pejorative terms are derived from
transmogrification, which they describe as
meaning "a grotesque metamorphosis." These
terms are described as "more accurate for
the abominable, dark beings called Morfphs™,
which were created by Alix Edison of Geneti-
Search Technologies and Laboratories, using
the unholy process of gene editing, to have
unnatural characteristics designed to please
and fulfill the lustful desires of their bonded
Godless Patroni."

# THE NEW TIMES

Editorial staff

August 8, 20**

### *The Mother of Morfphs. A fitting end to Alix Edison? Perhaps.*

*"O Brave new world, that has such people in't,"*

-William Shakespeare, The Tempest

By Morgan Murphy

The disgraced Alix Edison is now dead and gone, but what will become of her many "children"— over 3000 genetically engineered human beings known as Morfphs™.

Facts are coming to light about egregious and rampant abuses, abandonment, and even murder of these "Morfphs." Rumors, many salacious, abound. Geneti-Search Technologies, the company who engineered and distributed (some say sold), these genetically enhanced people, have been accused of culling and killing "defective" Morfphs. Other rumors speak of camps where runaway Morfphs are in hiding. These rumors have not been confirmed.

Geneti-Search announced that the Morfph™ program will now be shut down. The fate of the human beings already created and now in the process of growing to maturity but unpaired with Patroni is unknown.

Many people and organizations have stepped forward with offers of adoption. A group calling themselves The Morfph Caretakers has made a statement that they should be the ones to care for these people. Before maturity, all Morfphs™ were reportedly assigned one of these Caretakers who were employed by Geneti-Search and were tasked with raising and caring for Morfphs™ as they came to maturity and before being Paired with Patroni.

And what will be the fate of the Morfphs who have matured and been Paired? Or others who were Paired and then abandoned?

The courts will have these and many more decisions to make, and they will not likely be resolved soon. Morfphs™ themselves will hopefully be brought into the decisions made, but some argue that they do not have free-will and are not capable of making the best decision for themselves.

Nadia Kahl, the president of *The Society for the Protection of Morfphs and Other Genetically Engineered Human Beings (SPM)* said of this type of genetic engineering, "In my opinion, it is doubtful such a lucrative and powerful technology will completely end. Most likely it will go underground, grow, and spread around the world. It will probably grow into an even more malignant, unregulated form of creating 'special' human beings. Anything we can imagine, even nightmares, can and likely will be made real. We continue to work for the fair and humane treatment of these individuals."

So, whether this project ends or not, we have entered an amazing and terrifying new era.

# RIGHT THINKING NEWS

By Judea Soloman

August 9, 20**

Alix Hoffman Edison's life should be a cautionary tale for all God-fearing people and most especially for righteous women of this country. It should have come as no surprise that this woman, who has perpetrated such evil, has come to a well-deserved bad end as she burns in Hell. She, like Eve before her, has let loose a great evil into the world, and we will all suffer for it until it is completely purged from the land. She is the epitome of what happens when women are allowed out of their natural sphere and out of their ordained function in the world. The righteous hierarchy has been clearly written by the Almighty himself. Man is under God, and women, children, and the beasts are to be ruled by men.

*Exodus 22:15 Thou Shalt Not Suffer a Witch to Live.* There is no doubt Alix Edison was a witch. No woman is capable of accomplishing what she has done without the help of the Devil. And it must follow that all the creatures she has created, all these brown and black Mogs, are her spawn and thus, the spawn of the Devil.

From its inception, the "Morfph Project" and all its devil-spawn have been a corrupt abom-ination, a dark army of the most unnatural of females, and must be wiped from the face of the planet. Only cleansing flames will purge the evil this woman has wrought. The Bible leaves no doubt what we should do now.

# IV

# FROM THE ASHES

# CHAPTER 34

## *And, So It Ends*

### *Matthew*

Matthew was ready to finish it all and put "The Morfph Compendium and Handbook" to bed. He referred to it now as *The Morfph Bible*. He hadn't wanted this job that Alix had left for him after her death. No, he hadn't wanted to write it at all.

But truthfully, who better than he. The lies of Geneti-Search needed to be corrected for the Morfphs' sake, for everyone's sake. Reparations needed to be made as far as they could be. He had done the best he could gathering information, and he had, to his shame, been in on much of it. Geneti-Search continued to lie and withhold, but his information had come from many sources including, as many had suspected, Ruby and the Freed Morfph community where she now, seemingly quite happily, lived. He felt like he was coming out of a dark cave of obsession, depression, and guilt and emerging into the light.

His thoughts veered to Ruby's last email, and his face transformed into a wide smile. It had been a long time since he had felt this light joy. She hadn't said as much, but considering the timing, he was sure he was the father of the miraculous child—her child—that she had written about.

How could it be? How could she have gotten pregnant and then had a healthy baby boy? Morfphs were sterile, weren't they? Evidently not all; not anymore. Another way in which they had Transitioned, he guessed. He just didn't have all the answers yet. That was clear. The guilt he had been stewing in had blessedly evaporated with Ruby's news. He was now filled with a pure and giddy happiness.

And he now knew what he was going to do with this compendium, too— this *Morfph Bible*. He had decided right after he had finished off the last section. He would send actual paper copies of it to 100 different, all prominent, media outlets. He wanted everyone to know the truth of what had really happened. And to help make the case for the crucial importance of treating all the Morfphs with respect, humanity and fairness. He had first thought he would do it anonymously, then decided against it. Everything needed to be hit with the purifying light of day. No more secrecy.

There was one thing he had omitted, though. Discretion was necessary, at least for now. Fears must be dispelled, not inflamed. He did not include in the addendum to the Compendium that at least some Morfphs now had the capability of reproducing. No need to add the fuel of that knowledge. Fear had a nasty way of flaring to conflagrations and he had Ruby—and a son—to protect now.

———————

Weeks after the Morfph Compendium had been sent to the outlets, little else was talked about in the media and on social networks. The arrival of the compendium was met with pure glee by the media, as it was the juiciest story most of them had ever seen and more than a few careers were made on the coverage of it.

Editorials were written. Social media blew up. Twitcher storms caught fire. Online campaigns and petitions exploded. Internet forums talked of nothing else. There were protests on the street. Every end of the spectrum arose in outrage and fury. Human rights groups decried the treatment and fate of Morfphs. Religious groups branded Alix and the program evil incarnate.

The country was in an uproar.

And now the work to mend the damage must be done. He had recently found Sara Wilde's card in his pocket where Alix had put it. They would need good counsellors. Alix's therapist might just be the resource to tap.

# CHAPTER 35
## *A Pregnant Pause*

### *Sara*

Sam trotted into the room carrying Sara's buzzing cell phone. He'd been hovering over her solicitously for about a month now. Squelching her irritation, she admitted to herself that it *was* getting hard to heave herself and her very pregnant belly up from the couch once she had sunk into its cushions. Her center of balance was all off kilter. She couldn't wait to get this baby out of her belly.

Thankfully, all was well with her pregnancy. Her doctor called her an elderly primigravida. *Thanks Doc*, she thought every time he said it. But the tests still allowed were all normal... and it was a girl. Well, that's what the genetics said, anyway. Now they waited. But it wouldn't be long now.

Her divorce from Jack had finally come through, and she and Sam had gotten married in a very small ceremony with their good friends and family in the backyard of Sara's house. She and Sam had scraped up enough to buy Jack out, and he had readily agreed after their last face-to-face encounter. The wedding was lovely. Jack was not there. He had since separated from Jazmin and was on to another of his "cupcakes." Sara didn't know how old this one was, and she didn't care. *Good luck and good riddance.*

Sara took the phone from Sam and mouthed, "Thank you." She didn't recognize the number calling and was about to end the call and block the number, but she answered instead.

"Hello?"

"Sara Wilde?" A male voice she didn't recognize.

"Who is this?" she asked, wary.

"Dr. Wilde, this is Matthew Lawrence... actually I'm going by my real... uh, my whole name now... again... Devansh. It's even hard for me to remember," he said and laughed. "You don't know me. I called your work number, and a woman named Tania gave me your personal number. Not easily, but I finally convinced her."

"Really? Tania isn't supposed to... did you say Matthew Lawrence? I know who you are. Alix, um, I mean, a client I had talked about you. Also, you have been in the news lately... a lot."

"Please call me Devansh... or Dev. Yeah, I worked with Alix. She was the one who gave me your name before she... before she died."

"She did? Oh, Alix. Oh my god, what a shock..." Sara's heart rate increased. "But what is this about? Why are you calling me?"

"Well, I may have a proposal for you. Can we get together and talk?"

---

Several weeks before this call from Dev, aka Matthew, Sara had been shocked and horrified to read about Alix's death. She and Sam had been sitting on the couch together, her legs up on his lap. Their dog, Fergus, was on the couch with them and had his head on her lap. Sam was absent-mindedly rubbing her feet with his free hand as they both read news off their devices.

Suddenly Sara had gasped and fumbled with her phone. It fell from her hand and disappeared somewhere beneath her protruding belly. Alix Edison, her most troublesome client, was dead, and they were calling it a murder-suicide. Her Morfph had strangled her and then taken pills.

She hadn't heard from Alix for over two weeks now. As always, when Alix had left, she said she wasn't coming back, but this time she had settled her bill as she walked out the door. Sara knew things were blowing up with the Morfph program, but Alix seemed like the last person to kill herself. Well, technically, her Morfph had killed her, but it sounded very much as if Alix had planned it all.

When Sam saw Sara's shocked face, he reached over and quickly retrieved the fugitive phone. It was buried under a fold of fabric in what used to be Sara's lap, and the search prompted a surprised little yip from Sara. As Sam read what was on the screen, his eyes widened.

"She was your mysterious client, wasn't she? And it's all true. All the Morfph stuff you were talking about. It's real. Why didn't you tell me? We agreed, no lies," he said with no real heat.

"Well, I couldn't, could I? But, really, I shouldn't have talked about it at all. I'm sorry. I just needed to process it somehow."

It relieved Sara to see that Sam's initial irritation seemed to dissipate quickly as he hovered again.

"Are you okay, Sara? You look sick... like someone drained you. Can I get you something? Here, put your legs up."

"Yeah, yeah. I'm fine. Stop fussing. You're driving me crazy. It's just a shock. I can't believe she's dead." She felt dizzy, so she put her head down for a while.

"No reason I can't talk about it now, I guess. You interested?"

"Are you kidding me? Of course, I am."

---

During that first phone call, Sara and Dev had talked for a long time. She found what he had to say fascinating. At the end of the call, he asked if they could meet to talk further. She almost refused outright, but then changed her mind. *What's the harm?* So, they met for coffee to discuss his proposal. At first, Sara demurred.

"I can't help you," she said. "I have zero experience with this sort of thing. I'd just be making it up as I went along."

"Well, no one does, do they? There's never been this sort of thing before. You're more familiar with it than anyone else at this point."

Sara tipped her head sideways and nodded, ceding the point.

"I really need help, Sara. The Morfphs need help as the program shuts down. I think you could be integral with the healing and reparations."

"But me?" she said incredulously "I don't know..." She looked away and shook her head. "I just don't see it."

"I know it seems weird and *woo woo*," Dev said, "But they're just people. People who have been damaged by other people and the world... who need help."

"Yes, well, that I'm familiar with..."

"See? I know I'm right about this. Would you like to meet one before you decide?"

She looked at him with surprise but didn't answer right away.

"Maybe..."

"I could arrange it. We could just meet here again. Very low key. No pressure."

"Yeah. Okay. That is actually a good idea." Then she smiled.

"Matthew... Dev... whatever your name is, you are a very determined and persuasive man."

Dev smiled widely. "Sooo, we have a plan, then?"

Sara liked him. Sam had come along for this first meeting, but after the initial introductions, he had sat at another table. Later, he said he liked Dev, too.

———————

The next time Sara met Dev, an ordinary-looking young woman accompanied him. She was about twenty at the most, and she had matching warm-brown skin and hair. She kept averting her eyes—which were also warm-brown—and ducking her head as they talked. Her smile was shy and sweet, and Sara had to lean in to hear her soft voice.

They all talked for about fifteen minutes. Nothing of any import was discussed, but by the end of the discussion, Sara had decided. The Transitioned Morfphs *needed* help... her help. It might be just what she needed, too. An exciting new project. And so it was decided.

# CHAPTER 36
## *Lillianna*

### *Sara*

Sara and Dev met regularly after that and found they worked well together. For a meeting or two, they only talked about the planning of a program, but then the topics expanded. He told her more about the Transitioned Morfph named Ruby.

At first, he didn't say she had been *his* Morfph. He seemed embarrassed about it. But eventually, everything spilled out. He told her about Ruby's Pairing, her Transition, and her pregnancy. He also talked a lot about his wife, Lily. But it was Ruby Sara kept thinking about. Ruby, the young woman who had had the courage, the determination, and the strength to break free of her very genetics to become her true and unique self.

---

"Everyone talks about Alix like she was some kind of monster, even me at first. But now I'm just not sure what I think," Dev said at one of their meetings.

"I don't know either. She'd been treated terribly by her mother, by her mother's boyfriends, by her husbands, her boyfriends, by her coworkers." Sara was defensive about Alix—protective, even. "No one had ever been there for her. She figured out a way to deal with it. It was self-preservation, I guess. But regardless of how she got that way, maybe she was... a monster, I mean. By the end she may have realized it herself."

"What about Ruby? What do you think about Ruby?"

"Ruby is a hero—heroine—to me. She threw off her Morfphdom and has become her genuine self. She refused to be anything but herself. That took a lot of strength, I think."

"She's the reason I went back to my real name... Devansh. Look what she did to become her true self. The least I can do is acknowledge... embrace... where I came from and who I really am."

Sara nodded.

They sat for a while thinking their own thoughts.

"What about me?" Dev asked. "Am I a monster, too, then? We haven't talked about me—the widower who wanted to replace his dead wife... bring her back to life. So many bad—selfish—choices. Was I any less of a user than Alix, I wonder?"

Sara shrugged.

"I'm no one to judge, believe me. Really, though, most of us are pretty selfish. You're doing everything you can to make it right."

"I'm trying."

"What was Alix's Morfph's name? Adam? Or do we call her Pearl now? All these names... and genders... they're getting very confusing."

Dev laughed. "I know. Sorry. Let's just call him Adam."

"Okay, Adam it is." Sara worried at her lower lip. "Poor Adam. He couldn't break free from Alix and went down with her. He was destroyed by his allegiance, by his self-destructive loyalty, really. And especially, by his own inability to change—to become his own person. His inability to grow, to adapt—his rigidity—destroyed him. It wasn't his fault, of course. But Adam is a cautionary tale.

"I really feel for the Orphaned Morfphs. Their emptiness must be like the pain I felt when Jack walked out on me... only for the Morfphs it is magnified by a thousand... a million," Sara said. "It's an annihilation. You lose the self you were with that person. It sounds like even Ruby felt a sense of loss with her Transition and needed to be repaired and healed after."

"What about you, Sara? Have *you* repaired and healed completely?" Dev asked.

Sara smiled at him.

"Yeah. I'm happy with life. Nervous, though. Always nervous. I can hardly wait until this baby is born. I've waited a long time for her. She's strong... so far."

With some difficulty, she reached over her pregnant belly to tap three times on the wooden table in front of them. No use tempting those jealous gods.

At the end of the third knock, Sara groaned and then laughed. Briefly, the outline of a tiny foot pushed through the tightly stretched shirt over her belly.

"She's ready to get out of there," Sara said.

"Whoa, I can see that from way over here. We might need to take a break for a while very soon."

"Yeah, it looks that way. I'll be in touch, Matthew... *Dev*," Sara said and laughed as they both stood up. Before she walked out, she leaned out over her bulge and hugged him goodbye.

———————

Sara Wilde's Journal entry

> Matthew/ Dev has been telling me a lot about his Morfph... about Ruby. I feel a kinship with her. Like Ruby, something snapped and shifted inside me. She outgrew and transcended other's expectations to become truly and wholly herself. Ruby is who I want to be when I grow up. Ruby is my best and my fiercest self.
>
> I was considering naming my baby Ruby, but I won't. We will name her after Sam's mother. Like Sam, she's a lovely person. Our baby's name will be Lillianna. Dev smiled and teared up when I told him what her name would be. There's a story there, but we'll have to explore that later.
>
> Now, however, we need to get to the hospital. Lillianna's on her way and she seems quite insistent. S.W.

TWO YEARS LATER

# CHAPTER 37

## *Rebirth*

### *Matthew/Devansh*

Hopeful, Dev checked his email and smiled when he saw a new one waiting for him in his in-box. He had received a handful of emails from Ruby in the two years since she had left. All came from a different server. This one looked like it had come from Hong Kong, but Dev knew it most probably had not originated there. Somehow, Ruby would bounce it through many servers before it appeared in his mailbox.

He had been too busy, at least during the daytime, to be lonely after Ruby had left. First, he had been tasked with finishing Alix's "Morfph Bible" by writing a Forward and adding a fairly detailed Postscript. Then, there was the distribution of it to the media. And last, with Sara's help, he had been instrumental in putting together a program to make reparations to the Morfph survivors.

Initially, to mitigate their culpability, Geneti-Search had funded the program. A crow-eating Arthur Riche had actually come to Dev to run it. But ultimately, it hadn't helped. Geneti-Search was still underwater in lawsuits and would likely fold by the end of the year.

But now, he read Ruby's email eagerly.

```
My Dearest Matthew,

Things are volatile here, but don't fear for us.
We are safe and loved. The number of what you
call Transitioned or Freed Morfphs continues to
grow daily, both here and at nearby locations.
We now call each other f-Morfphs. I have already
told you that f-Morfphs are now having babies.
Miracle babies.
```

My beautiful little boy is now eighteen months old. He is growing and mostly developing like an 'Ordinary,' except for his enhanced intelligence. I am pregnant again and thrilled about it. The new pregnancy seems to be going normally in Freeborn terms, as well. I am well past the three-month gestation of un-transitioned or trad-Morfphs, so it looks like my pregnancy will be taking the standard Freeborn forty weeks. I, therefore, expect this child to grow and develop in close to normal Freeborn terms… and have an Ordinary life span, as well. Thank the Goodness.

There have been many babies born and even more pregnancies. Most are developing like mine—the differences we're seeing, however, are in their learning and cognitive stages. They learn to talk almost as soon as they are born, learn to read at one year of age, and are very coordinated at a young age as well, usually running by nine months. But, as I mentioned above, physically, *f*-Morfphs seem to age at a normal Ordinary rate and because our appearance is no longer determined by another's desires and most of us no longer have shape shifting abilities, we now visibly age, as well.

But there are a few pregnancies that are different. They are greatly accelerated, as we were as trad-Morfphs. These pregnancies last less than three months. One-year-old "babies" are the size of a four-year-old and look and act like (albeit brilliant) children that age. Many believe these children will be mature enough to be Super-Soldiers by five years of age. I will get to why the Super-Soldier sobriquet is applied and why it is so important to many here.

I have read the Compendium you sent to me. There are several things that are inaccurate in it. One of those things is that there are some bio-genic male Morfphs. Not many, but they are quite popular, if you know what I mean. And not just as sexual partners, also as sperm donors.

I have a regular partner, but share him, hap-pily, with others. We just can't be selfish or possessive here. He's quite happy with the sit-uation, of course. Luckily, he is a sweet and giving human being.

And it turns out that we *ƒ*-Morfphs are very fertile, indeed. Many came here already preg-nant. Some had become pregnant with their Patron before they left. Others got pregnant on the journey here, some from consensual relation-ships, some by rape.

Other pregnancies have occurred from relations with the male Morfphs here. In three- or four-years' time there will also be fertile males maturing among the fast-developing offspring. So, the Geneti-Search reassurance that Morfphs will all die out because they are female, short-lived, and infertile is completely inaccurate.

Another inaccuracy has to do with *ƒ*-Morfphs. Many are like me. They have lost all their special abilities, except high intelligence and rapid learning. All Morfphs keep that. Others have retained their ability to shape shift, but have lost their empathy and their desire to please others. They have largely learned to control their shape shifting. They can shift to any form or gender, just as they please. And they do please.

A few have kept their empathy and telepathy, but have lost their shape shifting abilities. Their empathy has generalized to sensing the feelings and desires of all people, not just one Paired individual. A smaller number have retained their overriding desire to please. Most have not, which is good. The ones who have are very needy and unhappy people. I don't expect them to last long. Maybe we'll find a way to Transition that extreme neediness out of them.

That brings me to the raids that have begun. You may have heard about them, but I believe they are trying to keep them quiet. We have retrieved a variety of individuals, including immature un-bonded Morfphs, mature un-bonded Morfphs, un-Transitioned Orphaned Morfphs (these are the hardest), and the Culled Transitioned Morfphs from holding facilities. The raids have been very successful.

They should just let us have them back without the raids. The facilities have been equally unsuccessful at helping the Orphaned Morfphs and at keeping the Culled Morfphs in custody. They claim they can save them, but they can't. Another lie.

We, on the other hand, have been very success-ful at helping Orphaned Morfphs to transition to *f*-Morfphs, if they are not too far gone into psychosis or coma. The Culled Morfphs are very pleased to be here—out of captivity and with their peers.

We laughingly call the Transitioning process Conversion Therapy. We borrowed the term from the unsuccessful, misguided, and cruel "ther-apy" of converting people's sexuality to some-thing supposedly more acceptable.

It's a big joke here because, although most *f*- Morfphs have physically hardened into one gender or another, usually female, we are still quite fluid in our sexuality, gender roles, and gender identities. And then there's the handful of shapeshifters who are gender fluid, flipping back and forth.

We have extraordinary facilities here—hospi-tals, laboratories, research facilities, and schools. Donors have been very generous and our hacking abilities have been lucrative. We also have a state-of-the-art shielding and defense technology that hides and protects our compounds from any sort of detection or threat.

But let's get back to the Super Soldiers. Why soldiers, you ask? Many of us (not me! my dear) are angry—very angry. We are also, as you know, intellectually and physically quite superior to Freeborns. The anger is drowning out pleas—mine and some others—who insist that not all Freeborns are evil. Many Morfphs have been severely bullied and abused, or worse—some much worse.

The stories of physical and psychological abuse, even torture, that many of these Morfphs have suffered at the hands of Freeborns are horrendous and heart breaking. Pleas for getting along and working with Freeborns are falling on deaf ears, I'm afraid. It certainly doesn't help our cause of peaceful coexistence when there are bands of assassins out to kill us.

The exact numbers are as yet unknown, but it is estimated that dozens of *f*-Morfphs who were trying to make it to us have been murdered—some in the most horrific ways. One was burned alive and left hanging from a tree with a sign around her neck. It said "Black Spawn of Satan."

So, I believe things will come to a head in the not-too-distant future. I will do everything I can to protect you—as you did for me. I'm not sure when I can write again, but I will do my best to keep you abreast of important developments.

As to your question about the paternity of my son, I will only say that he is beautiful and smart and perfect, and he is mine. And what a gift that is for a motherless child like me. For who is my mother… or my father? My Donators? My Gestator? My Caretakers? No, none of them. And I get to be all three for my children! What a wonderful thing that is. And just as it should be. I do so wish you could be his Heart Father— and for my new one when she comes. But I fear that will never be.

Take care and be safe.

Yours, Ruby

# THE NEW WORLD TIMES

*After the Fall: The End of the Morfph Project*

Op-Ed

**by Devansh Matthew Lawrence**

"The Morfph Project" of Geneti-Search Corporation came to an abrupt end two years ago when Alix Edison, the lead genetic scientist and designer of the specific gene sequencing that made it possible to engineer Morfphs, was found murdered by her own Morfph. They had been Paired for over two years. After her Morfph strangled Ms. Edison, s/he fatally overdosed on a powerful narcotic pain-killer and alcohol, in what appeared to be a planned murder/ suicide. There is little doubt in my mind that the plan was masterminded by Ms. Edison. It has been conjectured by the media that Morfphs or maybe only this Morfph in particular, may have had a genetic defect that caused the violent attack. This is just another example of hyperbolic fear-mongering. Either way, the murder triggered the ending of an already controversial and increasingly beleaguered project. After these two deaths, and the many other reports of abuse, torture, and even murder of Morfphs, chaos ensued.

Geneti-Search at first attempted to cover up the truth and the extent of the problems which are still coming to light. Once it couldn't be adequately covered up, their damage control changed tack with a show of compassion for the Morfphs. They declared that their chief concern was the well-being of all Morfphs.

Geneti-Search stopped hunting "runaway" Transitioned, a.k.a. *Freed*, Morfphs and declared an amnesty of sorts. The hope was to gather all Morfphs without force, thus minimizing the damage to the company. Geneti-Search has funded a large variety of programs with the purported goal of helping Morfphs, which includes their assimilation into general society.

It has turned out that very few Transitioned Morfphs would, then or now, come in for any sort of assistance from Geneti-Search. The predominant reason appears to be that they continue to have no trust in the people trying to gather them in or in the type of help they have to offer.

With their enhanced intelligence, Morfphs feel superior to us 'Ordinaries' or Freeborns. Many Transitioned Morfphs want nothing to do with normal society. Besides their mistrust of stated motives, many fear for their actual physical safety. They know Transitioned Morfphs, all Morfphs really, are still in danger from people who think they need to be eradicated. They have been dubbed "freaks", "dangers to society", and "dark spawns of the devil," to name just a few of the epithets. Calls for a Morfph purge are gaining momentum.

At the time of this writing, there are about three thousand Morfphs. What must be understood is that these Morfphs are in several different situations and conditions. Most of the Morfphs are un-Transitioned and are still with their Patroni, and most hope to remain with them. About twenty percent are Transitioned (Freed) Morfphs with freewill. They have attained this freewill or ability to choose, reportedly due to some sort of unresolvable and extreme stress that apparently results in a series of gene switches within them. Most of those Transitioned Morfphs have fled their Patroni to live in hidden compounds with other Freed Morfphs. A few Transitioned Morfphs have stayed with their Patroni. Others, who had been discovered earlier and Culled, are living in a separate wing of the facilities still run by Geneti-Search. Sara Wilde, PhD, has become a prominent therapist and advocate for Transitioned Morfphs who have stayed with their Patroni or are living in the facilities run by Geneti-Search.

Another group—the most unfortunate—are the Orphaned Morfphs. These are Morfphs who have lost their Patron for a variety of reasons and who have not Transitioned to become Freed Morfphs. Most Orphaned Morfphs haven't survived long, as they either chose voluntary euthanasia, commit suicide, or simply lapse into comas and die. A vast majority of those who are still living have been hospitalized and are being kept deeply sedated. They are in various states of decline.

It is estimated that eight to ten percent of Morfphs have been Orphaned. Some were unwanted and abandoned by their Patron and returned to Geneti-Search. Others have had a Patron who has died. There have been some attempts at Transition therapy for Orphaned Morfphs. See section below for a discussion of the status of the current attempts at Transition Therapy.

Finally, there are also immature Morfphs, not yet ready for Pairing and mature Morfphs not yet Paired. These individuals are still in the Geneti-Search compound. It is an especially precarious situation for mature, un-bonded Morfphs, as they need to be kept in isolation or constantly veiled until a method is developed for Transition. So far there has been no reliable success in forcing these Transitions. They may need to be temporarily Paired and then Transitioned which would be a very complex and risky procedure.

All the categories of Morfphs who are not in secret compounds of their own making are supposed to be monitored by what remains of the Department of Human Services. Because of the strain on the program, this is rarely happening.

Geneti-Search has, inevitably, ended up in court. Because of multiple lawsuits, and a court-ordered restitution, all the categories of Morfphs have been awarded very large monetary settlements. But to collect, they need to come forward and reveal their locations. Transitioned Morfphs are being offered help to find a life outside the Freed Morfph Compounds, but most have stayed and new ones arrive daily. Due to safety concerns alluded to above, the Freed Morfph Compounds are keeping their locations secured, shielded, and secret, even after they declared amnesty.

All Morfphs are in danger of purges by various groups. Their lives remain precarious. There continues to be an exodus of Freed Morfphs from the Geneti-Search facilities. They remove their chips and leave at night. They are not being actively stopped or assisted at this point. An underground railroad, of sorts, has emerged to help them get to the Morfph compound.

Transition Therapy, a new controversial and dangerous therapy, is being offered. Its aim is to force Transitioning. By its very nature, it is dangerously stressful, painful, and nowhere near a sure thing. It is believed that there have been a few fatalities from the procedure,

but there is still little transparency in anything pertaining to Morfphs.

Patroni need to be willing to help in the
process. Very few still-Paired Morfphs want
anything to do with it. The few who desire the
process are Morfphs who have retained some
vestiges of freewill, and who were therefore
not completely bonded to their Patroni. The
therapy is very rarely attempted and may soon
be outlawed.

It's my hope to humanize, and to inform the public about this group of people called Morfphs.
They, like the rest of us human beings, were
not asked to be born as they were. I believe
they were dealt a cruel and unjust hand as
they were created to be our slaves. It was a
doomed project from the start, and one that
I am deeply regretful of having been a part.
I am hoping to redeem myself and mitigate my
culpability by advocating for Morfphs in all
their states of being.

It says a great deal about the human spirit
and resiliency that many of these people have
broken out of their mental chains and have
freed themselves. This is not a criticism of
the many others who have stayed devoted to
their Patroni or to the Patroni who keep and
cherish them.

I end with a quote from Dr. Wilde, the therapist I mentioned earlier in this piece, who

specializes in treating Transitioned or Freed Morfphs:

*"I find very little difference between Freed Morfphs and my other clientele. Transitioned Morfphs are simply in search of their true and authentic selves. Aren't many of us in a similar search as we traverse and try to make sense of our, often-confusing, lives?"*

# CHAPTER 38

## *Domestic Bliss*

### *Sara*

A year after Dev had received what turned out to be Ruby's last email, Sara sat at her dining room table moodily gazing out the window at the overgrown garden. *Needs weeding*, she thought, and looked away.

Lillianna was napping, and Sam was at his office. The floor was strewn with toys and the remains of lunch littered the table. She took her phone out and texted a message. When finished, she read it over, and immediately erased it, jabbing the delete key over and over until all the letters disappeared.

She abruptly stood, walked to the refrigerator, blindly studied the contents, and closed the door with an impatient slam. After she paced back and forth for several minutes, she sat heavily in the chair at the table where she had left her phone. Sometimes she was surprised there was no worry path worn into the floor where she paced daily.

*What is wrong with me?* she thought. *I have everything.*

Well, almost everything. The program to help Morfphs had been defunded and Geneti-Search had risen again under a new name. Most of the law-suits and criminal prosecutions had been dropped with little to no media attention. The public had tired of them and had moved onto the next outrage du jour. So, her job with Dev and the Morfphs had evaporated.

Her private clients had dropped off to just a handful, as well. From the con-versations she had with those who had quit therapy—the ones with the courage to contact her, Sara sensed she had acquired some sort of taint from working so closely with Morfphs. They were now seen as little better, or maybe worse, than prostitutes.

But in the end, it turned out that none of that really mattered, because not much later, her license to practice was suspended. She was a "woman with a child and she needed to give her full attention to the care and raising of that child." That was the explanation given by the licensing board for her suspension.

After she lost her license, she had cried and raged in fear and frustration.

"Don't worry, Sara, I'll always take care of you. I'll take care of all of us," Sam had said. "I'll take more clients. We'll be okay."

"I don't want to be taken care of," she had cried. "I want my job... I want my *life* back."

"You have your life. With me and with Lillianna."

Lillianna *was* happy and healthy. And Sam, of course, was the perfect husband and father. Just perfect. *Perfectly perfect.* Except, they rarely talked now. True to his promise, Sam had more than doubled his caseload, and he was away from home much of the time. When they did have time together, Sam walked out of the room or changed the subject whenever Sara brought up her frustration or grieved her losses.

She finally stopped trying to talk about them—or about much of anything, except the mundane details of their life together. Many of Sam's new clients had been hers, but they didn't talk about that either. She felt like a ghost. Dread followed her in everything she did, leaving her breathless with its constant weight.

She lowered her head to the table. The motion nudged her phone off the edge and it clattered to the floor. She grabbed the phone and this time agitatedly tapped in a number to make a call. It was one she had deleted from her phone but knew by heart. She jumped when he answered. His voice had been seared into her brain and soul years before.

"Hello, Sara." No surprise in his voice.

She almost hung up. She took a deep, shuddering breath.

"I miss you."

"Well, of course you do," he said and laughed. "What took you so long to realize it, little darlin'?

"It's not funny. I really thought I'd exorcised you."

"Now, why would you want to do that? We belong together."

Sara groaned, and he laughed again.

"Don't be too hard on yourself, Sara. You needed something I couldn't give you. Now you've got it—got her. Right? We're not so very different, you and I."

"Oh, god," she whispered, and dropped the phone.

Sara could still hear Jack's voice and laughter coming from the phone on the floor. Horrified, she viciously kicked it across the room, where it hit the wall. Not hearing anything more, she cautiously walked up to it and shoved it once with her toe. Still nothing. *Thank god.*

In a daze, she walked to Lilliana's bedroom door and carefully opened it. Her daughter lay on her back with her arms spread wide, sleeping the blissfully untroubled sleep of a toddler. Long, dark eyelashes—Sam's eyelashes—lay against the pore-less velvet skin of her face. *So vulnerable, so precious.*

Sara's stomach lurched and waves of emotion flooded her: guilt, grief, and an overwhelming need to protect Lillianna—to let nothing bad happen to her... ever. Sara sat on one of Lillianna's chairs next to the bed and stared at her for several minutes. She inhaled, quick and deep. Those were the words Sam had used. *I'll keep you both safe,* he had said. *I won't let anything bad happen to you... to either of you.* But that was beyond both of their powers, regardless of how much they wanted it—no matter how hard they tried.

She walked slowly back into the dining room, retrieved her cracked, but still functioning, phone and called another, even more familiar, number.

Sam answered immediately—before she even heard it ring.

"Is everything okay?" His voice broke on the last word.

"We're fine."

She heard a relieved exhalation of breath.

"What is it then? I'm booked solid until eight tonight. Back-to-back. Then I need to write up my notes."

"Cancel tonight's appointments... please. Come home. We need to talk. Like before... like we used to. I miss you." *Not Jack, Sam.*

"Sara..." He sounded frustrated, exasperated.

"I'm struggling, Sam... really struggling. You need to listen... we both do. I know you can't fix everything that's wrong. I know that. It's too big. Please, Sam."

There was a long pause.

"I'll be home in twenty," he said.

With those simple words, she could breathe again. The tight bands around her chest—and around her heart—loosened their cruel grip.

# EPILOGUE I

## *In the Morgue*

The afternoon Dev had found Alix and her Morfph dead, after he had read her letter, and after he had talked to the two detectives, he watched as their neatly bagged and zipped remains were wheeled out the front door of the condo and loaded into the waiting ambulance. Their next stop was the morgue, where they were to be officially identified, autopsied, and released for cremation. So, it seemed at that point, Alix's fear of being burned was to be her ultimate fate after all. However, as it turned out, that was *not* the way it went.

———————

At the morgue, they finished up with the Morfph first—cutting her open from stem to stern, weighing her organs, taking samples of stomach contents and blood, and finally putting her back together and sewing her up tightly. The conclusion, not unexpectedly, was that she had died of an overdose of opioids washed down with whiskey.

Alix was next up. They cut off her red dress, bagged it, washed her body, and just as the forensic pathologist picked up the scalpel to do the Y incision, an assistant hurried in.

"New orders. Wait on this one. You're not to do the autopsy until tomorrow morning, earliest."

"Well, shit. I'm all ready to go. Why?"

"Didn't say."

The pathologist shook his head. "Okay, help me get her back into a body bag and the drawer. You can go home after everything is cleaned up. I'll close it down."

After they finished and he'd changed his clothes, he gathered his things, closed everything up, and walked to his car.

Hours later, in the early morning hours, an unmarked, white paneled van with no license plates pulled up into the loading dock. It was an old-model, driver-driven vehicle with no automation. The driver and passenger, both dressed in dark clothes, jumped out, pulled a collapsible gurney from the back, and wheeled it right into the morgue. Inexplicably, doors opened for them automatically and no alarms sounded. A few minutes later, they wheeled back out and now the gurney held a full body bag. After loading it into the back of the van, they sped away, spitting loose gravel out from under its tires.

By the time it was discovered the next morning, Alix was well gone. That her body disappeared from the morgue that night never appeared in the media. Arthur Riche of Geneti-Search made sure of this. He still had some pull in high places.

Ten miles away from the morgue, Jason Martin, Alix's ex-coworker, looked down at her lifeless body lying on a metal table in a white room lined with machines and instruments. Naked and exposed, her emaciated body, with its rows of visibly protruding ribs and jutting hip bones, looked uncomfortable even in death. Lucky thing they got her out of there before the autopsy had been done. That was a close call.

On a table next to her lay another body; a young man with his eyes closed and, even though this one lived, his smooth, unlined face was blank of expression.

"You're not getting away that easily, Alix," Jason said with a twisted smile. "I need your mind... just for a while. Just 'til I can get everything out of it I need.

# EPILOGUE II

## *Just Call Me Alex*

### *Alix/Alex*

I know this is the first you've heard my voice other than the little snippets of thought here and there, but I think it's about time. It has been *my* story all along and continues to be so.

When I died at the hands of my own sweet Adam, my soul did not travel down a long, dark tunnel. Nor did I see or hear any departed loved ones. Not that I have any of those. And I most definitely did not see a bright light beckoning me on. No, none of that.

What I felt, however briefly, was a profound sense of release and a floating peace. No more rage. No more fear. And then... well, nothing. I felt absolutely nothing. Nothing, that is, until that bastard brought me back, ripping me from my floating netherworld back to this shit show.

I did not choose it. I did not want it. But I got it anyway and since I did, I have endeavored, and will continue to endeavor, to make the most of it.

My name is... was... Alix Edison and my mind has been Uploaded.

But now you should call me Alex... Alex with an *e* where the *i* used to be. Because this time around, the Merry-Go-Round I'm traveling in is the skin and body of a man. This should be interesting.

**END**